Go Deep

Leigh Matthews

Praise for Don't Bang the Barista!

"[...] intriguing, endearing and utterly captivating throughout."

Kalyanii, The Lesbrary.com

"If smart, well-written theatrics are your thing, you're in for a fun ride with Don't Bang the Barista!"

Melanie Bell, Autostraddle.com.

"[...] in the small space of about 200 pages, this book manages to be fun and smart, complex and intensely readable."

Casey Stepaniuk, Caseythecanlesbrarian.com

"I devoured this book in two nights. Great story, great writing, an absolute page turner!"

Goodreads reviewer

Also by Leigh Matthews

Fiction

Don't Bang the Barista!
The Old Arbutus Tree

Non-fiction

Eat to Beat Acne: how a plant-based diet can help heal
your skin

For Julia.

Part One

ONE

Cass was in the bath re-enacting Macbeth with rubber duckies when Kate got home, so she poured them both a glass of wine and went to sit on the side of the tub. Kate's dog, Jupiter, had been asleep on the bath mat, but now stood briefly to say hello before padding to the living room to snooze on the couch. It was clearly Kate's turn to play lifeguard.

"How was your day?" Cass asked, after thanking Kate for the wine and giving her a wet, slightly soapy kiss.

"Fine, the usual for a Friday," Kate said, pulling off her stockings and rubbing her right ankle. "Anna's talking about leaving again, and Sami forgot to buy more coffee, so there was a bit of a crisis at three."

"Well, you can't run a company without coffee," Cass said gravely, reaching out to massage Kate's foot.

Kate smiled and leaned back, then realised that Cass was pulling her foot into the bath. She laughed and tried to retract her foot, but Cass wiggled her eyebrows, put down her wineglass and gently tugged at Kate's leg. "It'll make you feel better," Cass said.

"But I don't feel bad!" Kate said, standing up and staring down at Cass.

"So, it'll make you feel spectacular!" Cass began easing Kate's dress up her thighs, getting water all over the bathroom floor as she splashed around in the tub.

"Cass! Stop it!" Kate laughed and stepped away. "I'm going to go and make a start on dinner."

Cass sank down into the bubbles and pouted. "We can just order in."

"We got takeout last night."

"So? There's no rule against ordering in twice in a row. Hand me my phone and then take off your clothes and get in here with me." Cass put out her hand, but Kate took a towel from the rail instead and draped it over Cass's hand.

"How about getting out of the tub and helping with dinner?"

Cass gasped, "But I only just got in!"

"You're all pruny. You've clearly been in there for hours. C'mon, you can't spend all day in the bath, Cass." Kate watched Cass drop the towel on the floor. "You're such a brat."

"Well, you're not my mother, so quit acting like you are." Cass slipped down under the water and Kate knew better than to wait around for her girlfriend to resurface. Cass would rather asphyxiate than give Kate the satisfaction of meeting her gaze right now.

Kate went to scour the refrigerator to see what Cass had left after another day of grazing. There was a note on the refrigerator door: INK Hotel, room 303. Kate wasn't aware that Cass had friends coming to town, and she wondered if this would shake up their weekend plan to head out on their bikes to Bloemendaal with Sami.

Kate took a zucchini, pepper, and two carrots out of the refrigerator, along with some leftover chickpeas. She lit one of the gas burners and set a pan warming.

Cass crept up behind her and threw her arms around Kate's waist. "I'm sorry. I don't know how you put up with me," Cass murmured into Kate's neck.

Kate breathed in the fresh scent of Cass's skin and the hint of Old Spice Game Day and closed her eyes as she leaned against Cass's damp body. She wanted to get on with making dinner, so they could eat at a reasonable hour, but the heat emanating from Cass was hugely distracting.

"Did you miss me today?" Cass said softly. "Were you thinking about me, all alone at home in bed without you?" Cass licked Kate's ear lobe. "I was thinking about you."

"What were you thinking?" Kate whispered as Cass slipped her sweater over her head.

"I was thinking about how soft your skin is across your belly, and how amazing you smell when you're hot and wet for me." Cass took one of Kate's bra straps in her teeth and pulled it off Kate's shoulder. Kate shrugged off the other strap as Cass undid the clasp. She dropped the bra to the kitchen floor and cupped Kate's breasts, squeezing her nipples to make her gasp. Cass bit Kate's neck gently, making little humming sounds that vibrated through Kate's spine.

Cass's wet hair was cool against Kate's flushed skin and as she let her bath towel fall to the floor, Cass pushed her body against Kate's, leaning her into the kitchen counter.

Kate put out her hands to grip the cool quartz surface and her fingers bumped against the vegetables, knocking the zucchini to the floor. Cass laughed and said, "Don't give me ideas," as she unbuttoned Kate's pants.

A sizzling, popping sound and the smell of burning oil jolted Kate out of the moment and she pushed against the counter to force Cass back.

"The pan!" Kate cried, looking around for an oven mitt as she turned off the gas and tried to avoid splashing hot oil on her bare skin.

Cass laughed and wrapped a tea towel over her hand before carrying the pan to dump it in the sink. She threw that

3

towel on the floor too and grabbed Kate by the waist. She kissed Kate's breast and licked her nipple, murmuring, "Where were we?" Kate leaned back against the refrigerator, trying to recapture her mood from a moment ago, but her hair snagged against the magnet holding up the note about room 303.

"Who's staying at the INK Hotel?"

Cass mumbled something into Kate's belly as she sank to her knees and started tugging at Kate's pants. She bit the top of Kate's knickers and tugged at them playfully, but Kate was distracted.

"Who?" Kate said, feeling a shiver running down her legs, despite herself.

Cass murmured unintelligibly into the soft flesh of Kate's belly.

"Cass. Cass, just stop for a second." Kate pulled Cass up by the shoulders so they were facing each other.

Cass smirked, seeing how flushed her girlfriend's face had become. Kate pointed at the note on the refrigerator behind her. "Who's in town?"

Cass stopped smirking and turned to pick up the wet towel from the kitchen floor. She wrapped it around her shoulders and said, "Em. She called the landline this morning."

"Em? Em's in town?" Kate snatched at her phone and began searching for the number for the hotel.

Cass watched Kate for a second and then started walking towards the bedroom. She called over her shoulder, "I guess we're not going to the party later then, huh," before dropping the wet towel to the floor and slamming the door.

Kate put down her phone and started after Cass. She was about to call Cass's name, then she stopped. Why did she feel the need to placate her girlfriend even though Cass had neglected to tell her right away that Em was in town? Cass would have known that Kate would want to see Em as soon as possible.

4

Now that the blood was returning to Kate's head from elsewhere in her body, she realised that, if anything, she should be the one who was mad, not Cass. Kate looked in the direction of the bedroom and shook her head as she picked up her phone again. The damage was done, and Kate didn't want to spend the rest of the evening contending with Cass's mood. She wanted to see Em. She called the hotel.

TWO

The concierge at the INK Hotel stared expectantly at Kate as she entered the lobby. "Goedenavond, mevrouw. Hoe kan ik je helpen?"

"Goedenavond," Kate replied, "I'm meeting a friend. She's a guest here." She smiled at the woman in her sleek little black dress, who nodded and turned her attention back to the desk.

Kate sat down on the circular wooden bench in the atrium that served as the hotel reception. While she waited for Em, Kate looked around, examining the giant typeset letters that formed one wall, and, harking back to the building's days as home to a newspaper, the mural that read, "Where stories are yet to be written."

Em had great taste in hotels, Kate thought, and looked over at the very attractive receptionist, who had been joined by an equally beautiful colleague also wearing a little black dress. They were discussing something in Dutch and when one of them barely restrained a giggle, Kate tried to eavesdrop so she would know what was so funny. She could barely pick out any words, and she wished she'd taken the opportunity to practice her Dutch with the receptionist, who glanced up at her and caught her eye before looking back at her colleague and laughing again.

Kate had assumed that being in Amsterdam would be like Dutch immersion school and that after three months of living here she would be practically fluent and able to work out if gorgeous customer service representatives were talking about her. The problem was that everyone spoke English, making things far too easy, and making her feel foolish for even attempting to speak Dutch. Kate rarely had a chance to utter a single sentence before her Britishness was noted and the assumption made that she wouldn't know any language other than English. The fact that she didn't, in fact, know any language other than English was neither here nor there, Kate thought, making an effort to maintain her annoyance and deflect any possible blame.

Everyone in Kate's office spoke perfect English, aside from Sami, the enthusiastic office manager whose vocabulary was delightfully eclectic and not always appropriate for a business setting. Kate adored Sami, as did Jupiter, who Sami begged Kate to bring into the office every day. Sami's boyfriend was allergic to dogs and so Sami liked to take full advantage of having an office dog. In fact, Kate thought, Jupiter probably knew more Dutch than she did, given his long conversations with Sami.

Most of Kate's clients also worked in English, or made sure to bring along a fluent assistant, especially after having heard Kate mangle a few Dutch sentences. Kate's ambition to become a polyglot while back in Europe was looking a little unrealistic.

Cass had suggested that they learn Dutch together. She would need it for the documentary course she planned on taking next semester. Unfortunately, most of the things they had learnt to say to each other weren't really safe for polite conversation, and Kate wondered if there was a risk of developing a Pavlovian response to the language: a sort of

7

linguistic kink if you will.

The elevator chimed and Kate turned in her chair, half standing, anticipating the sight of Em. Instead, a janitor wheeled her cart out into the lobby, her elbows resting on the metal frame, dirty linens trailing on the floor where they'd tumbled unseen. The receptionist eyeballed the woman and, despite Kate's lack of finesse with Dutch, she quickly understood that the volley of words delivered in hushed tones was a serious chastisement for not having used the service elevator.

There was something to be said, Kate thought, for guests and staff having to ride the elevators together. Maybe people would think twice before leaving their rooms in complete disarray when they checked out. Kate always left hotel rooms as tidy and neat as possible, only to get back to her own apartment and discover it to be a complete mess as she'd left it while packing in a panic. Perhaps she should ride the elevator with herself sometime, she thought.

The elevator chimed again and this time Kate jumped up as Em strode out into the lobby. They ran toward each other and Kate scooped up Em and twirled her around, kissing her on both cheeks as she set her friend back down. Em was lighter than Kate remembered, and paler too. Probably just jet lag, Kate thought, holding her friend's hands in hers as she backed up a little and grinned.

"Surprise!" Em said, and they hugged again, laughing.

"When did you arrive? How long are you here for? Why are you at a hotel and not staying with me? You should check out and stay with me." Kate effervesced with the thrill of Em's arrival in Amsterdam, hoping that it wasn't a fleeting visit and that they'd actually get to spend some time relaxing together.

"Woah, monster. How about you get us to a good bar and I'll fill you in?" Em eyed the models masquerading as receptionists and said quietly, "The bar here's a little chic for my taste." Em slipped her arm into Kate's and they walked

8

out of the hotel into the cool night, the breeze from the canal bringing with it the smells and sounds of the city.

Half an hour later, Kate and Em were sitting at the bar at the Prik: Amsterdam's best gay bar, according to Sami, and a place that was rapidly becoming Kate and Cass's go-to drinking hole.

Kate slammed a shot of tequila and then slammed her fist on the counter and said, "Holy shit, Em! That's great news!" Kate ordered another round, and yelled over the music, "My friend is going to propose to her girlfriend!"

The barman cocked an eyebrow and mumbled what Kate decided to translate as 'congratulations', as she wasn't about to let anyone ruin the moment, especially not some sulky bear in chaps and hot pants. Kate hadn't realised it was a theme night, and she certainly hadn't expected her evening to involve that much thigh hair.

Em laughed and rolled her eyes. "Technically, I guess I'm proposing to Steve and Hanna. It's all a bit odd."

"I love that you're so queer, you've even managed to convert Steve to UHauling," Kate said, slamming another shot.

"Slow down, love," Em said, putting her hand on Kate's. "You don't have to drain the bar tonight."

"Just celebrating!" Kate hugged Em and said, "It's so fucking good to see you. I have missed you something rotten."

"Liar. You've been having too much sex to think about me and the East Van crew." Em winked at Kate, who groaned and took a sip of beer.

"Truth be told, Cass is getting on my nerves a little. She's so aimless. I feel like I'm living with a toddler, an academic, and a sex addict, and I never know which one I'll come home to."

"Which one do you want to come home to?" Em asked.

"Maybe none of the above?" Kate grimaced.

9

"Definitely not the academic," Em said, nudging Kate's elbow.

"Right? Nobody wants to be fucking Foucault."

"So, back to me..." Em raised her eyebrows.

"Yes! So when are you popping the question? Or questions? How will this whole thing work? I mean, you can't actually marry them both, so who is going to get married, legally?"

"So, here's the fucked up bit. Ready?"

Kate nodded and said, "Always."

"No, seriously. This is majorly fucked up, so steel yourself."

Kate made fists and scrunched her eyes, then clapped her hands and said, "Hit me!"

"I'm thinking Steve will marry Hanna and then they'll adopt me."

Kate tried to respond, but got no further than opening and closing her mouth several times, making no audible sound. A few seconds went by, then Em signalled to the barman to get them more tequila. "My friend here needs a stiff drink," Em said. "And bring the smelling salts," she added as the barman gave her a withering glance, either due to a lack of comprehension or a lack of caring. Em patted Kate's hand, seeing that she was still struggling to figure out the situation. "See, I warned you," Em said as she slid Kate's shot of tequila towards her.

Kate downed the shot and then managed to get some words out, saying, "So, I'm guessing that because you can't legally all get married, you're, what? You're going to do this adoption thing so you have some familial connection in the eyes of the law?"

Em nodded.

"But," Kate went on, "can you do that? I mean, I know your folks aren't around, but you're an adult, so can you be adopted? And, anyway, isn't it all kind of incestuous?"

Em nodded and laughed. "I guess so! I'm looking for

10

another way, but this is the only thing I can think of where the three of us have something akin to similar legal and financial rights and responsibilities in the relationship." Em picked up her drink and added, "And, as it turns out, now that we've all moved in together we're already pretty close to breaking the law."

"What? How so?" Kate asked.

"Well, there's this weird thing in Vancouver where it's not legal for more than three unrelated adults to live together in a household. Technically, we could be prosecuted if anyone comes to stay in the spare room, not that that ever really happens. It's some hang-up from when people wanted to stop Mormons from engaging in polygamy. Now it's just kind of fucked up because it means most of the people we know who live in co-op, community-type situations are actually breaking the law without realising it."

"Man, that is messed up. I mean, I know some people used to adopt their partners, like, back in the fifties or whatever, but, jeez."

Em nodded again. "Well, when it comes to plural marriages, we're pretty much in the same position as those closeted queers. I'm hoping we'll have a commitment ceremony that's more, ah, normal, but legally I think this is the only way to be a family, unless this lawyer here tells me otherwise."

"What lawyer?" Kate asked.

"So, a triad got married here recently, and there's been a few poly marriages in Brazil, so there are some legal precedents being set. Most of the time though, it just seems to be that the existing law can be interpreted so as to avoid prosecuting consenting adults, but the marriage isn't actually legal."

"But why do you even want to be married?" Kate asked. "I didn't think you and Steve were the marrying types."

"Well, yeah, Steve and I were both pretty anti-marriage. I'd rather keep state involvement in my affairs to a minimum," Em said, laughing. "But, realistically, it's a pretty decent institution for granting certain rights and conveying a sense of commitment, and it's a way of showing people that the three of us are truly committed to each other." Em shrugged and added, "Also, who doesn't want an excuse to eat sugared almond favours and get all those tax breaks? Am I right?"

"Well, obvs." Kate furrowed her brow and asked, "Can't you just have some kind of legal document drawn up that states the nature of the magical three-way relationship and have a unicorn-themed blessing in a forest somewhere?"

"I've thought about it. And I do want that, especially the unicorns, but I think I want to do things in a way that is actually legal, you know? So I'm hoping to talk to this lawyer in a couple of days. She specializes in odd family formations."

"Oh, so you're not just here to visit me then?" Kate laughed.

"I'd have come anyway!" Em said, laughing, "Honestly! But it is convenient that this woman is here. I mean, Steve and Hanna obviously think nothing of me coming to visit you, but hopping a flight to Europe would otherwise give the game away, wouldn't it?"

"What do you mean?" Kate asked.

"It's all a bit short notice really, that's why I didn't let you know I was visiting. I only got in touch with this lawyer a couple of days ago and she agreed to see me right away."

"So Steve and Hanna don't know what you're planning?"

Em shook her head and sipped her beer. Kate whistled softly and then said, "Yikes. That'll be a surprise."

"I hope so!" Em said, then turned squarely to Kate and asked, "Am I completely bananas to think this will work?"

"Yes. But I love you anyway." Kate hugged Em and suggested that she escort her back to the hotel as Em looked absolutely exhausted.

THREE

Scout nudged her baseball cap up her head slightly and flicked her hand over her scalp to smooth her hair. She swung her leg over the top tube of her new fixie and pushed off, working her hard-earned muscles to capacity on the hill beside China Creek Park.

Ahead of Scout, Alice lurched from side to side as she climbed the hill on her own bike. The dark patch of sweat on the back of Alice's softball jersey crept outward with each revolution of the pedals in the warm spring air. It didn't take Scout long to catch up to Alice and, after checking behind her for cars, she passed the labouring cyclist. Scout whistled jauntily as she cruised by, hiding the fact that her lungs felt like they'd been doused in absinthe and set alight. She had no intention of letting Alice know that she, too, was suffering.

Alice sighed as Scout passed her, then yelled "Screw you, Scout!" and carried on grinding her way up the incline. Scout hoped that at least Alice was enjoying the view of her superior physique as she worked her legs hard up the hill.

Alice was new to the softball team that season, and Scout had watched with amusement as Alice's boyfriend

13

skulked on the sidelines at their first two games. Scout hadn't figured out if he was there as a security blanket or a security guard, but whenever Jeff was in attendance, Scout revelled in the awkwardness of her new teammate. Jeff hadn't been at the game today, but at the previous game Scout had made a point of jostling Alice's elbow and wrapping her arm around Alice's shoulders. She had drawn the line at slapping Alice's ass as she ran out to bat, but that didn't mean that she hadn't been tempted.

Scout's face had hurt a little from smirking so much as she noted Alice's frequent check-ins with Jeff, especially when Scout was apprising Alice of all the league gossip - who was hooking up with who, including which of their teammates and opposition Scout had slept with, as well as who she planned on adding to her conquests.

Jeff's absence at the game that night had given Scout the opportunity for more overt flirting with Alice. She figured she'd sow some lustful little seeds in the woman, in case they'd sprout given a few months of summer sun, and regular watering with growlers of craft beer. To Scout, Alice seemed like the quintessential wannabe bisexual, the lesbian in hiding, a queer tourist. Because Alice seemed so sweet and kind, Scout couldn't help but want to blow her mind and shake up her worldview. She probably wouldn't stick around after though: Scout had already become embroiled too many times with women new to relationships with other women, and was tired of the messiness of all the feelings that came with them.

As she pondered the reasons why she so frequently hooked up with formerly straight-identified women – what was she trying to prove? – Scout sailed along the 10th Avenue bikeway, took Ontario St. south, and squinted as the sun set, shooting pink light at her from the right. She cycled up onto the sidewalk and slowed to a stop outside her front gate. She dismounted and propped her bike up against the wire fence, then used both hands to lift the rusty metal gate so she could swing it open without scraping the concrete path leading to

14

her front door.

She had moved into the garden suite three months earlier and had made a point of asking the landlord to fix the gate, but he'd done nothing to help. Scout decided that tomorrow she would go on a hunt at one of the numerous nearby construction sites to see if she could find a piece of rebar to prop up the gate. That'd be an easier fix than the mold issue in the bathroom, or the little huddle of mushrooms that had sprouted from the living room carpet earlier in the week. Scout's new housemate, Afra, seemed to be stoned out of their tree much of the time, and Scout had realised there was little point relying on Afra to do anything. Scout hadn't bothered telling them about the fungus. Afra would probably want to cultivate the mushrooms and see if they were hallucinogenic.

Perhaps she should just move in with Janice, Scout thought. They'd been seeing each other for six months now - or fucking at least - and Janice had an amazing place that had plenty of space for the two of them. Aside from the obvious perils of UHauling, there were a couple of problems Scout could foresee, though.

Firstly, Janice had just acquired an enormous cat called Thunderpuss. Scout hated cats, which made the world of lesbian dating a difficult place to play. Cats seemed to hate Scout just as much as she disliked them, so she had learned to keep her distance, cooing faux adoration from afar while feigning allergies. Scout had learned to pretend to be upset that she couldn't pet all her lovers' animal friends. Some dogs were tolerable, but even they put her on edge, so she rarely stayed the night unless the only animals in the bedroom were human.

Aside from the enormous cat, the other problem Scout saw with moving into Janice's place was its location in the thick of Kitsilano. Scout's throat began to close at even the thought of living among the Lululemoners and shirtless generic buff dudes. She'd probably suffocate in the toxic gas cloud of heteronormativity that blanketed the neighbourhood. Still, to have consistent hot water, even flooring, and a house free from possible neurotoxins growing in the carpet, Scout could probably learn to tolerate the seven-dollar raw almond milk lattes and five dollar gluten-free, organic, vegan croissants. Janice would probably treat her to all of those things anyway.

Scout forced open the swollen front door of the garden suite, swung her bag off her shoulder, and called out over the disco music that was shaking the saucepans with its improperly elevated bass. "Afra, you home?"

Scout heard no reply, so she went to turn off the music; her gut threatening something truly unruly as she approached the vibrating speakers and their brown noise. Afra was either asleep, stoned, both, or out. They worked as a volunteer at WISH on Sunday nights, and Scout wondered if they would show up later with one of the women Scout had slept with or briefly dated last summer when she'd first arrived in the city. Scout hadn't volunteered at the centre, figuring she didn't have much to offer. Instead, she'd gone to the volunteer orientation session for Women in Sheltered Housing largely to pick up numbers from the cute social justice do-gooders who had managed to put down their women's studies books for an evening.

Scout had considered signing up for a shift or two, but her schedule had filled up with camping trips, brewery tours, hook-ups, and hangovers, and then her fall fling with Janice had taken flight. When Scout met Janice she had intended to avoid being the woman's immediate post-break-up rebound. Instead, her plan was to set things in motion so there would likely be a hook-up a few weeks or months later. Scout was used to playing the long game, happy to wait someone out while she kept herself occupied with other trifles.

When Janice took the initiative, Scout had been genuinely surprised and had enjoyed seeing the older woman explore the thrill of recklessness. The two of them had gone

16

on a bike ride to Lighthouse Park, setting off in glorious sunshine and returning in a downpour, sodden and chilled to the bone. Janice had insisted that Scout come up to her apartment to take a hot shower and warm up while she threw all their clothes in the dryer. The hot water quickly restored sensation to Scout's fingers and toes, and as she began investigating the variety of hair products, Janice interrupted her by pulling aside the curtain and stepping into the tub. Janice pushed her naked body up against Scout and pressed her lips to the surprised circle of Scout's mouth. Scout had considered turning things around and backing Janice up against the cold tile, assuming Janice wasn't a top, but Janice had slipped her thigh between Scout's legs and began exploring her new lover's body with a soapy, slippery, surprisingly expert hand.

Scout stayed over that night, and the next. Janice's apartment was free from animals then, and so they had fucked themselves into exhaustion, only stopping to eat and top up either their alcohol or caffeine levels. It was a holiday weekend, so Janice waited until Monday afternoon to kick Scout out. She had kissed Scout lightly on the lips and pushed her out the door into the cobbled courtyard with its Mediterranean style potted palms and terracotta fountains. Scout grinned all the way home, happy at how uncomplicated the weekend had been, and how Janice hadn't said anything about making plans to see each other again. They did, though, spending the next weekend together, and the weekend after. Soon they were spending almost every weekend together, mostly indoors, mostly naked, and mostly drunk or high.

Somehow, six months had gone by, with Scout leaving Janice's every Sunday night to cycle over to the softball games, flirt with Alice, and make sure to leave an impression on at least one member of the opposition team. Now softball season was coming to an end and Scout's easy conquests would dry up unless she switched scenes. This left Scout thinking that it might be wise to move in with Janice and have a ready and willing body at her fingertips whenever she wanted.

She hadn't seen Janice this weekend as she was at a meditation retreat in Tofino. Scout wondered if Janice had done some thinking about the direction of their relationship while she'd been on the retreat, and the thought left Scout feeling distressingly ambivalent.

Perhaps, Scout thought, she should send Janice a text mentioning the awfulness of the mushroom-infected hovel in which she lived, and how difficult it was to find a decent place that was affordable. She'd at least get the idea of cohabitation lodged in Janice's brain, in case of future need. But maybe she didn't really want someone around all the time, however good she was in bed. And maybe Janice would see cohabitation as a step towards marriage and kids.

Truth be told, Scout and Janice hadn't really talked about the nature of their relationship. They hadn't actually talked much at all. But Scout was enjoying the casual consistency and how little Janice demanded to be in Scout's everyday life. Janice had never once asked if Scout was seeing anyone else, and Scout wondered if that would change if they moved in together.

Scout was also curious to see if Alice would ditch Jeff. Maybe Alice would need to find a new place to live, and Scout could suggest they move in together. She could sell Alice on the idea that living with a renowned queermo, and pretty much UHauling out of a straight relationship, would be the perfect way to fully embrace her lady-loving tendencies.

Scout mused on other housing possibilities as she knocked on Afra's door. There was no answer, so she pushed the door open to see if Afra was asleep. With no sign of her housemate, Scout returned to the kitchen, grabbed a beer from the refrigerator and slumped into her favourite squishy armchair in the living room. She dug out the remote control from the side of the chair and settled in for some brainless visual stimuli. Half an hour later, Scout was dreaming about

18

sapphire earrings and a sparkling pendant as the ululating sounds of The Shopping Channel slithered across her synapses while she dozed.

FOUR

As Scout's mind filled with shiny sapphires, Janice's mind was awash with peaceful clarity. She had let go of the persistent roar of the bigger questions in her life, and the soft burble of her internal narrative, and allowed herself to concentrate only on the sound of her breath: in and out, in and out, until even that awareness fell away.

This inner peace persisted for about thirty seconds, as the inner turmoil of the man on the mat beside her resulted in a loud and noxious release of gas. Janice opened one eye and looked over at the man. She watched his long ponytail swing from side to side as he settled himself in lotus, never once opening his eyes. He resumed his centred, calm pose, but Janice saw the creeping flush of embarrassment spread up his neck and into his cheeks. She closed her eye and tried to regain her previous stillness, but she knew the session was almost at an end, and the soft, blanketing calm evaded her.

This was the final session of the weekend, and Janice began to think about the drive home. She was carpooling with two other women from Vancouver, and she wanted to set off as soon as possible so that they could make the reservation for the last ferry. She had no intention of staying over on the island: she'd even thought about flying instead of risking the ferry being overbooked. In the end, Janice had decided that the drive itself would be meditative. The idea of immediately getting on a busy plane after a weekend of silent contemplation had just seemed overwhelming.

Fortunately, her two travelling companions had turned out to be quiet, introverted types, so most of their drive to Tofino had been spent in silence. The three of them had only spoken to introduce themselves and to work out the necessary stops for food, bathroom breaks, and the switching of drivers.

Janice got the impression that Selena was an old hand at these kinds of retreats, entering a silent space as soon as she packed her bag. Hanna, meanwhile, seemed to Janice to have something heavy on her mind. Janice had noticed the glistening slink of tears down Hanna's cheeks in the workshop that morning. She had watched, unnerved as Hanna remained motionless and quiet: a weeping statue.

As Selena and Janice organised their cases in the trunk of Janice's car, Hanna dug her cellphone out of her bag and turned it on. A flurry of messages burst forth, breaking the quietude of the retreat. Hanna dialled her voicemail and held the phone to her ear as she waited in the back of the car. Janice could see Hanna's posture change. Her shoulders crept upward and in as she listened to her messages. Hanna sniffed and wiped at her eyes, and Janice felt compelled to break the unacknowledged rule of their road trip and ask if Hanna was OK.

"I just got some bad news about my girlfriend is all. I'll be fine. Thanks."

Selena, as if speaking from the pit of her stomach, bypassing her brain, asked, "Is your friend sick?"

Hanna turned to look at the older woman, her eyes narrowed and brow furrowed. "Yes. My girlfriend has breast cancer and her chemo has killed her immune system, and now

21

she has an infection and the medication has damaged her heart and so she's in intensive care. And I, ugh, I won't be able to see her."

"Why not?" Janice asked. "Can't they just gown you up and have you wear gloves and a mask?"

Hanna clenched her fists and pursed her lips, then said, "I'm not family."

"But you're her girlfriend? Doesn't that count?" Selena asked.

"But I'm only her girlfriend, not her partner. We're polyamorous. Her common-law partner, Steve, is allowed to see her, but I'm nothing to her, legally at least."

Selena frowned, opened her mouth to speak and then closed it again. She slammed the trunk shut and got into the front passenger seat. As she buckled her seatbelt, Selena turned to face Hanna and smiled, "I'm sorry that you're all going through this. If you ever want to talk, please reach out. I know it's not the same, but I've had friends who've faced cancer."

Hanna thanked Selena and asked how her friends were doing now. Selena paused and Hanna looked away. "I'm sorry. I shouldn't have asked," Hanna said.

As Janice got into the car, she noted Hanna's dark, shoulder-length hair, her cut-off white t-shirt, and her muscular arms. Janice put the key in the ignition and started the engine, breaking the silence thick with the thought of death. As she eased the car down the gravel driveway back to the road, Janice said, "Are you the drummer? The barista? Em's Hanna?"

Hanna laughed and nodded, meeting Janice's eyes in the rear-view mirror.

Selena laughed too, turning to look first at Janice, then at Hanna. "Oh Vangroovy. Such a small world for all us weirdoes."

FIVE

The small silver bells that hung above the door tinkled as Steve entered the flower shop. A tiny florist emerged from behind a tall stand of bamboo and foliage, and a fluffy, goofy schnoodle wandered over to sniff Steve's legs.

"Looking for anything in particular? For a special occasion?" The florist asked, smiling. "Flowers for a special lady, perhaps?"

Steve shook his head and couldn't help but grimace. The florist's expression changed to one of detached politeness.

Looking around, Steve's gaze settled on some tall brown stalks with heavy, tight seed heads. "Can you make up a bouquet with the millet, and some of those white tulips, please? No, wait, sorry. White is death. It means death. I should remember that. So, maybe the yellow. No! Wait. Sorry."

"Sir, are you OK?" The florist reached across the counter and patted Steve's hand. His hand looked like a child's compared to Steve's giant mitt. The florist's hand was also delicate and manicured; as small as Em's hand, but missing the now all too familiar catheter IV and visible veins running at the surface of the skin as if desperate to exude their toxic blood.

This little man surrounded by beautiful flowers didn't have a bunch of toxic chemicals flowing through his body, Steve thought. There was nothing poisoning his heart, taking him away from his loved ones in slow, agonising increments. Steve pulled his hand away and wiped at the tears that had gathered in his eyes.

"I'm fine. Sorry. If you could just wrap these up, that'll be good." Steve picked up five red gerberas and placed them on the counter.

The florist added in some foliage, "No charge, don't worry. I could add daffodils to that if you like?"

"No, thanks. How much is that?"

"Are you sure? How about I just put a couple of these in there?" The florist picked up three yellow daffodils from a pot on the counter.

"No, no, definitely not those. They're the cancer flower. They're too bright, too full of hope."

The florist pursed his lips and nodded, understanding now. He rang up the total and handed Steve the bouquet: the green and red made Steve think of Christmas. Em might never have another Christmas. These might be the last flowers she'd ever see, but she probably wouldn't even notice them, Steve thought, feeling his legs almost give out beneath him.

Steve felt that there was something significant in the fact that it was Em's heart that was giving up. Em had always loved so hard, so fully, and Steve felt guilty, not for the first time, as he wondered if he had taken too much from Em.

She was always so generous, putting everyone else first. These last few months had stripped her of that ability to give all of herself to him and Hanna, and to her friends. Since they had moved her to the ICU, Em had struggled even to keep her eyes open. She could barely maintain a smile; her muscles and her motivation were both failing her now, and Steve had

24

been so alone, with Hanna out of cellphone range.

After two days of not knowing what to expect, Steve felt like it was time to tell Em that he'd be OK, that she didn't have to keep expending her energy trying to make him believe it would all be fine. He should tell her that it was OK to let go, Steve thought, but he knew he wasn't ready. It wasn't OK, and he wasn't fine. Steve was already missing her and she was still right there in front of him, still breathing, for now.

He was grateful that Hanna would be home that evening, but even feeling happy about that seemed wrong somehow. They would probably sleep in separate beds tonight. He would feel too weird lying there together, without Em, like they were both cheating, even though it had been almost nine months since the three of them decided to be a triad, a tryout, or a trifecta as Em had called them the first time they had successfully squeezed into Em and Steve's queen-sized bed.

Steve thought about how he should talk to the nurses and see if they would let Hanna in to see Em. It would help lift Em's spirits.

Steve shook himself and wondered when his internal monologue had become so trite. Em's spirits didn't need lifting, he thought, she just needed to kick this cancer's butt and get back to being the badass they all knew she was.

The florist coughed quietly, waiting for Steve to leave. He had no idea how long he had been standing there, buried in his misery. Had he been talking out loud? He really needed to sleep, and to eat something, and to shower, Steve thought. He took a deep breath, thanked the florist, and nodded politely at the dog, who was now on the counter beside the daffodils.

After closing the door behind him, Steve hesitated for a moment and looked over toward the North Shore mountains. Would he and Em ever head out there together again? He tried to smile, to armour himself with a veneer of cheer for Em's sake. Turning away from the hazy mountains, Steve started walking up the hill to the hospital. Official visiting hours started in ten minutes, and although Em would probably be asleep, Steve could always hold her hand and listen to her breathing. He could rub her back if she felt nauseous, and try to get her to eat a little food. He prayed that a miracle had happened in the four hours he had spent away from the hospital trying to gather himself back together. Steve felt ready to abandon his atheism if it would help Em get better. He imagined standing beside Em, waving goodbye to Richard Dawkins, and he laughed, shocking himself with the noise. If Em were able to read my mind right now she would never let me get away with such irrationality, he thought.

When Steve arrived back at the ICU, he could see nurses running to and fro. He heard the faint sound of an alarm muffled by the glass doors. It was agony to have to wait to be let in, but there was no nurse at the desk and no one cared that Steve had lost all sensation in his hands, his arms, everywhere but his chest, where it felt as though his heart was a grenade, its pin removed.

Em, Steve thought, I need you to put the pin back in. I need you to survive.

Steve clutched at the flowers, crushing their stems. He wanted to hammer on the glass door. If he could just get to Em, maybe he could do something.

The nurses came back into view. One of them laughed, and the sound quietened Steve's heart temporarily. The alarm must have been inconsequential, a mistake perhaps, a loose wire, or a patient pushing their alert accidentally. He willed himself to remember that there were other patients in the ICU besides Em. He didn't need to panic every time an alarm sounded and people started running with crash carts, yelling instructions across the normally quiet ward.

A nurse spotted Steve and nodded, walking toward the panel to open the ICU door. Steve didn't recognise her and she had to ask for his name and who he was visiting.

26

"Oh, Steve, yes," the nurse said, checking a chart. "Emilie's doing better, she had a rough spell earlier, but I think she's napping now. The medication's making her sick, and the anti-nausea meds aren't really helping as much as we'd like. But her heart's on the mend it seems, now that we've switched her medications." She put down the chart and looked up at Steve. "Maybe you can get her to try to eat something. She really needs to get her strength back."

"I'll do my best. Thanks, erm..." Steve craned to see the nurse's name badge, while trying not stare at her chest.

"Alice. Nice to meet you. I'll be on duty until seven. I'm on the day shift for the rest of the week – seven to seven – so let me know if you need anything."

Steve thanked Alice and walked down the hall to Em's room. He was surprised to see her awake, and she smiled as he hid the flowers behind his back.

"I already saw them, you charmer. Come here and kiss my toxic mouth."

"Gladly," Steve said, and bent down to give her a smooch. Her lips were dry so Steve poured himself some water and filled her glass. He took a gulp of water and watched Em.

"I know what you're up to, my love. It won't work. I can't keep a thing down, not even water." Em smiled, wincing as her lips cracked.

"How about I get you some ice chips?" Steve suggested, and Em acquiesced.

As he headed down the hall, he passed Alice and she offered to get rid of the vase of dying orange gerbera Steve was holding. Steve asked if Alice would mind bringing some ice chips for Em and Alice smiled, "Sure. Back in a jiffy."

When Steve returned to Em's room he found her trying to get out of the bed to reach for another blanket.

"Hey! What the hell?! Get back in bed, right now!" He took her by the shoulders, feeling how thin the flesh was over her bones. He was scared he would break her: his hands

27

enormous against her shrunken body. Alice entered the room with a vase of fresh water and a cup of ice chips. She tutted at Em and pressed a button on the heart monitor to silence the frantic beeping. Taking hold of the extra blanket, Alice tucked Em back under the covers, then handed Steve the cup of ice chips. She checked various wires and monitors and then started to arrange the new flowers, distracting Em with chatter about the other patients, the nurses, something about a softball team she had just joined.

Em took the ice chips from Steve and held them in her mouth. He watched her face, seeing how her jaw set and relaxed, letting him know when she was ready for another one. All the while, Em was distracted by Alice's chatter, and Steve could see that Alice knew what she was doing.

Alice understood that Em needed to not be seen as just another sick person. She didn't need any more attention on the frailness of her body, or the potential for catastrophe with every breath, every slight cough. Alice kept herself busy, monitoring Em's ice chip intake without obviously watching her. Steve felt like they were silent conspirators, never making eye contact. He wondered whether Em was in on the conspiracy too; did she feel that some of her autonomy was being eroded in this transaction?

This whole experience has been one of Em losing herself, he thought, wondering how Em would come back from it, if she came back at all. She had literally lost pieces of herself, and was barely recognisable as Em, but still she smiled and teased him for trying to deceive and manipulate her. She was still his Em. She was still in charge.

Once the ice chips were almost gone, Alice reached into the pocket of her scrubs and handed Em a small pudding cup and a spoon.

"Don't tell anyone," she said quietly, "I took a patient's pudding. His family brought him a giant box of chocolates so we need to do something to keep his blood sugar in check."

Em struggled to peel back the cover of the pudding, but

28

neither Steve nor Alice moved to help her. Steve bit his lip and looked away, fighting the impulse to reach out. Em was not a child.

Steve distracted himself by asking Alice about softball. "Are you any good?"

"I'm getting better," Alice said, grinning. "It's been a while since I played!"

Steve laughed and said, "I hear you. It's been ages since I swung a bat. Same for Em." He looked at Em and saw that she was struggling to keep the pudding down. He moved to grab a bedpan in case she was sick, but she shook her head and glared at him. Steve's hand remained poised mid-air for a second. Then he lowered it and turned back to Alice, who had maintained her calm, giving Em space to figure out what she needed.

Steve decided that he would be a terrible nurse. Although, he thought, perhaps it's easier with people that you don't really know. Maybe you can keep that necessary distance then: that professional confidence and aura of efficient care that Alice exuded so completely. She was probably killer at softball, Steve thought; she would be the quiet storm that took the opposition by surprise.

Alice laughed as she said to Em, "Even if you've not played in a while, I imagine you'd still be a better softball player than me. It's taking me a while to find my feet." Alice laughed, and almost added something about how she was struggling to find her feet in a number of ways, but thought better of it.

Steve and Em smiled at Alice, and he saw that Em was now looking less panicky, the nausea having passed. Steve said, "Maybe when Em is better we can come watch you in action?"

"Yes!" Em cried, "And Hanna too." She looked over at Steve and then back at Alice. "Hanna is our girlfriend. We're poly. She's been out of town, but she's back tonight and will want to visit." Em took a breath and continued, "But now that I'm in the ICU, I'm worried she won't be allowed in to see me as she's not technically family, at least not in the way that fits on a hospital visitation form." Em reached out to take Steve's hand, and he smiled at her briefly before looking away and frowning. Just for a second, Steve felt a stab of jealousy, then anger at Hanna, and he struggled to work out why. He concentrated on the sensation of Em's hand in his and let the feelings wash through him and become clearer. What he was really worried about was that Em was expending energy on something other than getting better. She gave so much to look after everyone around her, Steve thought, that she was at risk of having nothing left to fight the cancer.

Alice, whose face was now a little flushed, looked at Steve, seemingly avoiding Em's gaze. She asked, "What's your, er, girlfriend's full name. I will see about adding her to the visitor list."

Em told Alice the name and thanked her, then turned to look at Steve, saying, "Can you call Hanna and let her know she might be able to visit? She'll be on her way back from the retreat now and will have got your messages. She'll be worrying about me."

Steve nodded and kissed Em's hand. "She's getting a ride with a couple of people from Vancouver and they're trying to make the last ferry back. So she probably won't make it tonight, but I'll call her."

Em took a deep, laboured breath and Steve could see her body relax. He felt angry that they had even had to worry about this. He could recognise now that he wasn't angry at Hanna, he was just tired of needing to fight so much, for all three of them. He thought back to the florist and how the man had been trying to offer some comfort that Steve just couldn't bring himself to accept. Steve knew that he needed to shake off the anger so he didn't risk losing both Em and himself.

Em was watching him and she said quietly, "We're doing OK, you know?"

30

Steve smiled at her, and tried to see himself as Em's quiet, gentle giant once again, rather than as some perpetually furious high-wire artist.

Alice was watching Steve now too, so he smiled at her and said, "Thanks again. I'll go talk to Hanna. I won't be long."

"I'm not going anywhere!" Em said, grinning. She turned to Alice and asked, "So softball, huh? What's your team name?" She wiggled her brow, bereft of eyebrows, and for a second Steve saw his Em again, the little bit of devilishness having lit her face up momentarily.

Alice grinned and blushed. "It's a bit embarrassing really."

She laughed and Em said, "Hey, my friend used to coach a team called the 'Headfirst Sliders', so it can't be worse than that."

Alice's eyes widened and she said, "Oh! That's my team!"

"No way! So… you're queer?" Em asked, grinning.

"Em, -" Steve started to say she shouldn't make assumptions, but really he was just anxious that Em was going to spend her evening distracting Alice from her work and trying to set her up with all their single queer friends rather than getting some rest.

Em shot him a look and said, "Steve, I know what you're thinking, but it's good to think about something fun for once." She turned to Alice again and asked, "So, is there anyone on the team you like? You are single, right?"

Alice laughed and said, "No, well, not really. I don't know. It's a bit complicated."

"It always is!" Em said. "But now you have to explain." Em looked over at Steve, who was making frustrated noises as he tried to locate his phone. She laughed and pointed towards Steve's jacket, which he had thrown over the side of a chair.

"OK. OK. Now I am really going to go and call Hanna," Steve said, retrieving his phone from his jacket pocket.

31

"I'm not promising anything, but I'll see if I can make up a couple of cots so the three of you can all stay in here tonight," Alice said and Em's eyes shone. "I'll have to check with your doctor, but I reckon I can swing it. You're doing so much better now we've taken you off the medication that was affecting your heart. Like Dr. Chan said earlier, you'll probably be back on a normal ward tomorrow anyway."

"That'd be amazing," Em said. "Thank you!"

"No problem. I'm a firm believer in the healing power of happiness. Being surrounded by love is the best medicine in my book, Emilie. Well, that and actual medicine," Alice said, and she patted Steve's arm as she walked by him at the door to Em's room.

Em shouted after her, "Call me Em! And don't think you can dodge my questions that easily!" She began to cough and Steve took a step back into the room towards Em. She waved her hand at him and took a few shallow breaths and then said, "I'm fine. I forgot my limitations for a second, but I'm fine now."

Steve smiled at her. "My pragmatic little peony," he said. "I love you."

"I love you too. Now, go ring our girlfriend, and tell her I love her too, will ya, you big galumph."

SIX

Scout slid onto the barstool beside Afra and her housemate yelled to their friend behind the bar to get them another round of beers.

"Took your time in the washroom there, Scout. Run into an old friend and indulge in a long reunion?"

Scout cuffed Afra lightly across the back of the head and said, "No. I was just, you know, adjusting." She looked down at her crotch to check that her RodeoH shorts were still holding her soft-pack as intended.

Afra laughed and said, "Oh, you're having a boy day today, huh?"

Scout scowled and picked up her glass, downing the last inch of flat, warm liquid. She had been nursing the beer for about an hour, waiting for Afra to arrive so that her housemate would buy her another. Scout hadn't had any shifts at the store that week and Janice's absence over the weekend meant she had drained her bank balance to buy booze and burritos for dates. The essentials. Oh, and a new bow-tie, because it had beavers on it. It would be cheaper, thought Scout, if she just shacked up with Janice. Scout caught the eye of the petite blond woman at the other end of the bar and reassessed, again. Perhaps the price of cohabitation was just too high.

The blonde woman held Scout's gaze for a second, then turned to her friend to say something. They laughed and the woman finished her drink, stepped down from her stool, and made her way over to Scout.

"Hey," she said, and Scout raised her a hey and an eyebrow. The blonde laughed, her cheeks a little flushed from what Scout presumed was shyness rather than from the cocktail she just finished.

"You don't remember me, do you?" the woman asked.

Scout looked at her again and slowly shook her head. "Sorry sweetheart. If we'd met before, I'm sure I'd not have forgotten a babe like you."

The woman laughed and looked at her feet for half a second. When she looked back up into Scout's eyes she hesitated, struggling to extract a memory from some murky, alcohol-sodden vault. "We hooked up last winter," the blonde said, and Scout laughed and shrugged.

"Sorry," Scout said. "I really don't think I'd have forgotten you."

"I'm Amanda. I work at SFU?" The rise in her inflection was cute, Scout decided, and she wondered if she should go along with the story. It wouldn't be difficult to pretend that she was just toying with Amanda, and that of course she remembered her. Scout opted for the honest approach, though, deciding it was all too easy to get caught in a lie and have the drama just snowball.

"Sorry, Amanda. You seem super awesome and all, but I wasn't here last winter. I only moved to Vancouver nine months ago, so we've not had the pleasure of meeting, until now." Scout put out her hand, and Amanda took it, thoroughly scrutinising Scout's face.

"Are you serious? So, all this time I've been seeing you around and you weren't even you?"

34

Scout laughed and said, "I've always been me. But, yeah, I guess I'm not the me you think I am."

Afra guffawed loudly, so Scout introduced them to Amanda.

"Hey, Afra. I use they/them pronouns." Amanda looked a little taken aback, and Afra said, "I just find it easier to get that out up front, so you have no reason to misgender me."

Amanda looked even more shocked for a second, then recovered herself and put out her hand to shake Afra's. "Amanda. She/her, I guess. Not that I've ever really thought about it."

Afra smiled and shook Amanda's hand, then whispered to Scout, "And therein lies the privilege," as Amanda turned to look over at her friend.

Scout rolled her eyes at Afra, then looked back at Amanda and asked, "So who did you think I was? And, hey," she lowered her voice to a sultry whisper, "was the other me good?"

Amanda's face grew even more flushed and she nodded, "Um, yeah, actually." Amanda bit her lip, as Scout patted the empty seat at the bar.

After Amanda sat down beside her, Scout gestured to the bartender for another round of drinks and said, "Well, I guess my doppelganger's loss is my gain. Pretty sure you won't get me mixed up with her again though, not after tonight."

Amanda laughed and Afra groaned. "Seriously dude, how does this shit work for you?"

"Watch and learn my friend, watch and learn," Scout said, and turned to Amanda, who was waving her friend over. "Maybe it's your lucky night too," Scout whispered to Afra.

SEVEN

As they drove along Alberni Highway from Tofino to Nanaimo, Selena asked Janice if they had time for a quick stop at Cathedral Grove.

"The light in the Douglas firs will be just magical right now, and I'd love to get my camera out."

Janice checked the time, then turned to Hanna to see if she was OK with stopping for a few minutes.

"Sure. We've got plenty of time to make the ferry." Hanna looked out the window as they passed by the exit to Loon Lake and then approached MacMillan Provincial Park. It quickly became clear why the locals had taken to calling the place Cathedral Grove. The ancient stands of Douglas firs rose high up into the sky, creating a natural shrine.

Janice found a parking spot and pulled in just as Hanna's phone rang. Hanna answered the call as she got out of the car, then gestured to Janice and Selena to say she'd meet them back at the car in ten minutes. She set off down the trail at a quick march and Janice heard her asking Steve how Em was doing.

In the two hours it took to drive from Tofino to

Cathedral Grove, Hanna had filled Janice in on Em's diagnosis, her decision to undergo a double mastectomy to fight the aggressive cancer, and how tired and sick Em had been with the chemotherapy. Em's last chemotherapy session had been the previous week, and she had insisted that Hanna go on the retreat to have some time to herself after months of caregiving.

It was probably a good thing, Janice thought, that Hanna had been out of cellphone range when Em got taken into the ICU. That way, she had actually had a couple of days of silent meditation while under the impression Em was getting better.

Janice hoped that Steve was calling with good news about Em. It had obviously been a horrible shock for Hanna to get his messages once she had cell service again.

After Janice had realised who Hanna was, she had begun to wonder about Kate, Em's best friend. Kate was Janice's ex, and the last Janice had heard, Kate had relocated to Amsterdam for work. If Em was this sick, Janice assumed that Kate would have returned from Europe, and she was a bit surprised not to have heard from her. Maybe she shouldn't be that surprised though, Janice thought, realising that she hadn't spoken to Kate in months, not since Kate had broken things off with her after a brief fling when she first got back to Vancouver after travelling.

Janice and Kate hadn't exactly parted as friends. Initially, Janice hadn't felt too shaken up about the break-up; they had only been seeing each other again for a few weeks and their real break-up had happened almost two years before they hooked up for a second time.

The first break-up had been Janice's doing. She had desperately needed to shake herself out of the rut they had co-created over eight years together, so she split up with Kate and went travelling for a year. She returned to Vancouver with the idea that she had grown, that she was more spontaneous and better able to handle whatever life threw at her. Then, when Kate left for Europe, Janice had suddenly felt the finality of the break-up truly hit her. She realised that this was because, for the first time in a long time, Kate had made a significant life choice without even talking things over with her. Kate had left for Europe, and Janice was left to face the reality that she was no longer an important person in Kate's life. Despite having been away for a year, and having broken up again, Janice had just assumed that she and Kate would always be connected in some essential way, that they would always have some kind of special insight into how the other was feeling.

Then Janice had heard through the East Van queer grapevine that Kate had chosen to go to Europe in part to follow a woman, and she knew that she would never have inspired that passion in Kate. She had never prompted Kate to do anything remotely reckless or risky, and that left Janice with the sense that all the enlightenment and serenity she had stuffed into her backpack while travelling had simply evaporated. She felt adrift, unloved, unnecessary, and thoroughly uninspiring. That's when Janice had started going on these meditation retreats. She wondered if she would ever be like Selena, whose inner calm seemed unshakeable, despite the fact that she'd been fighting with the zip on her camera case for at least a minute.

A loud unzipping heralded success and Selena extracted her camera and hung it around her neck. She smiled at Janice and nodded toward the trail. As Janice followed Selena along the forest path, she tried to concentrate on the golden light filtering through the tall trees. She tried to see the light the way she thought Selena must see it, through the lens of her camera, capturing each moment. Selena told her that the Japanese had a word - komorebi – for this dance of sunlight through leaves and trees. She took a moment to appreciate the richness of the red ribs of the ancient cedars, and the dark contrast where the falling light had already crept away. Janice tried to get back to the warm, peaceful contentment she had felt earlier that weekend at the retreat, but she couldn't empty her mind of thoughts of Em, lying in a bed in the hospital.

Janice had never really been all that close to Em, but their shared love of Kate meant that they had spent a lot of time together. Most of their mutual friends had simply become Kate's friends by default when Janice left the city. She had made no claims to those bonds of friendship, and hadn't missed them while away. The queer scene hadn't really been her thing anyway, but Kate had provided a useful link to the community and so, upon her return to Vancouver, Janice had felt a little removed from her peers. It seemed like even in those ten or eleven months things had shifted slightly. It had been hard to decide if the queer scene had changed, or if Janice just saw things differently, now that she was single. She had made a point of spending time alone for a couple of months after Kate left, not wanting reflexive loneliness to prompt a desperate fling that only served to consolidate her inability to be at peace alone. After that, Janice had gone on a few dates with people she had met online, only to discover that those women saw her as a good option for marriage and kids and a quiet townhouse life. Between her early twenties, when she met Kate, and now, she had moved into a different dating pool, and she wasn't at all sure she was comfortable there.

As Janice tried to reconcile herself to being marriage material, she ran into Scout, literally. Janice was waiting in line for beer at 33 Acres, reading the list of beer names with amusement, when Scout turned away from the bar with a growler full of Life and bumped straight into Janice, almost knocking her off her feet. Scout reached out a hand and grabbed Janice's flailing arm, then grinned at Janice with such mischief that she figured Scout couldn't possibly want to UHaul. Scout didn't seem the type to start discussing potential sperm donors on a first date. So, although it was entirely out of character for Janice, she gave Scout her card and told her to call sometime. Scout took her card, gestured at the label on the growler Janice was about to get filled, and said, "You got it, Sunshine."

A week went by and Scout hadn't been in touch. Janice figured that this super hot, beer-toting queer hadn't given her a second thought, but then she got a text to say that there was a beach party and that she should come. It suddenly seemed perfect that Scout hadn't called right away, and that she hadn't invited her on a straightforward dinner date. It was just a party, with Scout's friends. Of course she should go. So Janice had made the effort to shake off the feeling that she should be in bed by ten and had cycled down to the beach with a six-pack and a mickey of whisky. She followed the glow of the fire and the sound of laughter and found a dozen twenty-somethings smoking and drinking and fiddling with various instruments. She didn't recognize anyone other than Scout, and it felt good to have no connection to these people, to be able to form her own opinion of them. After a couple of beers, she picked up the guitar and shakily played *Rocket Man*, with everyone singing drunkenly along.

Janice felt that sense of serenity and enlightenment creeping back into her as she sat between Scout and Afra. Scout was having a long conversation with the woman next to her and as Janice and Afra talked, Janice discovered that Afra had just gotten a job with the Queer Arts Festival. They revealed a few secrets about the upcoming festival programme and Afra told Janice she should volunteer. It was a great way to meet people, Afra said and Janice laughed as they told her how Scout had signed up to volunteer everywhere when she'd first arrived in Vancouver, figuring it was a great way to find easy hook-ups as well as a job.

Janice turned her attention back to Scout, but before she could say anything, Scout got to her feet and walked over to help a guy build a sandcastle using Mason jars. Janice was glad she had cans of beer, and made a mental note not to accept drinks from jars for the rest of the evening.

Someone from across the circle stumbled into the growing sandcastle, and Scout pretended to throw down,
40

then hugged her friend and disappeared into the trees to pee. In her absence, another woman joined the party and sat in the space beside Janice. When Scout returned to the circle she found a spot across from Janice. This gave Janice the perfect vantage point to spend the rest of the night watching Scout flirt with the women on either side of her. By midnight there was a clear winner, with Scout now completely ignoring one woman as she made out with the other. She had only looked at Janice once, raising her glass and smiling before resuming her flirting.

Janice talked to a couple of students about their grad school applications, promised to look up a Kickstarter campaign for a local bike co-op, and spent a while discussing with Afra the difference between narcissism and radical self-care. One of the guitars ended up back with Janice at around one in the morning and so she played one more song and then handed the instrument to the woman beside her, who claimed to be a folk musician, but whose talent seemed to have been drowned in cheap wine.

Janice donated her remaining cans of beer to Afra and zipped up her backpack. She looked across the circle and saw Scout pour out the last of a growler for her new friend. As she screwed the growler cap back on, Scout glanced up at Janice, looked at the woman beside her, and then turned back to Janice with a grin and a shrug of her shoulders. Janice laughed, waved goodbye, and went to retrieve her bike from the railing at the top of the steps. She had no illusions about Scout inviting her to another party, but it had been a fun evening anyway, and Janice had enjoyed talking to Afra. She was even considering volunteering for the QAF.

When Scout called Janice the following Saturday to see if she wanted to go for a bike ride, Janice was surprised, but happy. It was a beautifully bright day, with only a few tiny white clouds hanging in the sky, so Janice suggested they cycle across the Lion's Gate Bridge and over to Lighthouse Park. When they got to the park, they locked up their bikes and headed through the trees to sit on the rocks looking out towards Bowen Island. They ate a couple of granola bars that Scout had brought, and watched the sky growing darker to the west.

The wind picked up and Scout jostled Janice's shoulder and opened her eyes wide. "We're going to get pretty wet!" Scout said, grinning. She raised her hands to the sky as the first drops of rain fell, then they rushed back to their bikes and tried to out-cycle the rain.

The downpour caught up with them as they raced through downtown, and Janice had taken the opportunity to get Scout back to her place to dry off and wait out the storm. As Scout warmed up in the shower, Janice lingered outside the bathroom door. Scout seemed uncomplicated, unfettered by questions about wedding venues and baby names. Janice figured there was no danger of an actual relationship. Scout wouldn't get invested in Janice, she wouldn't want anything from her. Scout was nothing like Kate, and to Scout, Janice was not just Kate's ex.

Janice quietly opened the bathroom door, stripped off her wet clothes and reached through the steam to pull aside the shower curtain. She barely knew anything about Scout, but Janice felt pretty sure that there would be no entanglement here, no messy break-up or hurt feelings. It could just be sex.

Of course, Janice rationalised afterward, Scout knew nothing about her either, not really. Janice figured that either Scout wasn't very discerning, or she liked what she saw. The next weekend Janice called Scout to see if she wanted to come over, and they soon established a weekend routine. Weekdays didn't work for Janice, and that seemed to be fine with Scout. Janice had no time for hangovers during the week, and she needed her sleep too much to stay up all night having sex. Things were working out well. Everything was simple. The sex was fantastic, and Scout hadn't even mentioned leaving a toothbrush at Janice's place. For the most part, Scout didn't bother Janice between hook-ups, and they had not labelled whatever was happening between them, despite having spent almost every weekend together for the past few months. Aside from going to a handful of house parties thrown by Scout's friends, they had done nothing even remotely couply, instead spending most weekends in bed.

It all seemed delightfully easy and uncomplicated, and Janice realised, not without a degree of pride, that she hadn't thought about Scout at all this weekend. She was only now thinking about her lover because her mind had turned to Kate, and how acutely she had felt Kate's absence from her life just before meeting Scout. Now Janice felt happily single, and she let this idea settle for a few minutes. The feeling wrapped itself around her, as warming as the last rays of sunlight stretching through the trees. Janice closed her eyes and focused on the sweet smell of hemlock spruce. She let the whispering sound of the wind through the needles rush toward her ears, and then opened her eyes to see Selena taking her photograph and smiling beatifically.

EIGHT

The softball cut through the air, its parabola sending it directly toward Alice's nose. She braced her torso and swung out. The crack of the bat sent tremors through her ulnar nerve, and Alice's jaw dropped as the ball sailed away from her over the field. She was sure it would drop and be caught, but the ball just kept going until it had outstripped the farthest catcher.

"Run, idiot!"

Scout's yell drew Alice back into her body and she took off to first base, kicking up dust and gravel and loving the feeling as her ligaments strained with every stride, pulling her closer to home. She was about to reach third when the ball whizzed over her head, almost grazing her scalp, but the woman at the base fumbled and Alice looked to the bleachers to see Scout waving her home. She thought about sliding safe with panache, but just ran straight through and was ecstatic as her teammates slapped her on the back. Scout offered up a palm and Alice slapped it hard, enjoying the sound and the look on Scout's face.

"Yuhhh!" she yelled, "C'mon!"

Scout lowered her head and shook it, arms out, all the while laughing at Alice. "What the hell, dude? When did you become such a bro!?"

Alice swaggered, still feeling the adrenaline. "I'm certainly not a bro, but perhaps there is more to me than you think." She wiggled both eyebrows to make Scout laugh again. The sound was extremely pleasing to Alice. Scout's laughter burbled up from some locked down place that Alice wagered normally only released a calculated amount of mirth.

"You're up," Alice said, and put out a hand to pull Scout up off the bench. She was tempted to slap Scout on the ass as she walked toward the diamond, but Alice was relieved to miss her chance as the adrenaline was starting to subside.

She sat down and looked over to see if Jeff had arrived. She couldn't see him, and assumed he was still at the hospital. Her mother had warned her about dating a med. student, but Jeff had charmed her anyway. With thirty years of nursing under her belt, Alice's mom had a lot of reasons to dislike doctors. Fortunately for Alice, Jeff had also charmed her mom, and after three years together, he was like the son she'd never had. The question of them getting married had come up more than once in these past few weeks, and Alice suspected Jeff was planning something. She hadn't yet worked out if the intense knot in her stomach was excitement or apprehension.

Jeff was due to graduate in a few months, and Alice knew that he might not get matched to Vancouver. They had talked in loose terms about what that meant for them. Alice had grown up here, had trained here. Her family and friends were all in the city, and she couldn't imagine being some wife-sized luggage that Jeff simply packed up and lugged across to the other side of the country. Alice especially didn't relish the idea of being stuck in a smaller city where there was nothing even approaching Vancouver's queer scene. She had only just begun to question her sexuality: how would she explore that if they lived somewhere more conservative?

She turned her attention back to the game in time to see Scout scuffing her shoe into the dirt and spitting on the ground. Somehow, the gesture was charming rather than disgusting. Alice drummed her fingers on her thigh and looked anywhere other than at Scout. When the connection was made between bat and ball however, Alice's eyes were immediately drawn back to Scout as she tore around each base, finally sliding safe at third and shaking her head as she got to her feet. She looked over at the bench, caught Alice's eye, and shrugged, palms upward. Alice made a silent promise to herself that she wouldn't be charmed by Scout.

When the game was over, one of their teammates suggested beers and burgers at the Whip. Jeff still hadn't arrived, so Alice sent him a text to let him know where she'd be and that he was welcome to join when he was finally released from his shift.

Scout arrived at the bar first, closely followed by Alice and then Drew, the coach. As Drew put some money in the parking meter, Alice locked up her bike. Scout made her way inside to talk to one of the servers, a friend, to see if she could get them a patio table. Drew watched Alice watching Scout and she whistled quietly. When Alice looked her way, Drew shook her head and said, "Don't go there. Trust me. Women like that are trouble."

Alice laughed and asked, "How would you know?"

"Oh, I can just tell. I've seen plenty of players like that in my time."

Alice assured Drew that she had no intention of giving in to Scout's overtures.

"See that you don't. Turns out that you're a pretty good hitter, and I wouldn't want to lose you to some trifling little hookup and heartbreak."

Scout had commandeered part of the patio and so Alice and Drew stepped over the barrier and took a seat.

"I ordered us a pitcher," Scout said, "and some shots."

Drew rolled her eyes and looked pointedly at Alice, who said, "I've got the seven A.M. shift tomorrow, so I need to be in bed early."

Scout put her hand over Alice's and grinned, saying, "That can be arranged."

A couple more of their players rolled by on their bikes and then clambered over to join them, just in time for the arrival of the beer and a tray of shots.

"Did you break the bank, Scout?" Drew asked, "Or are you expecting this to come out of league dues?" She grasped the handle of the pitcher and began pouring the beers. "Because, let me tell you, I'm not picking up the tab this time. Not like at Strangefellows. I almost had to wash the dishes to clear that bill."

Scout said she had it covered, "But, just so you know, our server is a little spaghetti, so you can probably flirt your way to clearing any outstanding bill."

"Not my type. But yours, or so it seems," Drew said, glancing over at Alice. Scout feigned innocence and raised her glass.

"To girls who are straight until hot and wet!" Scout cried, eliciting groans from her teammates.

After two beers and two shots of tequila, Alice slipped Drew some cash and took her leave. She checked her phone again to see if Jeff had been in touch, but there was no message. As she leaned down to unlock her bike, she felt the tequila battling with the fries she'd eaten, and she knew she would need to drink a lot of water when she got home. The dehydration from the game, the alcohol, and the greasy and insubstantial food would all conspire to make her a poor bedfellow tonight.

A car horn caused Alice to look up quickly, and her unsecured bike helmet shot off the back of her head. It crashed to the floor and Alice felt a surge of annoyance. She'd have to find time to buy a new helmet now. She scanned to see which irksome driver had just cost her thirty bucks, and saw Jeff grinning at her from the truck. He leaned out of the window, and called over, "Hey pretty lady, need a ride?"

Alice saw that he was holding up traffic, so she waved at him to park. As she pushed her bike back past the Whip and her carousing teammates, Alice heard someone wolf whistle. Scout stood and saluted her, while Drew tried to pull her back down into her seat.

"Have a good night, Alice!" Drew called, clipping Scout gently around the back of her head, feeling the softness of the recent buzz cut under her palm. Drew poured herself another beer and stuffed a handful of fries into her mouth.

Jeff was standing by the truck waiting for Alice. He lifted her bike in and opened the passenger door for her. "You'll need a new helmet. Sorry," he said, and shut the door while grinning.

Alice poked her head out of the open window and pointed at her lips, "Apology kiss?"

"Happy to oblige," Jeff said, and kissed Alice's forehead.

"Hey!" Alice tried to bat at his arm but he had already backed away and was walking around to the driver's side.

As they drove back to their apartment just west of Cambie, Jeff told Alice about a woman he'd been asked to check on just before his shift was due to end. Alice listened contentedly as Jeff went over every detail of the last few hours, his initial impressions, the tests he'd ordered, the confusing results and the patient's increasingly bizarre behaviour. She knew that he was processing and filing away useful information, not just telling her a story. Happily, he and another doctor had figured out that the woman was having a bad reaction to some diet pills she'd bought online.

"It was only because Carl's taken speed himself that he recognised her symptoms. I didn't have a clue. I thought she was having a psychotic episode," Jeff said.

"You're so straight-edge. So well behaved," Alice laughed and squeezed his thigh.

"I think I might like this softball thing you've got going," Jeff said, sneaking a kiss as they waited at a stoplight. "Running around with a bunch of lesbians obviously gets you excited."

"Jeff..." Alice said, wary of where the conversation was heading. She knew that she was at a disadvantage, given the drinks she'd had, and she was also fully aware of her need to get adequate sleep before work tomorrow.

"I'm serious," Jeff said, kissing her again. "I think it's great that you're hanging out with people who are, well, batting for the same team." He laughed, and slapped his thigh.

"You really do amuse yourself don't you?" Alice said, grinning. "Anyway, I'm more of an equal opportunities batter. It does seem like most of my teammates are gay, though, maybe a few are even gold-stars."

"Gold-stars?"

"Women who have only ever slept with women."

"Oh," Jeff said. "So what does that make you?"

"The bi dipper?"

Jeff guffawed and Alice grinned at her joke.

"Well, you're my favourite constellation, Alice Peterson," Jeff said. He was silent for a moment, before asking, "Do you think if, you know, someday we, um, got married, if you would want to change your name?"

Alice stared at him, her eyes wide. She bit her lip. "Honestly, I'm not sure I want to be Nurse Ratchett."

"Ha! I hadn't even thought about that! Totally. Unless you got a transfer to be in charge of the Psych. Ward. Then it could work in your favour."

"Please, don't even joke about that. I'm happy in ICU. Although I guess it's all contingent on CARMS." Alice sighed, and Jeff took her hand as he brought the truck to a stop outside their building.

"We'll figure that out when it's time. Together. OK?"

"OK." Alice kissed him and said, "Now take me to bed, Dr. Ratchett."

NINE

Scout stepped out of the bath and snatched at the towel proffered by Janice, who was sitting on the toilet painting her toenails with red glitter polish. Scout wiped her eyes and then rubbed her hair vigorously, spraying water around the room. Putting down the bottle of polish, Janice looked up at Scout and frowned. Scout met her eye, said nothing, and walked out of the bathroom with the towel around her shoulders.

"Don't just leave the towel on the floor this time," Janice yelled after Scout. When there was no response, Janice muttered, "Yes, mom," to herself and then blew on her last painted toenail and twisted the top back onto the bottle of polish.

Scout yelled from the other room, "What time is our dinner reservation?"

Janice walked carefully out of the bathroom, toe-spreaders still in place, and joined Scout in her bedroom. Thunderpuss, Em's enormous cat, who Janice was looking after temporarily, was sitting licking himself enthusiastically on the towel Scout had dropped on the floor. Janice sighed and said, "7.30, so we need to leave in half an hour." She watched Scout wrap the binder around her chest and start to pin it in place. Reaching out, Janice asked, "Can I help?" but Scout quickly turned away and said no. "Doesn't it hurt?"

"What?"

"You know, compressing your boobs like that. Do you do it every day? Isn't it bad for you?"

"No."

"Only, I read that..."

Scout turned to glare at Janice. "What? What did you read about my body?"

"Not about your body, just about how there's a link between breast trauma and breast cancer." Janice smiled a thin smile and Scout's expression softened.

She walked over to Janice and hugged her. "I'm not going to get breast cancer like Em."

"You can't know that," Janice said. "You're so..."

"Young?" Scout laughed. "Yes. Yes, I am young, and you are ancient, but I am not going to give myself breast cancer by binding every now and again. OK? And Em got breast cancer even without binding. Now let's go and drink some beer and eat some food that might give us cancer. Deal?" Scout took Janice's hand and dragged her out of the bedroom, the toe-spacers throwing off Janice's gait.

"You think you're invincible, don't you?" Janice said, laughing.

"Nope. I just think I can roll with the punches, so I don't sweat it."

"I should try that sometime," Janice said, smiling.

"They don't teach you a 'roll with the punches' meditation at those retreats? I'd ask for a refund." Scout pulled on her shirt, which had been thrown across the back of the couch a couple of hours earlier, shortly after she had arrived at Janice's apartment. "Where did my pants go?" Scout crouched down to look under the couch and tugged on a pant leg, only to have Thunderpuss come crashing out, hissing in Scout's face. "Sweet Jesus! How long will that animal be

51

here?" Scout screamed.

"Until he can go home," Janice said. "I thought you liked him?"

"Sure, sure. Cats are great." Scout pulled on her pants and jumped as she tugged the skinny jeans up her thighs. All the cycling up hills this summer had built up her muscles. Her prairie pants might need updating, she thought.

"Actually," Janice said as she stepped carefully over to the couch, "I thought I might go to VOKRA once Thunderpuss goes back to Em and Steve."

"To where?" Scout asked, puzzled.

"To adopt a cat, or kittens maybe. VOKRA is a kitty adoption agency." Janice smiled and Scout waited for her to ask what she thought about adopting kittens together.

After a couple of seconds, Scout said, "Oh. Great." She wondered if she had misread the situation. Perhaps Janice had no intention of asking her to move into the apartment, or even of making this a lasting relationship. To test the waters, she said, "It's just, my allergies, you know?" She rubbed her eyes and nose and sniffed a little.

"Yes. I forgot. Well, if I do, I'll be sure to have antihistamines on hand for guests!" Janice laughed and bent down to pick up her dress from the armchair. "I'll just go and get changed, and then we're ready to go, right?" Janice didn't wait for an answer, and Scout sat down on the couch to lace up her shoes. She didn't feel at all hungry, and even if she was famished, she wouldn't have wanted to go for dinner with Janice now.

Scout walked past the bedroom to the front door of the apartment and called to Janice, "I'm not really up for dinner. I'll see you next weekend, alright?" She unlocked the door and was about to leave when Janice stepped into the hallway, half dressed.

"What's up?" Janice said, pulling the straps of the dress over her shoulders and adjusting her bra. She turned her back to Scout and asked to be zipped up. Scout let the door go and obliged, but said nothing.

"Scout? What's wrong? Did I say something wrong?" Janice peered at her, hands on hips.

"I'm just not stoked about having dinner at some fancy restaurant is all. I mean, it's not like we're dating, so why do I need to do the girlfriend thing, right?"

"We're not dating?" Janice said, bemused. "Do you want to date me?"

"Don't laugh at me," Scout said. Janice tried to stop smiling, but she was rather enjoying the situation.

"What do you want from me Scout?" Janice asked, not unkindly.

Scout dropped her bag to the floor and leaned against the wall. "I don't know. I guess it just kind of sucks to hear you talking about the future as if I'm obviously not going to be part of it. I like..." she gestured at the space between them, "this. Don't you?"

"I do. But I thought it was pretty clear we were just fucking. I mean, you're seeing other people, I'm seeing other people."

"Are you?"

"Well, no, but I would be if I had time." Janice smiled. "I don't think we're really cut out to date each other. We're pretty different, and, honestly, you are quite a bit younger than me."

"I'm 24, it's only 7 years."

"It's a big 7 years. A lot happens in those years." Janice reached out for Scout's hand.

"What, like you get wise and shit?" Scout frowned. "I'm pretty fucking wise, Janice, given the crap I've been through."

"Yeah, a real wise-ass," Janice said, "going through all those terrible experiences with all those women whose hearts you've broken."

Scout gaped at Janice and then said quietly, "You really don't know anything about me, do you? Except that I'm a good lay and not up to much else."

53

Janice took a breath and held out her hands again, saying, "I'm sorry. You're right. I don't really know much about you, but I do think you're more than just a good lover."

"Do you want to know more? Or is that where your interest begins and ends?"

Janice seriously considered this for a few seconds. "Honestly, I don't know. I got into this because it seemed simple, and that's what I needed after everything with Kate. Now, I guess things are different, but I just haven't really paid much attention to the idea of a relationship." She narrowed her gaze and asked again, "Seriously, do you want to date me? Because," she held up her hand to stop Scout interrupting, "because if you do, I'll seriously think about whether or not I am ready to date, and whether or not I am ready to date you."

Scout looked up at the ceiling and said, "Wow." She picked up her bag and opened the door again. Turning back to Janice, she looked her straight in the eye and said again, "Wow. What a charming invitation. Take care Janice."

"Hey!" Janice called after her, "Scout! C'mon!"

Scout crossed the courtyard without looking back, and Janice realised she was not only going to miss her reservation, she had totally lost her appetite.

TEN

"What's up with you today?" Alice asked Scout, while wiping mud from her sneakers. "You haven't flirted with me even a little."

Scout looked up at Alice and then leaned forward, propping her elbows on her knees and resting her head in her hands.

"Are you sick?" Alice asked.

"No," Scout said. "Just sick of people."

"Wow. Um, OK." Alice laughed a little and watched as the other team walked towards them across the field. "Any particular people you're sick of?"

Scout was quiet. Then she stood up and started stretching out her hamstrings. Alice waited for a response.

"I broke up with someone," Scout said quietly. Then, in an even quieter voice, she added, "I think."

"I didn't know you were seeing someone," Alice said. "At least, not seriously."

"Neither did she," Scout laughed. "That was the problem."

"So, what, you were dating casually and you thought it

was going somewhere?" Alice grinned, "Going deep, perhaps?"

Scout rolled her eyes and said, "To extend your metaphor, yes, I thought that maybe I'd get to pitch past the sixth innings, you know?" Alice laughed and Scout sat back down and began throwing the softball into her gloved hand over and over. "I thought that even if it looked casual, it still meant something, but it obviously didn't mean the same to her." Scout sighed and looked at Alice. "I'm just sick of the game, I guess."

"Softball?" Alice joked, digging her elbow into Scout's side and getting a slight smile.

"Yeah. I hate all these hot queers in tight pants." Scout looked up as the opposition's coach talked to Drew, who looked completely incongruous in her pant suit. She must have come straight from work, Scout thought, although she didn't know what Drew actually did for a living. She didn't really know much at all about Drew, come to think of it. She just sort of got on with things and no one ever questioned her choices because they all made sense.

Scout hadn't really even looked at Drew before. She was so assured in her role that she didn't bring any attention to herself, but Scout realised she was really quite striking. Tall, strong, and purposeful, with a naturally calm expression that also somehow communicated that she wouldn't take any shit from anyone. Scout realised that she had that same neutral expression as duty counsel. What Scout had come to call 'lawyer face.' She wondered if that was what Drew did for work. If she was a lawyer, Scout imagined she was damn good at her job, as she hadn't caused any of the team to defect or even object to a lineup. Not like Kerry, who seemed to start the season on the wrong foot, putting everyone's back up immediately as she went from being a solid teammate, or so Scout heard, to being a hard-ass as soon as she took on the role of coach. When she then tried to go back to being everyone's friend, no one was interested, and Kerry had jumped ship.

Scout was glad Drew was now coach, and she wondered if her not really noticing Drew before now was because of things with Janice or because Drew was quite a bit older than Scout and reminded Scout of the lawyers and social workers she'd spent so long trying to avoid.

"Why do you play then?" Alice asked, causing Scout to lose her train of thought.

She looked up at Alice and frowned.

Alice said, "The game, I mean. Why are you such a player?"

"Oh." Scout chuckled. "I don't really. You didn't get that yet?"

Alice shook her head.

"I don't lead people on. I fuck around. That's for sure. But I don't promise anything I can't deliver."

"So that makes it OK?" Alice asked, not smiling.

"Well, I don't think I'm unfair. I mean, I can't help it if people end up wanting more of what I've got, can I?" Scout held out her hands, the ball in one, and then pointed to herself before throwing the ball to her gloved hand.

Alice laughed and reached out to grab the ball before it landed in Scout's glove. She held it up between them.

"You don't think sleeping with someone is a promise of some kind?"

"Well, not really."

"But this woman you were sleeping with...she promised you something?"

Scout hesitated. "I guess she didn't."

"But you're angry at her anyway?"

Scout was silent. Alice let her have the silence for a few seconds, then dropped the ball into Scout's glove.

"It wasn't that I thought she promised me anything. And it isn't that I wanted things to get more serious, not really. I just didn't like how she made the assumption I wasn't worth getting serious about." Scout said, rolling the ball back and

57

forth in her glove.

"So, you set her up to think you're a player, and then get mad when she thinks you're a player."

"I guess." Scout looked at Alice, meeting her eye. "Stupid, huh?"

"I don't think so. It's been a while, but I remember how you have to adopt this persona when you date. Like nothing can hurt you, nothing can touch you, but it all does, in some way. Even the smallest slight is magnified when you're lonely. It all feels heavy when there's no one to laugh it off right away, to put it in perspective." Alice wondered if she and Jeff would get to the point of dating other people, and suddenly the idea scared her and she shuddered. "Are you lonely?" she asked.

Scout furrowed her brow. She opened her mouth to speak, but said nothing.

Drew walked towards the bank at China Creek where the two of them were sitting and motioned for them to get up. "Hey, hey, hey. Quit looking somber. We have a game to win. Let's go, let's go." She ran backwards for a few steps, clapping her hands, then pulled out the whistle that hung beneath her shirt and blew it as she turned around and ran to join the rest of the team.

They got their asses handed to them by the opposition team, and Drew said she'd buy everyone a beer to commiserate, but Scout was the only taker that night and she was about to duck out too when Drew asked if she wanted to just get a beer at her place. Drew lived just down the street, on Scout's way home, so she said yes, letting curiosity get the better of her.

When they got to Drew's apartment, Scout kept her coat on, her hands stuffed in her pockets and her shoulders hunched. Drew gestured to Scout that she could hang up her coat, but Scout just looked up from beneath her cap and said, "'S'alright."

Drew smiled, her eyes creasing in amusement as she turned to walk to the kitchen to get them both a drink. She bit her upper lip, willing herself not to laugh.

After assessing the beer content of her refrigerator, Drew called to Scout to ask, "IPA or ISA?"

"I'm fine with whatever," Scout replied as she headed to the living room to scope out Drew's vast collection of DVDs. She ran her fingers over the unfamiliar titles, then smirked as she got to *Better than Chocolate*.

Having padded up behind Scout, Drew handed her a beer and then reached for the DVD. "Have you seen this?" Drew asked, and her hand briefly touched Scout's hand.

Scout jerked her hand away and went to sit down on the overstuffed armchair at the far corner of the room. "Nope. I heard it's super cheesy."

Scout slouched into the chair and crossed her legs, ankle over knee. Her foot bobbed up and down as she looked around Drew's living room.

Drew watched Scout out of the corner of her eye, took a sip of beer and turned on the DVD player. She loaded the movie and turned to smile at Scout, saying, "It's a real travesty that you haven't seen this. Your queer Vancouver education isn't complete until you've sat through it at least once."

Scout blustered, "Oh, I think I'm educated enough in that department. Maybe I could even teach you a few things." She held Drew's gaze, grinning, then took a swig of beer as Drew laughed.

"There's always more to learn, I guess," Drew said as she sat down on the couch, taking the seat closest to Scout.

"Teaching an old dog new tricks," Scout pursed her lips and raised her eyebrows.

"Ouch."

Scout held her beer bottle by the neck, balancing it between three fingers and tipping her wrist to take a sip. Drew watched for a second, knowing Scout was watching her staring, then she turned away, feeling a slow, creeping flush rising up her chest and neck.

"Don't worry, young 'un," Drew countered. "I've got

plenty of tricks."

They sat quietly for a minute as the title sequence rolled, then Scout said, "I can't really stay for movies."

Drew took a moment, giving Scout space to add, "I've, er, I've got work in the morning."

"That's fine," Drew said. "Leave whenever you like. I'm going to watch this anyway. It'll help me fall asleep." She smiled at Scout and then turned back to the movie.

"It's weird you have DVDs. Like, who even owns a physical copy of anything anymore? Movies, music, books." Scout looked at the shelves that held Drew's extensive library and thought about her own meager collection of thrift store sci-fi novels she had thrown out when she had moved to Vancouver. Just as well, Scout figured, as they would probably have mold or mushrooms growing on them by now, perhaps creating a whole new species to add to the fantastical plot.

Drew sat up and leaned over the arm of the couch towards Scout. She smiled and said, "I get that it makes me look uncool, but while you might feel OK about downloading or streaming everything for free, if I get caught doing that, it's my job."

Scout frowned. "I don't get it. You'd lose your job just for streaming a movie?" She laughed, then said, "Is it like that for all lawyers? You are a lawyer, right? "

Drew nodded and said, "Yep. And, oddly enough, lawyers have to actually follow the law, or we can get disbarred. So, yeah, downloading one cheesy movie could lose me my job." Drew watched Scout shake her head in disbelief.

Scout grimaced. "Practice what you preach, I guess." Scout laughed. "I bet you break a bunch of other laws without even knowing it, though."

Drew laughed and held out her hands, turning them upwards. "Probably. But I try not to!"

Scout grinned at her and held out her bottle to clink

Drew's, saying, "Don't worry. If you lose your job, I'll put in a word with my boss." She winked at Drew as Drew shook her head, laughing.

"Yeah? That'd be great. Thanks!" Drew laughed again and said, "Although, I'm not sure minimum wage will help me pay for daycare."

Scout waved her hand to gesture across the room. "Um, hate to break it to you, but your kid must've escaped." She raised her eyebrows at Drew and then looked pointedly at Drew's bottle of beer. "And, I'm guessing you're not pregnant, given that you're drinking."

"Correct. No kid yet. You're quite the detective."

"Why do you think they call me Scout?" She mock-saluted and laughed.

"Oh, I figured it was a reference to the book. No?" Drew asked.

Scout looked at her and shook her head, "What book?"

"To Kill a Mockingbird. You must've read it at school?"

"Nope. All I remember is Catcher in the Rye, with that psycho. Oh, and some book about birds in northern Ontario."

"Gabrielle Roi?"

"Sounds about right." Scout nodded, then asked, "So what's the other bird book about?"

"To Kill a Mockingbird? Oh, it's about racism in the southern US. There's a character called Scout, a real tomboy. I figured that's where you'd taken the name from."

Scout smirked and shook her head, closing her eyes for a second. "Nope, it's 'cause I was lookout when -" she stopped and bit her lip, then smiled and shook her head again.

Drew narrowed her eyes and smiled back, then asked, "Hey, have you got a quarter?"

After taking a second to stare at Drew, Scout fished in her pocket and dug out ten cents. Drew held out her hand and took the coin.

"Great. Now you're protected by attorney-client

61

privilege."

Scout tipped her head back and laughed. "I'm still taking the fifth."

Drew shrugged and asked, "Sure?"

"It ain't me anymore," Scout said, her expression suddenly neutral. "People change."

"No doubt," Drew said quietly, smiling. "So you're not going to play the bad girl card? The soft-hearted loyal gang member? The con with a heart of gold?" She spoke softly, taking care not to laugh.

Scout remained serious, saying, "That ain't me either. I just grew up is all."

Drew nodded, and they both turned back to the movie, sipping their beers.

After a little while, Scout asked, "Cool if I get another?" She tapped at her bottle and then gestured at Drew's beer. "You want one?"

"Sure, thanks." Drew held out her empty bottle and watched Scout walk over to the refrigerator. "I thought you couldn't stay," Drew said, smiling to herself while Scout flipped the tops off two fresh bottles.

Scout handed Drew another ISA and said, "Another drink's fine." She sat down on the opposite end of the couch to Drew and pulled up her feet to sit cross-legged. Without looking away from the screen, Scout said, "So, seriously, you're looking to have a kid?"

"Yeah," Drew replied. "I've got a hot date with some sperm on Saturday."

Scout gagged. "Gross."

"That's how miracles are made," Drew laughed.

"I guess. Still though, ugh."

"If there was another way...." Drew sighed.

Scout turned to look at Drew and said, "So, what, you're not tempted to head down Granville tonight, buy a guy a few drinks and get to it? Free baby, y'all." She laughed as Drew gave her a disapproving glare.

"I'm pretty sure neither of us have much experience with an actual cock attached to a cis guy," Drew said, then she apologised, saying, "Sorry, I shouldn't make assumptions."

They were both silent for a moment, then Scout said quietly, "No, you shouldn't." She gulped down her beer, avoiding eye contact with Drew. Scout shifted in her seat and crossed her legs ankle over knee again, her foot bobbing until Scout gripped it with her hand, closing the circle of her body while simultaneously appearing relaxed and open.

"I'm sorry," Drew said again, turning her eyes back to the screen. She swallowed and opened her mouth as if to speak, then shut it again and gritted her teeth. She licked her lips and took a breath, but stayed silent, watching the movie. Drew realised she was digging her fingers into her hand hard enough that even her neatly clipped nails were leaving marks. She made a conscious effort to relax her muscles and was about to apologise again when Scout stood up.

"Oh!" Drew said, involuntarily, and she jumped to her feet. "Hey, Scout, I -"

Scout shrugged, saying, "It's cool. I'll see you at practice, yeah." She killed her beer and nodded at Drew in thanks.

Drew followed Scout to the door, frowning as she tried to think of something to say. "I'm sorry I upset you," Drew said softly as Scout turned in her direction while pulling on her Blundstones.

"Nah, it's cool. Who's upset?" Scout half-laughed and gave Drew a smile. "I've just got to get home is all." She handed Drew the empty beer bottle.

"Don't leave just because I overstepped," Drew said. "Please?" She put out a hand to touch Scout's shoulder, but Scout tensed at the touch and shrugged her off.

Drew flushed, withdrawing her hand and taking a breath. "I'm sorry, I don't know what to -"

"Stop it!" Scout looked directly at Drew, her eyes wide and her jaw set. "Just stop apologising. I don't need you to be so fucking sorry. Alright?" Scout twisted the latch and pulled

63

open the door behind her. She took a step back while turning, but stumbled over Drew's boots and fell into the wall. Drew reached out to steady Scout, but pulled back her hand before making contact. She bit her lip again and held her hand to her chest, feeling the heat of her skin and the rapidity of her breathing.

Scout righted herself and held the door open with her foot. She looked up at Drew and said, "Hey, Drew, I know you didn't mean anything. And I know you're trying to be nice and all. But, you know what? You're not my mother. Don't worry about it, OK." Scout walked backwards, leaving the door to swing closed behind her, but Drew jumped forward to grab it and called after Scout.

"I don't want to be your mother, Scout." Drew closed her eyes for half a second and said again, softly, "I seriously do not want to be your mother."

Scout had stopped five yards down the corridor, her head hanging and her hands stuffed in her jacket pockets. She was quiet for a couple of seconds and then she raised her head and cracked the joints in her cervical spine before turning.

"So what," Scout said, "You want to fuck me? Is that it?"

Drew swallowed and didn't respond. She just stared at Scout, wondering where the anger came from that she had triggered so unwittingly.

Scout tapped two fingers to her temple and said, "What do you think is going to happen here, Drew? I'm not stupid. I see how you look at me, but I'm not your last freedom fuck, and I'm not some dumbass kid who needs you to take care of me."

Drew took a breath and said in a whisper, "That's not what I'm trying to do." She gestured for Scout to come back inside the apartment and glanced over at the neighbouring apartment doors, frowning slightly.

"Oh," Scout said, grinning and putting her arms out as she walked slowly backwards. She laughed and shouted, "Good luck with that sperm!"

64

Drew watched in silence as Scout turned to strut down the corridor to the elevator, then she quietly closed the door. Leaning against the wall, Drew held up her half empty beer bottle and stared through the brown glass, slowly focusing her eyes on the whorls of her fingerprints, magnified by the liquid. She walked over to the sink and tipped the bottle, then rinsed all the empties and put them with the rest of the recycling.

She filled a glass with water and drank it down slowly, closing her eyes and going over what had just happened. She had touched on something still raw for Scout, some emotional landmine, and she hadn't known how to react. Maybe there wasn't anything she could have done. Maybe this was just something Scout had to work through on her own. Drew could still feel the effects of the adrenalin in her blood. She had felt it all evening, making her hands cool and clammy, her heart race. The line between lust and fear was so fragile, so ephemeral when getting to know someone new, and it had been a long time since Drew had even felt close to that line.

She thought about Saturday and leaned back against the kitchen counter. Maybe this had been her last chance, and she had blown it. She had let the easy banter carry her away, enjoying things feeling natural and simple. She had felt like she knew Scout. They were so similar in some ways, but Drew knew it had been foolish to think that meant she had some great insight into Scout's past or present reality. She should have realised that there was more than just the fifteen-year age gap that made them different, but Scout's smile, her laughter, and how it felt to run her hand over Scout's shaved head had pushed aside Drew's sense for once, and it had felt good to let it go, at least for a little while.

Part Two

ELEVEN

Kate walked up to the yellow line near the edge of the platform and positioned the shiny red points of her boots just shy of the mark. Cass joined her, overstepping the line as she turned to face Kate.

Cass's hazelnut brown eyes danced wildly under the flickering artificial light of the train platform. Kate knew that Cass was trying hard not to blink, desperate to contain her tears. Kate reached out and pulled Cass towards her, taking a step back.

"You have to be behind the yellow line. Otherwise you might get pulled onto the tracks, by the vacuum created by the train, you know?"

Cass laughed, then blinked, then turned away and wiped her sleeve across her face, mopping up the lachrymose escapees.

"Don't you want to push me onto the track anyway?" Cass said, laughing again.

"Cass. Don't be melodramatic. I have to go, you know that."

"But, that's just it. You don't. You could stay right here,

with me. There's no point going now. What good will you do if you go now? She already had chemo. It's just all about waiting now, isn't it?"

Kate closed her eyes, not wanting to have the conversation again: not wanting to think about how Em had gone through this whole thing and Kate hadn't been there to support her. Kate had been having the same circular discussion with Cass all day, since Kate had bought her ticket back to Vancouver. Em had already had surgery and finished her first round of chemo, but Kate only knew this because Grace had called to ask Kate when she was coming home.

Em had kept her diagnosis a secret from Kate for almost three months, maintaining a masquerade of business as usual. When the news had finally sunk in, Kate felt terrible for having spent the past few weeks bitching about Cass, about work, about how Jupiter had gotten into the neighbours' apartment and chased their cat around for several frantic minutes until Kate had managed to corner him and drag him out. Em had simply listened and laughed and murmured supportive things just like normal. It had all been just like normal. Em had given Kate no reason to think there was anything wrong. Or had she? Why hadn't Kate thought more about how Em's webcam had suddenly stopped working, or that Em had cut some of their calls short? Why had Em not mentioned the wedding again? Why had Kate not noticed that something was seriously wrong with her best friend? She thought back to Em's visit, and how pale and tired Em had looked. Kate had assumed Em had been working too hard, had lost some weight and was jetlagged. Maybe if she'd talked to Em then, her friend might have gone to the doctor sooner, before the cancer had really taken a hold. But Kate had been too busy managing Cass's jealousy during Em's visit. With Cass and Kate both new to Amsterdam and neither making much effort to make new friends, Cass had gotten too used to having Kate all to herself and had thrown a couple of tantrums when Kate had taken a day off work to show Em

68

around. Kate had protested that she had blown off work numerous times to spend the day in bed with Cass, but Cass's memory could be highly selective.

It was all too easy for Kate to blame Cass for her not noticing that Em was sick. And, as hard as Kate had tried to resist the temptation to lay everything at Cass's feet, she couldn't shake off the feeling that she had become detached from reality since coming to Amsterdam and finally getting together with Cass. Kate had been so caught up with the tempest of their relationship that the rest of the world had been but a subplot to their ongoing drama.

The sex was amazing, of course. As were the good days, when they'd meet up after Kate finished work, have a few drinks, head to a party, have some more drinks, and spend the night surrounded by the intrigue and wonder of Amsterdam's queermos. Then they would get into a fight about the way Kate had looked at some other woman, or the way Kate had looked at Cass while she was talking to another woman, and Cass would accuse Kate of controlling her or would worry she wasn't enough for Kate and they would go home angry and sleep that drunken sleep of dissatisfaction, facing away from each other.

The next day Kate would have to ignore her hangover and go into the office, while Cass spent the day on Kate's couch, working herself into a fit of self-loathing. Cass would send flirty, then dirty texts to Kate hour after hour, seemingly trying to claw back a little of her arrogant charm. The first time this had happened, Kate had squirmed in her office chair, trying desperately to concentrate on the file in front of her, until giving in and rushing home to fuck away the afternoon.

In those moments, Kate felt like she knew Cass and that things would work out. The sun would set as Cass lay in Kate's arms, their fingers laced together, and they would talk about the documentary Cass was working on, her harrowing footage of an interview with a queer sex worker who had been

69

beaten up by a client, or the class in Film and the Body Cass planned on taking next semester at Amsterdam's University College. They would talk about Kate's work too, but only briefly. Kate would worry about how Cass would react to a story about an office joke, or news that Kate had landed another client. Last time she had come home feeling elated at having brought in a big project, Cass had sunk into a depression, saying that Kate worked too hard and was never home. Kate wondered if things would be different if Cass had something, other than Kate, that she was passionate about.

After they ordered in takeout again one night, arguing over what to eat, Kate couldn't help but feel that something wasn't quite right. Should the highs and lows really be this pronounced? Maybe she just needed to wait things out, to get into a rhythm with Cass, like she had with Janice. Still, shouldn't things be easier, less fractious, this early in their relationship?

Perhaps, Kate thought, this was why Em hadn't told her about the cancer. Perhaps Em hadn't been able to get a word in with Kate detailing every fight with Cass, and every bout of fantastic make-up sex. Of course Em hadn't told her anything, not when Kate was so full of her own self-importance. Kate began to wonder if Em had already been suspicious that she was sick when she visited. Perhaps that's why she was so keen to go ahead with such an unorthodox marriage proposal. As always, Em had been worried about everyone else and how they'd handle things, rather than worrying about herself.

After talking to Grace, Kate had called Steve and asked him to give his phone to Em in the hospital. She told Em that she would be on the next flight to Vancouver and Em had admitted she was sick, but still insisted that she was fine, really, and that there was no need for Kate to come. There had been a sense of defeat in Em's voice that Kate had never heard before, and never wanted to hear again.

Kate had opened up her browser and booked a flight

70

while Em was on the phone, prompting Em to finally stop pretending she was fine. As Kate heard all the fear and confusion of the past few months tumble out of Em, she couldn't wait to wrap her arms around her friend, to just hold Em and give her the silence, the space, that Kate had denied her these past few months.

Now Kate stood on the platform at the train station, hoping that Cass wouldn't make a big scene. Cass had insisted on coming to see Kate off, despite having made it plain that she didn't understand why Kate was going now, when Em's treatment was done and they were just waiting to see what happened. She asked Kate what good she could be, given that Em had Steve and Hanna and all her other friends who had been there when she was diagnosed and undergoing chemo: all the friends she had told what was going on, unlike Kate. "Some friend, huh?" Cass said, and Kate didn't know if Cass meant her of Em, because she'd been asking herself the same question since she'd found out.

"Are you trying to be hurtful?" Kate asked Cass, braving an argument just as she was about to leave. "You do get that I'm not here purely for your amusement, your pleasure - that I have a life outside of you?"

"Jeez Louise. Don't get your knickers in a twist," Cass said. "You're being so dramatic."

"Cass. If you don't get that this is serious, that Em might die, and that I feel like a shitty friend for not having been supportive these past few months because we've been too busy fucking and fighting each other and ignoring the world, then that's a really big problem for us. I can't be your everything, and you can't be mine. That's not how relationships work. It's just not." Kate closed her eyes and took a deep breath. As she let the breath out slowly she tried to quell the rising nausea accompanying the idea that she might just be about to break up with Cass. There was an unfamiliar silence. Cass hadn't reached out to touch Kate, to bridge the gap in understanding by bridging the gap between their bodies.

The silence continued and Kate opened her eyes, half expecting Cass to have disappeared.

She was still standing in front of Kate, but was looking down at her Blundstones, quiet tears dripping onto the brown leather. These weren't toddler tears or tantrum tears. These weren't tears designed to manipulate Kate. Something had changed, and Kate knew that whatever happened next there was no going back for them. Cass remained silent for a few more seconds, then swallowed and wiped her face with her sleeve before looking up.

"But you are my everything," she began to say, but the words drowned in tears and it took a few moments for her to regain control. "I just don't want you to go. What if you don't come back?"

"I will come back. I'm just visiting," Kate said, trying to quell her frustration.

"But it's like you're saying someone else is more important than me," Cass said, her voice getting louder.

"Cass, that's not what I'm saying. I love you, but I love Em too, and right now I need to be with her to make sure she knows that. I will come back, but only if you understand that it's because I want to make a life with you, not to have you be my life."

Cass looked down at her feet and stuffed her hands in her pockets, but Kate reached out her hands to hold Cass's shoulders and gently raised Cass's chin. "Did you hear me," Kate asked. "I want to build a life with you, just not like this."

Cass sniffled, but held Kate's gaze. "I don't know how to do that. I've never done that."

"So this is a new challenge, a new adventure. You can learn to trust me, and I can learn to trust you. Things have to change though."

"But you'll come back and help me figure it out?" Cass said, her eyes swimming again.

"Of course. We'll figure it out together."

"And you'll forgive me when I fuck up?"

"How about you don't assume you'll fuck up?" Kate said.

"But we both know I will," Cass said, "and then you'll leave me."

"Stop it."

"I can't help it."

"You can. You just aren't trying, because it's always been easier this way. To cut and run. To make someone angry so they end up being the bad guy and you get to take the high ground." Kate set her jaw and stared at Cass, who shifted her gaze for a second to look down the platform.

"OK." Cass looked back at Kate. "I'm sorry."

"Thank you," Kate said. She exhaled slowly, feeling some of the tension dissipate. "When I'm back we can talk more, but while I'm away I trust that you won't fuck up, because I believe you want us to work."

"Me too. I love you. I'm just shitty at showing you."

Kate kissed Cass gently, unlike almost all of their previous kisses which had merely been a prelude to sex. She pulled Cass into an embrace and held her until the platform shook with the arrival of her train.

"I'll call you tomorrow! I love you!" Kate called over the noise of the train, and Cass let her go.

TWELVE

The server hesitated, looking back and forth at Drew and Scout before placing the bill in the centre of the table, saying, "Thank you, er, folks."

Scout smirked, enjoying the awkwardness. She reached out to take the bill wallet, but Drew quickly placed her hand over Scout's and then slowly slid the bill over to her side of the table.

"Hey, this was an apology dinner," Scout said, having called Drew that morning to say sorry for storming out the other night. Scout had explained that she apparently had a problem with authority, and Drew had laughed and thanked her for the apology but said that maybe Scout just had a problem with people meddling in her business, which was totally understandable. Scout apologised again, but when she mentioned one especially awful foster family, and then quickly skipped to talking about how she had just broken up with Janice, Drew cut Scout off and suggested dinner instead. That way, Drew explained, I can actually get to know you instead of upsetting you by making assumptions about your life history.

Drew smiled and did some quick arithmetic before slipping some cash into the black bill wallet. She pushed it to the edge of the table and Scout made to top up Drew's wine glass, but Drew covered it and shook her head. "You finish it. I'm driving."

Scout poured herself the last of the wine and took a big swig.

She looked over at Drew and grinned, her teeth stained red. She ran her tongue over her teeth and licked her lips. "I'm drowning my sorrows, remember?" She sighed dramatically then drained the glass and dabbed her mouth with her white napkin. Drew had half expected Scout to belch and throw the glass over her shoulder.

"So it was serious with this woman?" Drew asked.

"Yeah. I suppose. We were thinking of moving in together," Scout said, avoiding Drew's amused stare.

"Seriously?"

"Well, I guess I was thinking of moving into her place. It doesn't have hallucinogenic fungus growing from the carpet. So that'd be a step up, right?"

Drew laughed. "Yeah, I guess it would." She took a last sip of wine and placed her glass gently on the table, smoothing out the ruffle in the white linen.

"Hey, aren't you supposed to, like, not be drinking at all, or whatever?" Scout asked as they both stood up to leave.

"That was my last glass of wine, hopefully, for at least nine months," Drew said, smiling. "Second to last shot this weekend. Then I'm out."

"Out of sperm, or out of money, or out of time?"

"All three really. It's tough work getting knocked up without the knocking."

Scout looked puzzled and Drew said, "The knocking of a headboard against a wall when guys and dolls make the beast with two backs."

Scout looked even more puzzled.

"Never mind. It's Shakespeare. You should read a book

sometime," Drew said.

"Didn't Shakespeare do plays?" Scout wiggled her eyebrows. "And anyway, shut up. I read plenty."

"Beer bottle labels don't count," Drew said.

"Ha ha." Scout smiled, then said, "Maybe I should quit the booze too and be a sympathy teetotaller with you. I can grow as a person while you grow a person."

Drew laughed and ruffled Scout's hair, leaving her hand resting on Scout's head as she pulled the shorter woman into her shoulder. "I'll hold you to that. You're a real charmer."

"Oh, I know." Scout was enjoying the feeling of being held by Drew, but was also a little unnerved at how much she liked it. "How do you think I got this far. What with being a sad orphan and all. A child of the state. A waif and stray." She mimed wiping away a tear.

"They should've called you Annie," Drew said, "and bring on the violins.

"How do you know my name isn't Annie?" Scout pulled away from Drew and grinned. "Do you really think my name is Scout? Who in their right mind would name a kid Scout and then give them up for adoption? I mean, clearly any kid called Scout is going to be awesome."

"I thought you were a foster kid?" Drew asked.

"Not originally. I was supposed to be going to some family. Then they backed out and I landed in the system. Thus began my illustrious education in being a charmer."

They walked to the bike rack by the restaurant, where Scout's fixie was tethered with two heavy motorbike locks. Drew gestured at them and said, "And your education in keeping hold of your possessions, it seems."

"Seriously. I can't even count the number of bikes I've had stolen, not to mention the other shit that goes missing when you move homes every few months or weeks." Scout ran her hand over the top tube of her bike. "This beaut is going nowhere. I saved for this and if some punk comes and steals it, well, I'll not be a nice person to be around."

76

"So you aged out?" Drew asked as Scout unlocked the bike.

"Yep. And then I was gone. Saved up enough to get a deposit on a place, was living there until I moved here a few months ago."

"You were renting the same apartment all that time?" Drew looked impressed, then slightly apprehensive. "Wait, how old are you?"

"Twenty-four. Six years I'd been in my place, and it was awesome. And the rent was super cheap because the landlord could only raise it a tiny amount each year. I paid under five hundred a month."

"So why on earth did you move to Vancouver?"

"It was time." Scout wheeled her bike free and they started walking down to Drew's truck. "I started to feel like I was stuck, you know? Like I'd built this home, but just for the sake of having something feel permanent. Everything else was still shitty, and I realised it didn't matter if I came home to a place with perfectly painted walls and nice tiles if I still lived somewhere I couldn't be myself outside of my house."

"That makes sense," Drew said. "I felt like that for a while. Stuck, you know?"

"When was that?" Scout asked, navigating her bike onto the road to get around a group of people wearing Hawaiian shirts and party hats. She exchanged a look with Drew once the oblivious revellers had passed by.

"When I was married. When I was perfectly, blissfully married." Drew sighed dramatically and Scout laughed. "It was all just so goddamn perfect, so I felt horribly guilty for just not being happy. It wasn't even really about Kathryn; it was just that I felt like I'd stepped outside of convention to just land myself back into the same box."

"I think I get it. Not that I've ever been married, or even close."

"Would you want to be? Married, I mean?" Drew looked across at Scout then looked down at the sidewalk.

"No. It's not for me, I don't think. I'd feel trapped, like you did, I guess. And I'd feel this terrible need to be mean to whoever I was with, even if I really did love them, just so I could get some space." Scout held out her hand to stop Drew walking into the street. "Light's changing," she said.

"What about kids and stuff," Drew asked. "You think you want kids some day?"

"I'm pretty sure I don't. I definitely don't want to carry them. It'd creep me out too much. Change how I feel in my body, you know?" Scout smiled, adding, "But I would love to have lots of other people's kids in my life. They're great as long as I can give them back at the end of the day."

Drew grinned. "I'll sign you up for babysitting then."

"Seriously. Please do!" Scout laughed and nodded at Drew. "I just don't feel like that's where I want my life to go, my energy to go. I haven't quite figured it out yet, but there are other things that I want to do, and having kids just isn't on my list. When I talk to my straight friends, I actually feel pretty lucky that I don't have that constant anxiety about an accidental pregnancy, for the most part at least."

Drew nodded. "Yeah, I felt like that when I was younger. Now though...." She laughed and patted her belly. "All I've had the past few years is a food baby, and now I'm pretty set on the real thing. I never really thought I'd want kids, but it was just that I didn't see myself raising them with anyone else!"

Scout laughed. "You're a control freak then?"

"Not really! I just want to parent on my own. I'm not really sure why. I just do."

They walked in silence for a few seconds and then Drew put out a hand to touch Scout's arm and said, "Hey, sorry. I just realised that -. Well, just, I didn't mean to suggest that I think you'll change your mind about the kid thing, that it's just because you're younger than me."

"Oh, I know. I know." Scout smiled. "I get it."

"Seems like you know your own mind pretty well, for

such a young 'un." Drew grinned.

"I'm getting there," Scout said. "And, hey, I'm sure this time you'll get, what did you call it, 'knocked up' - god, that's a horrible term."

"It really is an awful euphemism. But I'm not much of a baker, so no one would believe I have a bun in the oven," Drew said, smiling.

"Wait, is it a euphemism?" Scout frowned and said, "I thought a euphemism was when you come up with a way of describing something bad. So, like, being dead is pushing up daisies."

Drew raised an eyebrow. "Did someone take a class in English lit. recently?"

Scout rolled her eyes. "Nope, I just learnt that in a small town there are a lot of ways to say dyke without teachers thinking anyone is being bullied."

"Oh yeah?" Drew said, "I can probably add a few to your list, along with a whole slew of racial slurs that fly under the radar and hit you where it really hurts."

"No doubt," Scout said. "What's your favourite lesbian euphemism, if you can choose?"

"Oh my, I don't know. I think gay men really have the best ones. I once heard someone say that they had a friend who was 'punting from the Cambridge end," Drew said, laughing. "No, no, wait, how about 'artisanal donut puncher'?" Drew snorted as she laughed and said, "I mean, I just love how easy it is to turn them around and make being gay sound like the most delicious thing ever, you know?"

Scout looked at Drew, her jaw slack, then said, "Seriously? Artisanal donuts? Woah." She shook her head then grinned and said, "You know what my favourite one is that I've heard here?"

Drew shook her head, "Go on, please."

"Having shares in Blundstone," Scout said, laughing as she stopped walking and looked down at her shoes.

"Ha!" Drew said, turning to face Scout. "I heard that one

a while back after a game. There were five of us all wearing the exact same Blundstones and Kate said she should switch her shares in Birkenstock to Blundstone to get with the current market conditions."

"Sounds like Kate knows her investments," Scout said, grinning. She set off to walk again and asked, "There's no Kate on the team this year though. Did she suck?"

Drew laughed as she walked alongside Scout. "Nah, she was only there because of one of the other players, Cass." Drew stopped walking and reached out to grab Scout's arm. She stared at Scout, searching her face for something. Scout stared back, wondering what Drew was looking at.

"Uh, hi?" Scout said. "What's up?"

"I just realised that you totally look like Cass. It's uncanny. Even some of your mannerisms are similar. I don't know why I didn't notice before." Drew began to wonder if the immediate familiarity she had felt with Scout, and, if she was honest, the inexplicable sense of annoyance she had felt at her when she joined the team had to do with the stunts Cass had pulled during the previous season. How had she not noticed the similarities? How had no one else in Mabel League mentioned it?

"Cass? Did you say Cass?" Scout furrowed her brow, trying to dredge up some memory from the murky depths of a night involving many many beers.

"Yeah. She was on the team last year. A great player but a huge flirt. Like you!" Drew laughed.

"Did you, you know...?" Scout smiled and wiggled her eyebrows.

Drew shook her head. "God no. She was a mess. Hot, but a mess. Her and Kate were doing this stupid dance of not hooking up, when everyone could tell they were into each other. Cass was just sort of working her way through the team to prop up her ego." Drew laughed, remembering Cass's hollering and posturing on the field.

Scout smirked. "So, you thought she was hot?"

80

"Yeah." Drew raised her eyebrows.

"And I look just like her?" Scout said.

Drew laughed and rolled her eyes, but Scout poked her gently in the shoulder. She asked again, "Huh? Yes?"

"Yes! Well, a bit friendlier maybe."

"So...?" Scout smiled and Drew shook her head, laughing and turning to carry on walking.

"Not so fast there, coach," Scout grabbed at Drew's hand and pulled her back. They stood face to face, both making tiny, almost imperceptible movements toward each other and back, until Scout reached out to cup the back of Drew's head and draw her in to kiss her. Drew slipped her hand beneath Scout's jacket and around her back to pull their bodies together. She gripped the soft flannel of Scout's shirt and breathed in the slight citrusy smell of her hair. The scent overwhelmed Drew's senses as the citrus mixed with the oaky taste of red wine on her lips and Scout's.

Scout broke away first, checking in, but Drew pulled her back in, shaking her head, "Don't stop." She kissed Scout again and walked them both backwards into the alley.

Drew felt Scout laughing as she pushed her gently against the cold wall of the alley and kissed Scout's neck.

"Well, well," Scout said, before gasping as Drew grazed her teeth against Scout's earlobe. Drew stopped and pulled away slightly, keeping her hands on Scout's waist.

"Sorry! I -" Scout silenced Drew by kissing her quickly. She nodded her head in the direction of the street.

"How about we take this somewhere less, well, cinematic?" Scout laughed as she looked around the alley, complete with its abandoned pallets and dumpsters.

Drew took a breath and nodded, her legs feeling a little shaky beneath her. "How about I take you and your precious bike home? I can drive."

"Can you?" Scout laughed again as she swung Drew back onto the sidewalk and then pulled her in for another kiss.

THIRTEEN

Kate walked down the cold tunnel from the aeroplane and felt a sudden heaviness in her heart that spread to her whole body. It was as if she could actually feel the slight increase in gravity now that she was no longer thirty thousand feet up.

While she was on the plane it had been like time had stopped and life was in stasis; Em's life at no greater risk than before. Now Kate had landed and would see her friend in just a few hours, the situation felt urgent, desperate. What if Em had died while Kate was over the Atlantic?

She turned her phone on as she headed toward the security lines. As she was waved through and welcomed home, her phone started buzzing and Kate sat by the empty luggage carousel steeling herself to check the messages.

There was a message from Steve just after Kate's flight had taken off. Em had spent a couple of nights in the hospital after more heart problems. He hadn't wanted to tell her so she didn't spend her whole flight worrying. Kate was already worrying, but she appreciated the thought, knowing that she wouldn't have been able to sleep at all if Steve had told her Em was sick enough again to be back in the hospital. She checked a later message from Hanna, from that afternoon, and was relieve to see that Em seemed to be doing better. She would probably be back home in a few days, so Kate's visit wouldn't be spent entirely at the hospital.

Kate tried to figure out when Hanna had actually sent her the message. Had her phone automatically updated to her new time zone? Kate looked out of the huge bank of windows offering a view of the airport runway bathed in a golden light. She couldn't remember if it was dusk or dawn. She had left Amsterdam at noon, changed in Toronto at five and it was now almost seven in the evening, or four in the morning in Amsterdam.

Kate thought about texting Cass to say she'd arrived safely, but she didn't want to wake her. Cass would be asleep, with Jupiter snuggled in next to her and, for a second, Kate wished she was snuggled up with the two of them. The thought of bed made it even harder to drag her feet across to the luggage carousel, so she missed grabbing her suitcase the first time around. She watched it circle the carousel again, on its way back to her for another attempt, hidden intermittently behind the other passengers on her flight who were lunging for their own luggage.

Kate checked a message from Grace, asking when her flight got in. Did she need a ride from the airport? Grace sent the same message about eight hours later, then said she'd check the flights. Kate had told Steve roughly when her flight would land, but hadn't expected anyone to pick her up.

Oddly, there was a message from Janice, which Kate almost didn't read, wondering why her ex was messaging her. She was even more confused when she saw that the message said Janice would be at International Arrivals in - Kate looked at her watch - twenty minutes. Grace had worked out her flight number and told Janice. Kate wondered what had been going on in her absence. Had all her friends ended up being friends with Janice again?

Whatever the situation, Kate was very glad of the ride as

83

she was exhausted. With no clue as to what kind of car Janice was driving these days, Kate peered at all the drivers pulling up at the arrivals area. Finally, she saw Janice smiling and waving as she parked. She jumped out and gave Kate a hug, saying, "Em is going to be thrilled to see you. We're all glad you're back." She put Kate's suitcase in the back seat of the Subaru as Kate got into the passenger seat. "How was your flight?"

"Fine. Exhausting. Thank you for picking me up. You didn't need to." Kate smiled at Janice as they drove away from the airport.

"It's no problem at all. It's nice to see you. I'd say you look well, but you look like you've been travelling for a whole day, so I'd be lying." Janice laughed. "I haven't seen Em, but Hanna and Steve are with her now. The doctors figured out that she has an infection, so they're giving her meds. I think Steve almost ended up having a heart attack this time. They just got her home!"

"How's he holding up?" Kate asked. "I can't even imagine how awful the last few months have been, for him and Hanna."

"It's been rough, that's for sure. But you know Em; she's pretty great at putting a brave face on everything. She's probably more worried about you flying out here than she is about herself." Janice smiled and put out her hand to pat Kate's leg.

Kate smiled across at her and covered Janice's hand with hers, giving it a squeeze then turning to look out of the window. She was excited to see Em in the morning, and happy to be back in Vancouver. As the familiar sights of south Granville whizzed past her, she closed her eyes and leaned her head against the window, enjoying the cool feeling of the glass against her cheek.

Janice, having returned her hand to two o'clock on the wheel, said quietly, "It's really good you're here. How's Amsterdam? How's Cass? You must have so many stories to tell!" She smiled and turned to look at Kate, then laughed softly. Kate's eyes were closed.

"Kate?" Janice said gently. She heard Kate's breath fall into the rhythm of sleep so familiar to her, even now, and said quietly, "Welcome home."

"Are we at the hotel?" Kate woke up with a start as Janice turned off the engine. They were in a parking garage. She must have slept the whole way back from the airport.

Janice shook her head. "Nope. This is my parkade. You're welcome to stay at mine tonight and for however long you're in town. It's near to the hospital and this way you get to see Thunderpuss."

Kate wiped the sleep out of her eyes and thanked Janice. "I'm so tired. I feel like I haven't slept in days." She got out of the car and asked about Thunderpuss as she grabbed her suitcase.

"Here, let me get that. You're the walking dead right now. And I know that feeling. Long haul flights really make you feel the haul sometimes." Janice took the suitcase and led Kate to the elevator. "Thunderpuss is my house guest right now. He was a bit much for Em to handle after the surgery, given his size. Even when she gets home she's not going to be able to lift that beast of a cat. He weighs about as much as Jupiter these days."

Janice held the door open for Kate and then followed her into the apartment. Thunderpuss came careening down the hallway and almost knocked Kate over as he tried to weave in and out of her legs.

"Crikey, he really has grown again hasn't he?" Kate bent down to tickle the enormous cat's enormous belly. "Maybe it's just relative. I've only made one cat friend in Amsterdam, and she's pretty small."

"Oh, no, he's grown alright. I think Steve and Hanna were overfeeding him. They weren't too organised about who was on food duty while Em's been having chemo and everything, so I reckon this lucky kitty has been eating twice as much as he should."

Thunderpuss stared up at Janice and meowed. She shook her head. "Nope. You already had dinner, remember?" He meowed again and Janice rolled her eyes.

Kate looked around Janice's apartment. The last time she was here was when they had rekindled things one last time. It felt like years had passed since then. "I like the new colours. This wall was white before, right?"

"Oh, yeah. I painted it green as my meditation wall. And the yellow is to help me start the day feeling cheery and energised while I eat breakfast in the kitchen."

Kate laughed and said, "I should probably sleep in the yellow kitchen then, to reenergise."

Janice smiled and pointed Kate towards the couch. "Or, you could sleep on this wonderfully comfortable sofa bed. I have to head out to a dinner thing, but I'll be back around eleven. I'll try not to wake you." Janice manoeuvered the sofa bed into position with Kate's assistance and then lay down blankets for Kate to organise. "Help yourself to anything you need. Food, more blankets, whisky, whatever. There's also a spare toothbrush on the side in the bathroom. I know how you always forget yours."

"Not any more! I learnt my lesson, thank you very much. Now it's the first thing I pack." Kate smiled and sat down on the couch, quickly realising that this was a mistake and that she wouldn't be getting up again any time soon. She took off her shoes and socks, wished she had the energy to have a shower, and then lay down. "Janice," she called, and the woman she had shared eight years of her life with came out the bathroom with one earring in and the other in her hand.

"Yes? You OK?"

"Thank you," Kate said.

"You're welcome. I figured a friendly, familiar face was better than some anonymous hotel, and I know things are a bit chaotic at Em's place right now. I'm happy to help." She got the other earring in and then scribbled something on a sticky note and stuck it to the refrigerator door. "This is Em's new room number. Visiting hours start at eleven. If you're awake earlier, we can go for breakfast nearby. I'm meeting Steve and Hanna at ten to pick up food for Thunderpuss. He eats some fancy stuff that they can only get in the States." Janice laughed as Kate rolled her eyes and Thunderpuss jumped up beside her on the sofa bed. "No prizes for guessing who's big spoon." Janice pulled on her shoes and wished Kate a good night. "It's good to have you here. Sleep well."

Kate fell asleep almost instantly, slipping into such a dreamless, heavy slumber that not even Thunderpuss's sudden urge to chase shadows could wake her.

FOURTEEN

It had been dark when Janice drove Kate to her apartment from the airport, and Kate's eyes had been closed almost the whole way anyway, so when she drew up the blinds in Janice's living room the next morning she got her first glimpse of the mountains. She had missed those white peaks while in Amsterdam, and she wondered, not for the first time, if it had been a mistake to take that job and go after Cass. It was silly to think that things could have been any different for Em if Kate had stayed in town, but Kate couldn't help feeling guilty that she'd left her friend just before the diagnosis.

Kate's excitement about seeing Em was laced with apprehension. She didn't know how she'd react to seeing Em looking so... so unlike Em. What if she said something insensitive? She was still tired from travelling and her brain felt unprepared to deal with the realities of life, and death, right now.

It was still early and Janice hadn't yet emerged from her bedroom, so Kate showered and took some time to catch up on emails she had missed the day before. Once she had replied to a few questions from colleagues, Kate sent Cass an email to let her know she had arrived safely. She took a selfie with Cypress Mountain and the two snowy ears of the Lions in the background. She sent this to Cass, saying, "The mountains and I miss you!"

As Kate had boarded her train to the airport in Amsterdam, she knew that the timing was terrible. Cass had just made herself painfully vulnerable and now Kate was going to be thousands of miles away for at least a week. Before they had started dating, Kate had heard so many tales from Cass about her random hookups and seeming inability to be alone for too long. When she was hurt and when she was angry, Cass found solace in sex and Kate couldn't help think that Cass might be angry enough at Kate for not being her priority right now to engage in a little revenge fuck with some stranger. She had to trust that Cass wouldn't cheat while she was in Vancouver, but it was hard to make that shift in expectations from confidante to girlfriend. It wasn't the cheating, *per se*, that Kate found hard to deal with, it was the deliberate act of weaponising sex to hurt someone.

Kate knew that at least one of her exes had cheated on her, but they had never told her and had not done it with the intention of hurting her. It had been a mistake, and while the betrayal had hurt, it hadn't felt malicious. With Cass, though, Kate knew her girlfriend could use her charm to seduce almost anyone, giving her a special kind of power.

The flip side was that this endless parade of potential partners prevented Cass from committing to a deeper relationship with other kinds of rewards. She was like a kid in a candy store who refused to leave, getting locked in night after night while the other kids went home to a cosy house with families who loved them.

When Cass had admitted that she didn't know how to change, Kate felt like those had been the first real tears Cass had cried since they had been dating. That had to mean something.

This peculiar dance within a relationship, the push and pull, the two-stepping over boundaries and back, was exhausting, especially when two partners seem to be hearing a different song and when neither wanted to commit to being the lead or follow. To Kate, it seemed that Cass had almost a pathological need to call the shots, acting out whenever anything didn't go her way. The problem was, Cass didn't seem to have any clear direction, but wasn't willing to spend any time reflecting on what she really wanted and working out a plan to get there. Everything had to be spontaneous and fun, but that felt so limiting to Kate, who was better able to be spontaneous and relax when she was confident of an underlying stability.

She suspected that Cass didn't even know what that kind of stability felt like, and for a while she had thought it foolish to try to build something with someone so hell bent on being a kid forever, with no responsibilities that couldn't be shirked at a second's notice. But it really did seem that Cass wanted a life with Kate, wanted something more meaningful than a few months of sex and parties, followed by an explosive, dramatic breakup.

Conversely, Kate knew that a certain kind of stability could also spell the death of a relationship. After all, she and Janice had gotten so comfortable with the status quo that they had just stagnated: their relationship fomenting fear of shaking things up, until it had imploded quietly and with bitterness.

Kate had changed since she had broken up with Janice. She knew that, and she knew it was for the better. She had thrown herself into work, creating new opportunities for herself and taking them, even if that had put her firmly outside of her comfort zone. She had moved countries, again, and even pursuing Cass had been contrary to her usual habit of waiting for people to come to her and assuming they weren't worth dating if they didn't.

90

There had to be a healthy middle ground that she and Cass could build a life on. She needed to find a way to talk to Cass about important things that didn't immediately antagonise her girlfriend and end the discussion. Recognising that and actually working out how to do it were clearly two very different things, however. Kate wondered if it might be worth seeing a couple's therapist when she got back to Amsterdam. Even if Cass agreed, there was the problem of potential language misunderstandings with a Dutch therapist. Kate wondered how easy it would be to find a queer-friendly, English-speaking therapist in Amsterdam. Considering that the whole point was to be able to talk to and listen to each other more easily and effectively, it seemed like a bad idea to throw in another confounding factor.

Kate was about to start googling therapists when she heard Janice stirring in the bedroom. It was just after nine and they were meeting Steve and Hanna at ten for brunch. She hoped they had good news about Em.

FIFTEEN

"I don't understand. Why's Em in the ICU? I thought it was just a minor infection. Don't they just give her antibiotics?" Kate put down her coffee cup and looked at Steve. Hanna placed her hand over his and gave it a squeeze.

"It's a bit more complicated than that now," Steve said. "Em's immune system is pretty shot, so even a little infection is a big deal. The last one really weakened her heart. Well, that and the reaction she had to the drugs."

Steve sighed and Hanna said, "They moved her to ICU last night. Her doctor said it was just a precaution really. She's worried about Em's heart again. She'll be in ICU until tomorrow at least, and could be there for a few days."

Steve moved his hand away from Hanna's and took a sip of coffee, then looked up at Kate and said, "ICU is immediate family only, Kate. I'm really sorry."

Kate looked from Steve to Hanna and back again. "But I've known Em for almost a decade. How is that fair?"

Hanna began to say something, but Steve interrupted, saying, "None of it's fair. Not a damn thing is fair right now." He took Hanna's hand in his, and then reached across the table to grasp Kate's hand too.

"But they're letting you see her?" Kate said to Hanna, who nodded without meeting Kate's glare.

"Kate," Janice said gently, "It's not a competition." Kate closed her eyes and nodded.

"I know, I'm sorry Hanna. I just wish there was something I could do. I just want to see her and, and to tell her -."

Kate began to cry. Janice put her arm around Kate's shoulder and pulled her close. When Kate composed herself, she said to Hanna and Steve, "Tell Em I'm here? Tell her I love her and that she needs to get better because if she dies I'll kill her." She broke down again and waved away Janice's attempts to comfort her.

Kate wiped at her tear-soaked face with the sleeve of her sweater as she ran to the washroom. She pushed open the door of the first cubicle and sank against the wall, sobbing as the full force of the idea of Em not being around finally hit her.

They had gone through so much together. All the drama and chaos of their twenties. School, career choices, the excitement and dread of new relationships, and of old relationships falling apart. The idea that Em wouldn't be around to grow into a hilarious old lady was too hard to swallow. Kate had always imagined they would end up as old curmudgeons, playing ukuleles on some porch somewhere, waving at the neighbourhood kids, and making pies from the blackberries growing in their backyards. Kate now saw herself mumbling sadly on that porch swing by herself, the image of Em and the sound of her laughter fading away.

She had never lost anyone like this before. Em was too young to die. She had stuff to do, and people to love. Kate just couldn't imagine a world without her. Who would be the voice of reason when Kate had a harebrained idea, or when she was too cautious to chase her dreams? Em was the one who had made it seem possible to leave Vancouver and head to Amsterdam. Em had given Kate the confidence to be bolder at work, without which the opportunity to relocate and be with Cass would never have come about. And now Em had two partners who loved her, who lived with her, and who would be utterly devastated if she died. And she hadn't even had a chance to have the bizarre wedding she was planning.

Kate knew she was talking herself into a spiralling sadness. Em wasn't dead. She could still beat this. But it seemed so dangerous to hope. She wanted someone to tell her it was all going to be OK. She wanted Cass to be there to hold her and tell her that Em would be fine. Cass could sound so sure, so comforting, like there was nothing in the world that she didn't have control over, and Kate needed that now.

She wiped her eyes and blew her nose, then Skyped Cass. She answered after four rings, but it wasn't Cass's face that filled the screen as a gruff voice said, "Herroo, where's my dinner?"

Kate began laughing through her tears. "Hi Jupes. Did Cass not feed you?"

"Cass? Who's Cass? That good for nothing layabout you left me with?" Kate's dog licked his lips and yawned, unsure as to why he could hear Kate's voice when she wasn't in the room. He tried to look behind the phone, revealing Cass right behind him, grinning widely.

"Hey you." Cass grimaced. "How's Em? You look tired."

"She's back in ICU."

"Shit. I'm sorry." Cass scrunched her nose and said, "So you can't see her, I'm guessing?"

"Nope. Not until she's better. If she even gets," Kate couldn't finish her sentence.

"She'll get better, Kate. Em's strong like an ox. You know that. This is just a setback and the extra care in ICU will just mean she gets better faster. That's how that works. Trust me." Cass gave Kate a goofy know-it-all grin.

"I forget that you're omnipotent."

"That's me. Em will be juuuust fine. You watch and see.

94

Now I've proclaimed it." Cass laughed, saying, "And how fucking happy will she be to see you when she's out of ICU?! So fucking happy, that's how fucking happy."

Kate laughed. "I'm going to give Steve a peace lily to give to Em."

"Of course you are. You champ. To remind her of death? Nice one." Cass chuckled. "You goof."

"Hey! Em would find it funny. And it purifies the air."

"I know! I called you a champ, didn't I!?"

"I can hear the interrobang in your voice," Kate grinned, setting Cass up for a punctuation pun.

"I'd interrobang you right now if you were here." Cass licked her lips. "Seriously, you make it too easy sometimes."

"You're too easy sometimes."

"Oh, damn," Cass said, then lowered her head and looked up at Kate from under her cap. "I'll make myself hard for you, if you'd like that."

Kate's eyes widened and she shook her head, still laughing. "How did this happen? I call you to tell you my best friend is possibly dying and within minutes we're flirting."

"Sex and death. It's a thing. Ask Freud." Cass moved the phone away from Jupiter, who was once again investigating the source of Kate's laughter.

"Is Jupes OK? Missing me?" Kate asked.

"He's all good. We're both missing you, but we'll survive. Right Jupes?

Kate's dog licked Cass's face then ran away, returning moments later to stand behind Cass with his leash. He wagged his tail hesitantly, then faster as Cass looked over her shoulder.

"Um. Looks like I've got to go, but you call whenever you want to, even if it's late here, or early or whatever." Cass blew Kate a kiss. "I love you," she said softly, as if it were the first time.

"I love you too. I miss you."

"It's only been a day! You'll see me soon enough. Once

Em is fighting-fit."

"That'll be a while yet." Kate sighed.

"But it will happen, Kate. I decree it." Cass nodded authoritatively.

"Well then, I guess I should go and send Steve and Hanna off to visiting hours so they can report back and let me know which marathon Em has signed up for."

"You go do that. And Jupes and I will go terrorise some squirrels. He likes to yell bad Dutch at them. Filthy beast."

"I wish I was there with you."

"Me too. But you just focus on Em now, and look after yourself. You're awesome, but you look awful." Cass laughed.

"Thanks! I guess crying and being exhausted isn't top on that list of winter skin care tips, eh?"

"Back in Canada for a day and you're already 'ehing' again, eh?"

"Eh? Whatchoo talking aboot?"

They said goodbye and Kate washed up, splashing cold water on her face before returning to her friends.

After paying the bill, they all headed out into the cold Vancouver air. The sun was still low in the sky, but bright and blinding as it reflected off the glassy buildings on Broadway.

As they started walking towards Vancouver General Hospital, Kate pulled Hanna aside and said, "Hey, I'm really sorry for what I said earlier. I know this is awful for you and Steve, and I'm glad that they're letting you see Em. She needs you, and I shouldn't have questioned your right to be there. I think I'm just feeling..." Kate trailed off as Hanna took her hand and then hugged her tightly.

When Hanna released her from the embrace, she asked softly, "You're just feeling... guilty?"

Kate nodded. "I was so wrapped up in everything, I didn't even see what was going on, even when Em visited and was talking about all the legal stuff and the wedding."

"Wedding? What wedding?" Hanna grinned and said, "Woah! Are you and Cass...? No way! That's fantastic!" She hugged Kate again, before Kate could correct her, then she dragged Kate to catch up with Steve and Hanna and yelled, "Hey, hey! Kate and Cass are getting hitched!"

Janice and Steve stopped and turned, their mouths hanging open.

"Thanks for looking so alarmed rather than elated," Kate said, then realised that she was taking offence over something that wasn't even happening.

"Kate, is this for reals?" Steve asked, frowning. "I mean, I know things with you and Cass are pretty full-on, but marriage? Is she even into that? Are you even into that?" He glanced at Janice, who still hadn't said anything and was looking at her feet, her hands stuffed in the pockets of her parka.

Hanna lightly punched Steve on the arm and said, "C'mon, it's been, what, like six months? They're way behind on the UHauling. They should be buying sperm soon, right Kate?" She laughed, but Kate didn't say anything and they all fell silent for a second.

Steve broke the silence by asking again, "You really want to marry her?"

"I don't know. I think so. I guess." Kate waved her hands to stall interruptions. She turned to Hanna and said, "But I wasn't talking about me and Cass. We're not getting married. Not yet at least. Sorry, I -" She stopped, trying to figure out how to avoid letting Em's secret slip, now she knew it was a secret still. "I meant, um, Lindsay and Madison's wedding. Em asked me about it when she visited, to see if Cass and I were coming back for it in spring. We still haven't met their kid."

Hanna laughed, and Steve looked visibly relieved. He asked Hanna who Lindsay and Madison were, and she caught him up on Cass's friends and their new baby as they all carried on walking in the direction of the hospital.

Janice bit her lip and then smiled at Kate. "I can't really see you in a big white dress with a boutonniere."

Kate laughed. "No, I guess not. More like jeans and a comfy sweater."

They walked in silence for a minute, then both spoke at the same time, asking, "Why did we never -"

Janice stopped laughing first and said, "Do you think we would have stayed together if we had gotten married? Do you think we would have tried harder to fix things?"

"I think it would have been harder to break up, yes, but that doesn't mean that we shouldn't have broken up. I mean, we're both happier now, right?"

"Right. Yeah. I guess so." Janice furrowed her brow, squinting into the low winter sun. "So, Cass makes you happy?"

"She does," Kate said slowly. "When we're not fighting, yeah, she does make me happy. Really happy. And I think things are getting better. We're getting better."

"You think you might marry her some day?"

"I hadn't really thought about it, but maybe. I don't even know if she's into that. Her family is pretty traditional. I mean, her dad's a preacher! I think the whole thing would be really hard for her. It's not like her dad would walk her down the aisle or anything, and her mom is still pretty shitty about the whole gay thing." Kate grinned, "And can you imagine my folks at my wedding? My mother would flirt outrageously with every man in sight, and they would have an enormous fight and it'd be another decade before they spoke to each other again."

"They're still not speaking? Wowzer." Janice said. "It was a flamenco dancer, right?"

"Merengue! Close!"

"God, that was so funny, watching your mom cavorting with that guy at your aunt's wedding. He was, what, like twenty?"

"Please, let's never speak of this again," Kate said, trying to banish the image of her mother sexy-dancing with a man younger than Kate. "My parents are clearly not a good model for marriage. Although I'm still pretty impressed that my dad actually said something finally."

"Maybe it wasn't the best moment to choose though, eh?" Janice laughed. "I mean, the look on your aunt's face when they had that big fight right on the dance floor. That was amazing. I'd never imagined your dad could get that fired up."

"It was something, that's for sure. I guess he reached his tipping point with such brazen public flirting."

"Your mom totally fucked that flamenco guy after. You know that, right?" Janice raised her eyebrows and grinned.

"Oh god, shut up. I don't even want to think about that." Kate shook her head and laughed. "But, hey, you know, at least it's easy to see where I get my fun, spontaneous nature from."

They both grinned and Janice said, "Don't forget your fear of commitment, and your love of weddings."

"Hey!" Kate smiled at Janice, "Not fair!"

"So, will I get an invite to your wedding? I would love to see what your mom gets up to this time."

"Sure. When I pop the question and set a date, you'll be first on the invite list," Kate said as they arrived at the entrance to the hospital. She grimaced at Janice and said, "Thanks for distracting me. I wish I could go in and make Em laugh too. She once harangued me for having no shoddy home video footage of my mother's dirty dancing escapades. I bet my aunt destroyed the tapes."

"Are you coming back to mine now, given that you can't see Em yet? I'm going to drop off this cat food and then head out to work."

"I think I'll hang out here for a bit, just in case something changes. Will you be around later? Maybe I can buy you dinner somewhere as a thanks for letting me crash at your place?"

"Sure, that'd be lovely. There's a new vegan-friendly place right by mine that I've been meaning to check out. Let's go there. Seven thirty or so? After I'm done CrossFit." Janice widened her eyes and said, "Want to join me at CrossFit?"

"Hell no. But I'm definitely up for eating after." Kate smiled and said goodbye, taking the spare apartment key Janice proffered.

Hanna and Steve waved goodbye to Janice and thanked her for looking after Thunderpuss, and Kate held out the plant she had bought for Em. "Can you give this to Em. Will they let her have it in ICU?"

Steve took the potted plant and nodded. "It should be fine. Thanks. What kind of plant is it?"

"Oh, she'll know. It's a peace lily, but deadly to cats and dogs. I know Em loves them, so I figured she finally has a chance to have one around without Thunderpuss eating it. And it purifies the air! I remember Em saying she hates the smell of hospitals, so maybe this will help."

Hanna hugged Kate and then took the plant from Steve, saying, "Death flowers. Em will love it." She put her hand on Steve's chest and laughed, "Steve's been studiously avoiding white flowers - lilies especially."

Steve kissed the top of Hanna's head and then wagged a finger at her, saying, "Hey, the flowers are basically the only thing I can control." He looked at his watch and motioned that they should head inside. "Will you stick around for a while, or are you heading back to Janice's, Kate?"

"I'll go find the cafeteria and get some more coffee. I'm feeling that jetlag. Let me know how Em is and if there's any chance I can come up and see her, though, yeah?" She hugged Steve as he promised to let her know.

"Em will be so happy you're here, even if she can't see you in person. Thank you for coming."

"Of course. Now go give her a big sloppy kiss from me, both of you."

Steve and Hanna gave her a salute and walked away, and Kate fished her phone out of her pocket to check the messages that had come in while they had been walking.

100

SIXTEEN

"Wait, so... you're not a top?"

"No. Not really. And you, you're not a top?"

"Me? Hell no!"

Scout and Drew had spent the last few minutes trying unsuccessfully to get underneath each other on Drew's bed, having progressed from alleyway makeouts to fumbling in Drew's car, to a few days of cooling off and then a real dinner date that ended up leading them back to Drew's apartment.

Now, lying next to Drew, Scout called a time-out, resulting in a fit of breathless laughter from both player and coach.

"So... what do we do now?" Scout asked, as she sat up and looked at Drew.

"Flip a coin?" Drew said as she unbuttoned the remaining few buttons of her shirt.

"Seriously."

"I am serious." Drew reached into the pocket of her jeans and found a quarter.

"Wait," said Scout, incredulous. "Have you done this before?"

Drew laughed. "Um, this?" she gestured at the bed, "Or this," she said, holding up the coin.

"Flipping a flipping coin!"

"Yeah. Maybe." Drew grinned. "So, heads you're in charge. Tails you get to pin me down."

"Sure," Scout said, shaking her head and then shrugging her shirt off her shoulders.

Drew paused, waiting for Scout to wise up.

"Heyyyy!"

"Ha! OK. OK." Drew adopted a mock somber expression. "So, heads you're in charge. Tails I'm in charge. Tonight at least."

"Oh, you think there'll be another night like this, do you?" Scout pushed at Drew's shoulder and then kissed her.

"Oh, I think there might," Drew laughed as Scout grabbed the coin and flipped it, but Drew didn't wait to see how it landed. Instead, she tackled Scout and straddled her, then bent down to kiss Scout's neck and whispered, "Can I take off your pants?"

"Yes, yes!" Scout wriggled out of the jeans and kicked them off the bed, then ran her hands up Drew's spine and asked if she could unhook her bra.

Drew nodded and moved her hand slowly down Scout's torso, her eyes locked on Scout's as she slid her hand into her briefs. Scout closed her eyes and arched her back as Drew's fingers flicked across her clit.

"Woah, slow. Slow," she said, reaching down to hold Drew's hand still. She moved Drew's fingers to make her palm flat and said, "Like this."

Drew pushed the palm of her hand against Scout's body and moved slowly in circles, causing Scout to tilt her pelvis into the bed as she said, "Fuck," over and over.

"You like that?" Drew asked, watching Scout's face contort as she writhed beneath her. "You want me to -"

"Get inside me," Scout said, "Now, please."

Drew slipped two fingers inside Scout and slowly moved her hand back and forth, feeling the slickness, the heat of Scout's body.

102

Scout stroked Drew's thighs, the muscles taught as Drew sat atop her, riding her. She moved her hands up Drew's belly and across Drew's breasts, grazing her nipples, a soft purple against the deep, dark brown of her areola. Scout wanted to sit up again to kiss them, but she was unable to stop pushing her body harder and harder into the bed as Drew's fingers moved inside her. She was so wet and so close to orgasm already, and she didn't want Drew to stop. She dug her fingers into Drew's flesh and opened her eyes to see Drew biting her lip and nodding. She liked it hard. She was playing top for Scout, just for tonight, and Scout revelled in it, wanted to know how far she could push Drew.

"Flip me over. I want you to fuck me from behind." Scout held Drew's stare, then Drew grinned and sat up a little, releasing Scout's legs so she could turn on her stomach. Drew pulled off Scout's boxers and pushed her legs apart, then pulled her to her knees. Scout gripped the headboard and clenched her jaw as Drew fucked her harder now, one hand on her belly and the other three fingers deep inside her.

Drew could feel Scout tensing and then the waves of pleasure as she found that sweet, soft spot that made Scout sink her head to the pillow and moan.

After riding out the climax, Scout shifted her body and Drew slipped her fingers out, then planted soft kisses up Scout's spine, causing Scout to sink down into the bed, spent. She lay there for a little while, feeling the blood pulsing in her clit, the last muscular spasms as she got her breath back. Finally, she opened her eyes and reached behind her to find Drew's hand, pulling it to her mouth and kissing it.

Drew lay down on top of Scout and rested her cheek against Scout's cheek.

"Fuck," said Scout.

Drew smiled and kissed her neck, enjoying the sound of her braids snagging slightly against Scout's buzz cut.

Scout wriggled under Drew so that she lay on her back. She moved her hands slowly up the back of Drew's legs and

103

then lightly stroked the skin on Drew's lower back. Drew kissed her and felt Scout slip one hand beneath her belly.

Scout used her thigh to move Drew's legs apart and teased her fingers over Drew's pubic bone and between her labia. Her breath still ragged, Scout whispered, "Your turn."

SEVENTEEN

"You're just in time for jello!" Em said as Kate walked onto the ward bearing a giant bouquet of clementine coloured gerbera.

"Jello?! Woah!" Kate said, "Now this is what I came back to Vancouver for!"

Kate placed the flowers on the bed and went to embrace Em, then paused. "Wait, am I allowed to hug you? I'm not going to infect you or anything?"

Em waved her arms out to Kate to beckon her in, causing the IV line to dance around manically. "Come here and hug me, damn you."

Kate gripped Em tightly, the hospital gown did nothing to cushion Em's thin frame and Kate began to cry.

"Oh, Em." Kate sobbed into Em's shoulder and Em smiled at Steve who was arranging the gerbera on the night stand.

"Don't worry, sweetheart. The doctors say that if I just eat this magic jello, all will be well." Em grinned as Kate loosened her grip and then stood up and wiped her tears away. "Look," Em gestured at the meal tray, "Magic jello comes in raspberry and orange flavours today!"

Steve swiped the orange jello pot and stuck his tongue out at Em, who gave him a mock frown. "I guess I'm looking better, if you're stealing my sustenance."

Steve kissed Em and grinned. "You do look better today actually. Alice said you slept well."

"Alice from the ICU?" Em looked at Steve.

"Yep. She was at the nurses' desk when we came in. She said she likes to check up on patients in their first few days out of ICU." Steve offered the orange jello to Em, who declined.

"Alice is so lovely. I do hope things work out with that doctor of hers."

Kate laughed and said, "Oh, Em, making friends wherever you go. How many of the nurses have you been counselling while you're meant to be getting well?"

Em smiled. "Hospital is a pretty boring place to be, you know, when you're sick. But there are some really interesting people here if you can stop throwing up long enough to actually have a real conversation."

"Curiosity, the best anti-nausea drug." Kate laughed.

"Totally," Steve agreed, "with a half dose of helpful meddling three times a day."

Em licked her plastic jello spoon clean then threw it at Steve just as Hanna walked around the curtain.

"Woah! Do I need to intervene?" Hanna said, before giving everyone a hug.

"Ah, another benefit of a triad," Em laughed. "There's always a deciding vote or an umpire when you need one."

"How's the magic jello today?" Hanna kissed Em and licked her lips. "Raspberry, right?" Em nodded. "Yes!" Hanna fist-bumped Em. "I'm getting good at this."

Em shuffled in her bed, moving a pillow to prop herself up better. She looked up at Steve and then at Hanna and said, "So, I've seen enough of your faces for a while. Why don't you go find me something amazing in the hospital gift store?

Or, better yet, go do something fun and non-cancer related for once? Jeez." She grinned. "Kate and I have some serious business to discuss."

After a little protest, Steve and Hanna left, saying they would be back in an hour. Kate watched Hanna slip her hand into Steve's as they walked through the automatic doors, and she smiled.

Turning back to Em, Kate said, "It's still a bit weird."

"What is?" Em asked.

"Seeing Steve and Hanna. Your Steve, and, well -"

"Your Hanna?" Em laughed.

"I know. I know. We only dated for, like, two weeks. But I was crushing on her so hard for months."

"Ah, the never-ending barista crush." Em sighed dramatically.

Kate shook her head, laughing. "I don't have a crush on her now, obviously. And she's clearly way happier with you and Steve, but it's still kind of a headfuck, you know? Especially because I always thought I'd be super mad at anyone who got between you and Steve."

Em snorted and widened her eyes, saying, "Little do you know." Kate rolled her eyes and Em said, "I guess it must be pretty strange, yeah. I mean, you left just after we all got together. You haven't really had a chance to hang out with us as a triad."

"A trifecta?" Kate raised her eyebrows. "Wasn't that what you called it once?"

"Ha! Yes. A trifecta." Em shimmied across to one side of the narrow bed and patted the small space beside her. "Come snuggle."

Kate obliged, nestling into Em's shoulder and laying her arm across Em's torso. They both closed their eyes and Em said, "I missed this. I missed you."

"Me too. So much."

Em felt Kate's body start to shake and she kissed the top of Kate's head softly. "No crying. We've all cried quite enough

107

this year."

"I'm so sorry I wasn't here, Em. I'm so sorry I didn't even see you were sick."

"It's OK. For the longest time I wouldn't let myself believe that I was sick either."

"But you knew. Right? When you came to Amsterdam. You already knew?" Kate looked up at Em, who bit her dry, pale lip and nodded.

"I had just had a biopsy. I was pretty sure."

"So the talk with the lawyer? About the wedding and stuff. That didn't go anywhere?"

"That happened. Just, don't tell Steve or Hanna."

"They still don't know?" Kate exclaimed. "But, weren't you all planning a wedding?"

Em laughed. "I was. They had no clue. I just wanted it to all be easy. I was going to ask them a couple of weeks after I saw you, but then everything just sort of fell apart." Em smiled, then looked down at her chest and patted it. "Good job I didn't buy a dress." She laughed, and Kate laughed too.

"Is it weird?" Kate asked. "Sorry. That's a stupid question."

"It is. It's really weird. Some mornings I wake up and I'm all like, 'where are my boobs?', then I remember and it's like grieving for a dead person. Well, for two dead people I guess."

"Is there, I don't know, like some sort of counselling thing you can do?"

"Oh, yeah, I am totally going to do that! Can you imagine? I mean, I get to sit in a room with a bunch of super sad women talking about their boobs and how they nearly died. It'll be the best!"

"Em. Maybe it's a good idea?" Kate held onto Em's hand, stroking her fingers softly.

"Seriously. I will do it. I will go to the support groups. I just got that first infection right when I should've been getting back to something approaching normal. Then the side-effects

108

of the medication screwed with my heart, and now another damn infection put me right back in here. All in all, I've had plenty of thinking time in ICU, and I'm doing pretty OK with it all. Really. I'm lucky."

Kate scoffed, "Lucky? How'd you figure?"

Em paused for a second, before saying, "Well, I have Steve and Hanna. So, twice the love most people have to see them through this. And my job covers healthcare, so money isn't a big deal for me right now. And the staff here are awesome. And there's magic jello."

"So I heard." Kate laughed.

Em lowered her voice and said, "Kate, you know, statistically speaking, lesbians and bisexual women have a greater chance of dying from breast cancer."

Kate frowned, "Seriously? But, I mean, aren't we more likely to be, erm, obsessed with our boobs?" Kate laughed awkwardly. "What's the deal?"

"Well, one of the nurses here – the one Steve mentioned, Alice - told me that one of the reasons is that queers are less likely to have a family doctor, so we don't get check-ups as often," Em pointed at herself and said, "*Mea culpa*." She went on, "And lady queers generally don't have the fancy earning power of dudes, or a cushy spousal health insurance policy. Oh, and we drink more, smoke more, have poorer mental health and don't use the Pill as much as straight ladies or have babies as often or as early, which increases our risk of breast cancer."

Kate whistled softly. "So, all in all, it's bad news bears for me?"

Em nodded her head. "And throw in a little estrangement from family so you don't know your own health risks and have no support if you do get sick."

"Great. That's just awesome," Kate said. "Aren't I supposed to be here to cheer you up? Got any vegan magic jello?"

Em shook her head, laughing. "I'm working on it," she

said, then nodded towards the woman in the far corner of the ward, by the window. "I don't know what her situation is, but I haven't seen a single person come to visit her since I moved to this ward out of ICU. Not one. She just watches that TV hour after hour with the same sad expression, and keeps her curtain mostly closed so no one really feels like they can talk to her." Em sniffed. "I got the nurse to take some of my flowers over to her yesterday. I was drowning in flowers anyway. She was asleep, and then I was asleep when she woke up, so I don't even know if she knows where they came from. It's so sad."

"Do you know her name?"

"Therese. And the woman to her right is Abigail. Then there's Brigitte, Sarah, Melanie, me, another Sarah, and Andrea."

Kate craned her neck to see the bed at the other end of the ward, across from Therese. "Who's in that bed?"

Em was quiet for a second. "That was Sonia's bed."

"Where'd she -" Kate began, then fell silent. After a heavy couple of seconds, Kate was shocked when Em bust out laughing.

"Jeez. Morbid much. Sonia was discharged." Em shook the bed with laughter, and Kate, eventually, joined her.

When Em stopped laughing, she said, "It was really sweet actually. Sonia's husband and kids came in yesterday with balloon animals and escorted her home like it was Canada Day." Em coughed and took a sip of water.

"You OK?"

"Yeah. Yeah." Em waved away Kate's concern. "I just haven't talked this much for a while. I'm out of practice!"

"Not now I'm here! Tell me all the things." Kate said, kissing Em's cheek.

Em put her hand to her cheek and frowned, then moved her fingers to her brow and said, "Seriously, Kate. Don't get cancer. There are easier ways to get rid of unwanted facial hair. The ads on the hospital TVs tell me this every day now.

110

If only I had known."

"Noted."

"I'm serious."

"So am I."

"No, Kate, I really am serious. You worry me sometimes."

Kate sat up to look at Em. "What do you mean?"

Em hesitated and then said quietly, "I mean, you're pretty much always worrying about something, and you're known to like a drink or two, and things with Cass, well, that seems to have upped your booze intake even more, and I know she smokes so you're probably getting some passive smoking in there now too. We're not immune to everything, you know, and we're getting older."

Kate looked away as Em spoke, turning her gaze to the empty bed by the window. She saw herself lying there, her body frail, her face pale, sickly and gaunt. She blinked to force the image aside.

Em went on, "I don't mean to be negative, and yay veganism and all, but I think it's important not to see it as an absolute guarantee to a long and healthy life. At least, not when there are other, er, toxic things happening."

Kate swung her feet down from the bed and stood by the chair, looking at Em. After a few seconds, she sat down and said, "Are you saying that you think Cass is toxic?"

"No! No! Well, not exactly." Em held Kate's stare. "I don't know. You just don't seem to have been all that happy since you followed her to Amsterdam. You're always fighting the same battles, and then having a big boozy blowout when you make up. And it always seems to be on her terms. I just worry. I mean, I don't see how that's love, and I want you to be happy, Kate. And I -." Em trailed off, then said, "I just don't see how you can ever end up happy with Cass, is all."

Kate was silent for a few seconds, thinking how she had come to the hospital to see Em and to apologise for being so self-absorbed these past few months. Now Em was counselling her about Cass and seemingly suggesting that they break up.

"I don't think you should worry about me and Cass right now. You should concentrate on getting well," Kate said, without meeting Em's eyes.

"I can do both," Em said, softly. "Kate. Honey. You know I love you and I will support you, whatever you do, but I just don't see what you see in her, and, yeah, I'm going to play the cancer card: Life's too damn short to be wasting it on someone who's not good for you. I'm sorry."

"You know if this was coming from anyone else, I would've walked out by now, right?" Kate said, finally meeting Em's gaze.

"I know." Em swallowed some more water. "That's why it's coming from me and not from someone else."

Kate laughed harshly. "Someone else? Like who?"

"We're all worried about you," Em said. "It's hard, you know, when you're so far away. We don't feel like we know what's going on with you, and then you tell us about another fight you've had and another hangover and, well, we're not young and infallible and I worry what would happen if you got sick. I mean, do you really think Cass would step up and be at your bedside day and night?"

Kate imagined Cass holding her hand while a doctor gave her some bad news. The image did seem odd somehow, but not because Kate couldn't imagine Cass by her side. Maybe it was just because Cass looked so young in her baseball cap and hoodie. The Mickey Mouse bowtie didn't really help either. Cass just didn't fit the typical image of the doting partner, Kate figured. But was that all it was, or did Em have a point?

Cass could certainly be tempestuous and was hardly ever serious. Kate could only really see Cass playing nurse in a sexy way, but maybe that was unfair. After all, the two of them hadn't faced any real problems so far, so how could Kate know how Cass would react?

112

When Kate had left Cass at the station in Amsterdam she had promised to come back and build a life together. Now that she was away from the sort of Cass-induced dream state in which she had been living for the last six months or so, Kate had time to really think about the future. Did she truly want to build a life with someone who seemed to focus only on having fun and avoiding growing up? Steve, and now Hanna, were Em's anchors. Who would Kate's anchor be when she got old or sick? Was it enough that Cass had said she would try, or should Kate have not even had to ask?

She looked back at Em with a thin smile. "Cass is trying, Em. I can't explain why, but I just know that I need to give her a chance. I love her. I really do. And I -" Kate paused, frowning before saying, "I know she loves me too. It just doesn't come easily to her. She's got so many walls up all the time. And she doesn't see things the way we do."

Em reached out for Kate's hand and nodded. "I'm sure you're right. I just wish things were easier for you, is all."

"She makes me really happy most of the time, you know? Like, she just sort of wormed her way into my heart and knows right where to prod and poke."

"That's gross," Em said. "Let's not talk about things prodding and poking hearts."

"Uh, yeah, sorry. Bad metaphor. But what I mean is that Cass just gets me. She knows how to make me laugh and smile and, yeah, that also means she knows exactly where to strike to really hurt me, but I don't think she does it maliciously, she just expects stuff to blow up, so she's always on the defensive."

"It sounds like you're legitimising abuse," Em said, stroking Kate's hand. "And you know that's not cool."

Kate bit her lip. "It's not like that. She just goes too far sometimes, and she's used to having her way."

Em raised her eyebrows and Kate said, "Yeah, OK. That sounds like I'm making excuses, but I'm not. If I didn't think she was fundamentally a good person, I wouldn't have even

113

started dating her. She's figuring her shit out, and I want to be around for that, because I think she's golden, I really do." Kate smiled. "So, for example, the other day Cass woke me up by jumping on the bed with a leash in her mouth."

Em grimaced, "Do I want to hear this story?"

"Hush. Not like that. Although...." Kate looked up at the ceiling and blushed. "Anyway. No, so Cass jumps up on the bed with Jupiter's leash in her mouth, just like he does. And she's making these stupid little barking noises, and starts turning in circles like Jupes does when he's trying to make me take him out. And poor Jupes is standing in the doorway, absolutely aghast. Then Cass jumps off the bed and runs out into the kitchen and I follow her and it turns out that she's already taken Jupiter out for his walk, and fed him, and let me have an enormous lie-in. It's, like, eleven and Cass has made pancakes and coffee and there are mimosas and she just sits me down and lets me ramble about work, which was horrible the day before, which was why I was so exhausted." Kate smiles, and thinks about how Cass presented her with the little heart-shaped pancakes and some maple syrup, 'just like at home', and how Kate had resisted the urge to tease, because she knew that this moment of cuteness was such a vulnerable thing for Cass to be sharing.

Kate looked at Em, who was biting her fist again, trying not to laugh.

"Hey! It was freaking adorable. Shut up."

Em smiled and squeezed Kate's hand. "It sounds lovely. It really does. But I want to hear more of that stuff, and that there's less of the fighting and the weirdness. OK?"

"Deal."

"Don't just stop telling me about the other stuff, but remember to tell me the good things too, because otherwise I just don't get why you're with her."

Kate nodded. "I can see that. I get it. I guess it's just easier to bitch about something and keep all the good things to myself."

114

"Well, whatever the other story is with the leash, feel free to keep that to yourself," Em said, smirking, and Kate grinned, blushing again.

Part Three

EIGHTEEN

Cass took a gulp of beer from the plastic cup on the plastic tray that hung at an angle from the plastic seat back in front of her. She thanked the hostess, who hadn't charged her for the second drink.

"No problem. Let me know if there's anything else you'd like," the woman said, and she cocked her head to one side. "You know, to help distract you from your fear of flying."

"I'm not..." Cass was about to say she wasn't afraid of flying, but then realised that the hostess was flirting with her. She frowned. "Yeah. Thanks." Cass turned to look out the window at the blanket of cloud below them, waiting for the woman to walk away.

The North Atlantic was down there somewhere, an enormous body of water ready to swallow the plane whole should anything go wrong. Great, Cass thought, now the hostess had started her thinking about the plane crashing. If she had just gone along with the flirting and finally joined the mile-high club, Cass wouldn't have had to think about her impending death in the dark, cold waters between her and Kate.

She knew she shouldn't feel like congratulating herself for turning down the advances of an attractive woman. There was more to being a good girlfriend than that, Cass thought, but it was a step. She wanted to get to the point where that was a given. Where Kate would be able to trust her, and where she could trust herself not to fuck up when offered an opportunity to do so.

Cass had given Kate every reason to break up with her before leaving, figuring it was easier to crash and burn on that train platform than to pine over Kate in her absence and go through the inevitable slow fade of their relationship. And yet Kate hadn't broken up with her. She had weathered Cass's storms and promised to come back. She had checked in when she arrived in Vancouver, just like she said she would, and Cass had to believe that Kate would stay true to her promise to build a life together.

For once, it seemed to Cass that she was dating someone who actually believed that she was worth coming back to. The memory of Kate shouting from the train that she loved her made Cass grin into her plastic beer cup. Kate made her feel like the things she had pretended not to want for so long were actually things she could have. With Kate, maybe she could start to expect better of herself. Now someone really had her back, maybe Cass could allow herself to think about what she wanted to achieve, instead of continuing this pretense that life was just a series of fun exploits that never amounted to anything real.

Most of all, Cass wanted Kate to feel she could rely on her to be there when things got bad. She had returned to the apartment from the train station and found Jupiter waiting for her, his leash at his feet. Cass realised in that moment that Kate had trusted her to take care of him, and she had crumpled to the floor with that realisation. Jupiter padded over to lick away her tears, which were both joyful and sad. She hoped he was happily snuggled up with Kate's co-worker, Sami, who had been thrilled at the opportunity to hang out

118

with Jupiter while Cass flew out to join Kate.

As Cass stared out the window over the white expanse of cloud, she became aware of some kind of disturbance at the front of their section of the plane. The man in the seat across the aisle stood up to see what was happening. Cass unbuckled her seatbelt and glanced at the man, meeting his eyes as she also stood.

"What's going on?" Cass asked him as she looked at the group of passengers amassing near the curtains to the first class area.

"I don't know." The man stepped out into the aisle and said, "I'm going to go and check."

Cass saw the man dab at his forehead with a handkerchief, mopping up beads of nervous sweat. She wondered if not being afraid of flying was stupid. Maybe something was wrong with the plane. Maybe the pilot had died and the co-pilot was drunk, or screwing a flight attendant in the washroom. Cass looked at the rows of seats behind her and met several pairs of eyes all looking down the plane, trying to gauge a level of panic.

"It's not the plane. We're fine, for now."

Cass looked at the man in the seat behind her. He was still seated and had just glanced up at her momentarily.

"What do you mean?" She asked him.

He looked up from his laptop and shrugged his shoulders. "They'll make us land in Halifax or somewhere like that. Maybe even turn around if we're not too far out."

"So there is something wrong with the plane?" Cass asked, a slight crack in her voice.

"Probably not. But they're grounding all flights. There's been a terror alert in Amsterdam. No bomb or anything, but they'll want to ground all the flights and make us go through extra security."

"No shit," Cass said, and whistled softly through her teeth.

"Yeah. I hope no one is waiting for you at YVR. It'll be

a while until we're home."

"Hey, how do you know this? And why are you so calm about it? Are you like a security expert or something?" Cass frowned.

The man laughed and shifted in his seat, closing the lid of his laptop. He extended his hand over the back of Cass's chair and introduced himself. "Guy, Homeland Security." He waited for Cass to take his hand and then laughed again as she shook it slowly, her eyes wide. "Just kidding. I'm a nurse, I was just in Groningen."

"A nurse? Oh."

"Yeah, boys can be nurses too. Surprise." Guy rolled his eyes.

"Wow. Mind that chip on your shoulder doesn't ruin your posture." Cass raised an eyebrow. "I was just wondering, A) why a nurse would be in Groningen, and B) why you'd know about a terror attack -"

"Alert," Guy interrupted.

"A terror alert - before anyone else."

Guy shuffled across to the empty window seat and gestured at his now vacant aisle seat. "Come and sit, staring up at you is what is ruining my posture, not the chip on my shoulder."

Cass moved to sit down, bringing her beer with her.

"A), I'm helping to organise a diversity in nursing panel for a conference, and, B), some of my colleagues were on a later flight. One of them emailed from the airport. Everything's on lock-down."

"You've got email access?"

"Yeah. I forgot to turn my phone to airplane mode and I just got an alert. I guess we just flew under a satellite or something."

Cass rummaged for her phone.

"I wouldn't bother. The Wi-Fi takes a while to set up and is hideously expensive. I only have it because there's so much to do for the conference. It's costing me a fortune."

"But, what if..." Cass took a couple of deep breaths to try to calm herself. She had just realised that no one even knew she was on this flight. If they all died, right now, on this plane, blown up by terrorists, would anyone even be looking for her? Kate would think she was still in Amsterdam. She hadn't talked to her sister or her mom and dad in weeks, and everyone in Amsterdam would think she was just skipping class (which she was, given that she was flying to Vancouver). When would anyone start looking for her?

Cass opened her browser and got redirected to some small print terms and conditions. She started to scroll through, waiting for the check box that said she agreed. She just wanted to send an email. She should tell Kate that she loved her, that she was sorry they never had a chance to make things work. And she should email her mom to say that she was sorry she was such a disappointment, such a fuck-up, that she was just starting to figure stuff out. She'd never see Hobbes again, her dog that she had left with her sister before moving to Amsterdam. Hobbes and Jupiter, Kate's dog, had brought the two of them together, and now she'd never again get woken up by him sneezing on her feet. And she should email her sister, Caroline: twelve years older than Cass and living the picture perfect life in PoCo with her husband who was one of the most boring men Cass had ever met. Cass had always railed against Caroline's constant imploring that she got her life in order. Right from being a teenager, when Cass had come out and stopped giving a shit about what her parents and their congregation thought, Caroline had continued to ask her to stop smoking, stop drinking, get a real job and settle down and stop pissing off their mom and dad. Cass had hated it, but maybe Caroline had just been looking out for her and really thought that Cass would be happier living in a freakishly neat bungalow in the suburbs. If this plane went down, Cass would never have a chance to build a real relationship with her sister, as an adult.

"Hey, are you OK? Here...." Guy held out his napkin

and looked at Cass who realised with horror that there were tears coursing down her cheeks. What was wrong with her? She never cried in front of people, let alone a complete stranger on a plane.

"I'm sorry," she sniffed and quickly wiped her face. "I'm sorry, I just, I'm too young to die."

Guy burst out laughing, then steadied himself and swallowed the guffaws. Cass looked at him in shock, watching his face contort with the effort of maintaining a serious and concerned expression. Then she also started laughing, repeating to herself, "I'm too young to die! I'm too young to die! Oh man."

Guy gave Cass a little punch on the arm. "Dude, way to have a little meltdown." He poured half of his beer into Cass's empty cup and raised his in a toast. "To dying young, for 'tis better to burn out than to fade away." He went to drink, but Cass put her hand on his wrist to stop him.

"No, no, I don't think it is," she said softly, holding his gaze and feeling overwhelmed with an unfamiliar and unpleasant feeling that she had something to lose.

"OK," Guy said, "how about 'To a long and happy life'?"

They both drank, then Cass raised her cup again and said, "And to kismet, for introducing me to you and for giving me an idea."

Guy drank, holding Cass's gaze while she sipped thoughtfully.

"What kind of an idea?" Guy asked, raising an eyebrow and adding, "I should tell you that I'm not really interested in getting married and settling down right now."

Cass laughed. "Don't worry dude, I'm super gay. But, hey, I do want to ask you something."

NINETEEN

"The game's tonight! And Drew has me batting first!" Alice laughed as she pushed Em in her wheelchair to the conference room on the eighth floor.

"So you're not at all excited, I take it?" Em said, grinning up at Alice. "Is your fella going to be there?"

"Nope. He's on call until," Alice looked at her watch, "until midnight. So only another eight hours."

"Doesn't that mean he's just asleep in one of the on-call rooms?" Em asked.

"Not today. He's on his obstetrics rotation and he's got a bunch of women who are expected to pop tonight." Alice laughed and said, "Sorry, that's gross and unprofessional. It was just something his supervisor said to him a while ago, and it sort of stuck."

Em laughed and asked Alice how softball was going.

"I'm getting pretty into it actually. And I'm not half bad!" Alice stopped outside the door to the conference room and mimed pulling down her baseball cap and swinging a bat.

"And what about the other stuff? Getting into that too?" Em grinned. "There are a lot of very attractive lady queers on your team if I recall."

Alice blushed and looked down at her feet. "You know, I'm not too sure about all that. The more I think about Jeff not getting matched to Vancouver, and us or him having to move somewhere else, the more that scares me."

"How so?" Em asked, looking up at Alice from the chair after a quick glance down the corridor to see if the man she was meeting was on his way.

Alice followed her gaze, but the corridor was still empty. "We're a little early for your meeting. What's it about anyway? Why the secrecy?"

Em wagged her finger at Alice. "You're not dodging my question that easily."

Alice smiled and leaned against the wall, folding her arms across her chest. "I may have gotten a little too excited at the idea of being queer. I mean, I find women attractive. I really do. But, I just sort of don't really actually want it to go anywhere, I think, maybe." Alice chewed her lower lip and then looked at Em and asked, "I just don't want to lead anyone on."

Em nodded and smiled at Alice. "I can't really see you doing that, but I get it."

Alice sighed, then said, "You were gay first, right? Before Steve?"

Em laughed and then coughed, turning bright red. Alice rubbed her back and looked around to see if she could get some water, but Em recovered and wiped the tears from her eyes.

"I'll be pretty happy when this cough is done with. I miss being able to talk forever!" Em swallowed and smiled. "To answer your question, no. I wasn't gay, as such. I just only had longer-term things with women up until meeting Steve, so the community mostly just assumed I was gay. 'Coming out' when I started dating him was not the best. A few friends made some terrible dick jokes. Some just couldn't handle me bringing him to queer events. And one person actually yelled

124

at me for upholding the patriarchy when all I was holding was Steve's hand at an art show." Em raised her eyebrows.

"Seriously?" Alice blinked at Em. "That's bizarre."

"It was pretty odd, yeah. I mean, for the most part, my friends were great. They could see I was happy and that Steve's awesome. There's always bad apples in any community, right? I just became a bit of a peculiar target."

"And now you're like the poster woman for polyamorous bisexuals!" Alice laughed.

"Totally. But probably still not allowed on the poster for breast cancer survivors. They'd need a wider angle lens for that happy family photoshoot."

Alice asked, "That's not what you're doing today, is it? A publicity thing for the hospital?"

Em shook her head, and then peered past Alice at the sound of a door swinging open just down the corridor. A man in brown corduroy pants and a red and green sweater vest over a white shirt was walking jauntily up to them and grinning.

Em looked up at Alice and said quickly, "Let's talk more about you and Jeff later, yeah? Sounds like you could use someone to bounce some thoughts around with, and I'll miss you once I'm discharged."

Alice nodded and smiled, "I'd really appreciate that. Thanks Em."

The grinning man stuck out his hand and said, "Angus O'Donnell, Community Outreach Team Manager. You must be Emilie? I hear you have some questions about our programmes."

Em shook his hand and introduced herself. She realised that Angus's vest featured reindeer and penguins, and she figured that this was going to be a much more entertaining meeting than she had anticipated. Any man who can rock that kind of vest in spring, or ever, was someone she wanted to work with.

Em thanked Alice for wheeling her about the hospital

and helping her find the meeting room, and promised to enlighten her later about what she was up to. As Angus wheeled Em into the meeting room, she called over her shoulder, "Good luck at the game tonight!"

TWENTY

Steve, Hanna, and Kate piled into a cab and headed to China Creek park, passing by Kate's old apartment on the way.

"Miss it?" Steve asked, looking at Kate.

She turned away from the window and smiled at Steve. "Yeah. A lot."

The cab's wipers screeched against the glass as the first few drops of rain reached critical mass.

"Even the rain?" Hanna said, smiling.

"It rains in Amsterdam! Vancouver doesn't have the monopoly on precipitation."

"Vancouver does have a rainforest though," Steve said, stroking his beard.

Kate reached out to tug gently on the beard and said, "This doesn't make you wise, you know?"

"Ah, but it makes me devilishly handsome."

Hanna turned to look at Kate from the front of the cab, rolling her eyes.

When they pulled up to the park, Steve handed the driver some cash and they all stepped out onto the sidewalk.

"I don't see anyone," Kate said, looking for any sign that

they were in the right place. "Um, I also don't see a softball field." She turned to Steve and said, "Isn't this China Creek south?"

"There's a China Creek north?" Steve said, prompting Hanna to groan and run into the street after the cab, waving her arms up and down. The cab stopped and started reversing slowly until Hanna was safely back onto the sidewalk, whereupon he sped back to them.

"Um, can you take us to the other China Creek park please?" Steve said as they all got back into the cab.

The driver laughed and shook his head. "You pay. I drive."

"Hey, where are you from?" Kate asked, hearing something familiar in the man's voice.

"Bloemendaal, Holland, originally. Been here five years. You're British, yes?"

"Originally, yes. I'm living in Amsterdam right now though. I went to Bloemendaal last week. I was missing the water!" Kate grinned at the driver in the rear view mirror. By the time they had arrived at the correct China Creek park, Kate had learned of a whole bunch of new places to check out near Amsterdam and had sadly informed their driver, Jens, that his favourite bar in Amsterdam had closed last month.

"I knew I should have visit sooner!" Jens cried, as he gave Steve his change and refused to take a tip.

He looked at Kate and said, "Have a drink back home for me."

Kate promised that she would and shook his hand, then they all ran across the field to the crowd of people gathered by the diamond.

Alice waved at Steve and Hanna as they found a spot to stand behind the netting. She smiled at Kate and then turned back to listen to the coach, who Kate realised she had met the previous season, when she had attended a couple of Cass's
128

games.

Kate smiled to herself, remembering how much of a fangirl she had been, without Cass ever even realising. It must have been so obvious to everyone on the team, Kate thought, and started looking to see if there were any other people she recognised from last season.

A couple of players looked familiar, but Kate couldn't remember their names. One woman she knew through Grace and Kerry, and she wondered where Kerry was. Hadn't she intended to coach the team this year?

Kate's eyes were drawn to a figure who had just moved to stand by Alice. The woman had her back to Kate, but there was something in the way she carried herself that held Kate's attention: her repetitive tapping of the bat against her shoe; the way she lifted her cap and ran her hand over her hair. The player, perhaps feeling Kate's intense gaze, turned and looked in Kate's direction.

Momentarily thrown, Kate reached forward and clutched at the netting, mouthing, "Hey, what the -"

"Kate?" Steve put a hand on her shoulder and she turned to look at him while pointing back at the field. Steve looked and asked what was wrong.

Kate looked back at the field and saw that the player had turned her back again and was walking over to Drew. The opposition team still wasn't ready, so Steve yelled over to Alice to come and say hi.

"You're all so sweet for coming to watch!"

Alice stood awkwardly and then Hanna hugged her and said, "I promised Em a blow-by-blow account of the game, so you'd better make it memorable!"

Steve hugged Alice and thanked her for the invitation. "Em wishes she could be here."

"Maybe she will be, by the end of the season," Alice said, and turned to Kate to introduce herself. "It's going to be a fun game if it carries on raining. Lots of muddy slides!" Alice said, grinning.

Kate smiled and started to ask, "Who's your teammate? The player who -" Drew's whistle drowned out Kate's question, and the coach clapped her hands and beckoned to her players.

Alice grinned manically and said, "Gotta go!" before running to join her team. Kate was perplexed. Alice's teammate clearly wasn't Cass, that was ridiculous. But the similarity was bizarre. Kate told Steve and Hanna that she was going to walk around a little to stay warm. The rain had continued and she did feel a little chilly, but she really just wanted to get a closer look at the unnerving doppelganger.

Kate walked around the netting, watching Alice swing the bat and connect first time. There were woops and howls from the rest of the team as Alice sprinted from base to base. As she was about to reach third, the ball flew over her head, so Alice stopped at the base and did a little dance on the spot. The player who looked like Cass was sitting on the bench, laughing at Alice. As Kate drew close, she heard the same childlike glee as with Cass's laughter. Then the woman stood up to take her turn to bat and Kate walked a little further.

A woman was walking her dog just ahead of Kate on the running track that circled the park. The sight of the young-looking Great Dane gave Kate a stab of anxiety about Jupiter. She knew Cass would take good care of him, and Sami from Kate's office was taking Jupiter for his afternoon walks on the days Cass had class until late, but she missed Jupiter nonetheless.

The Great Dane, who Kate figured was probably only about a year old, kept turning to look at Kate as the woman dragged him away. Kate decided to walk the track, allowing herself a little time to reminisce about the afternoons she had spent there with Jupiter: the hangouts with friends on the benches at the top of the park; the picnics she and Janice had shared there. Kate had even been on a few dates at the park, drinking wine on the steep bank that rose up above the field, which offered a grand view of the mountains and the city out

130

east.

Watching the light change across the city as the sun dipped, Kate wondered if she would be back, to live, in Vancouver any time soon. Cass seemed pretty set on staying in Amsterdam for the academic year at least and it seemed like the charity Cass did video editing for had another project slated for the fall. Kate's job was also going well, but she didn't know if she really wanted to be there for the longer term. If anything, her new position was much more managerial than she had expected. She barely did any actual design work, she just arranged for someone else to do the interesting stuff and fielded clients' worries and questions. She missed getting her teeth stuck into a project and taking it from the first inkling of an idea to a full-fledged brand and website.

Kate looked up at the sound of barking ahead of her. A little Boston terrier puppy was bouncing around the dog that had just passed by Kate. The Great Dane was straining at his leash while barking and wagging his enormous tail, and the woman was clearly struggling to keep hold of the massive dog as she looked around to try to locate the puppy's person. When the Great Dane's tail went down and he started growling at the puppy, Kate decided to hurry ahead and help the woman. She thought she might be able to get hold of the puppy and separate the dogs to prevent the Great Dane going ape-shit. Before Kate reached them, though, the woman slipped, letting go of the leash as she fell into a muddy puddle.

The puppy took off and the Great Dane sprinted after it, heading in the direction of the softball game. Kate quickly checked on the woman, who was annoyed but otherwise fine, then she turned and ran after the dogs, hoping to steer them back in the direction of their owners. The dogs were now too busy chasing each other to bother barking, meaning that the outfielders didn't hear them coming. The pitcher was also unaware and tossed the ball at the batter, who connected and sent the ball sailing out across the field.

Kate lunged for the Great Dane's leash as he ran past her after the puppy, who had finally realised that the other dog might not be a playmate after all. She caught the end of the leash but the hundred-pound dog yanked her forward and then everything suddenly went black.

TWENTY-ONE

"Cass?"

"She's waking up!"

"Kate? Kate? Can you hear me?"

"Cass?" Kate tried to shield her eyes from the rain, but there was something wrong with her arm. She couldn't feel her arm. "Oh god. Oh god." She tried to sit up, but that made her dizzy, so she closed her eyes.

"Kate. Don't try to sit up, but open your eyes if you can hear me."

Kate tried to speak, but the blinding pain at the back of her head was making her feel horribly nauseous and she didn't want to open her mouth. She opened her eyes and saw Alice bending over her.

"Kate. Do you know who I am?"

Kate tried to nod, but could barely move her head it hurt so much.

"Kate. Do you know where you are?"

"Home." Kate managed to say, then realised that this wasn't right. Where was she?

"Oh god. Is she OK?" Kate heard Steve's voice and

133

opened her eyes again. "Why is her arm at that weird angle? Oh god." Steve covered his mouth and turned away.

"Steve, stay calm. She'll be fine." Alice's voice was steady as she explained to Kate, "I'm pretty sure you've dislocated your right arm, so you probably can't feel it right now. Don't worry, we'll get it fixed. You also got whacked on the head pretty good by that softball, so you're most likely concussed. Again, don't worry. We'll take you to the hospital and get you checked out. OK?"

"Woah. Is she dead? Did I kill her?" A voice Kate didn't recognise broke through over the babble of voices and the increasingly distant sound of dogs barking. Why were there dogs? Was Jupiter there? Did someone have Jupiter?

"Steve! Steve! Where's Jupiter?" Kate started to cry, but Steve crouched down next to her and put his hand on her left shoulder, very gently.

"Why's she talking about planets? Damn, that ball hit her good, hey. Why was she even on the field?"

"Hey, everyone," Alice said, standing up. "Back up please and give Kate some air. She's going to be fine." She knelt down next to Steve and asked quietly, "Why is she asking about Jupiter?"

"Jupiter is Kate's dog. And he's in Amsterdam, with Cass. He's just fine, Kate." He patted her good shoulder. "Should we, I don't know, get her to the hospital?"

"Yes. Did you drive?"

"No, we all took a cab."

"You can borrow my car if you like," Drew spoke up. "I should stay for the game, but take the car and we can figure it out later. Best she gets that head checked out right away."

"Thanks Drew," Alice said, taking the proffered keys. She whispered something to Steve, who grimaced.

"Can't you just, you know, put it back into its socket or whatever?" Steve asked Alice quietly.

"Not without risking tissue damage or nerve damage, no. It's not really my field of expertise, so I might do more

134

harm than good." She held out her hand and asked for Steve's jacket, having nothing of her own to use.

He nodded and took off his jacket. Hanna handed Alice her bandana and nervously rubbed at her bare neck.

"Kate, I'm just going to stabilise your shoulder and arm, OK. You might feel some pain, but I'll be as quick as I can. Try not to move."

Kate nodded, then winced, then screamed as Alice used the jacket and her softball bat to splint Kate's arm and tie it to her body. She clutched at the ground with her left hand, her fingers sinking into the mud as her head started spinning again.

"OK. Done. Steve can you -" Alice paused and smiled at Steve, gesturing at Kate. "Kate, Steve is going to carry you to the car. It might hurt a little when your arm is moved, but Steve will be as gentle as he can and they can pop it back in when we get you to the hospital."

Steve slid his hands underneath Kate's legs and back. As gentle as he tried to be, he couldn't help knocking her arm. Kate felt an intense jolt of pain, then a persistent roar behind her eyes. She blacked out again.

When Kate woke up and opened her eyes, she immediately closed them again. Hospital lights were so incredibly bright when you were staring right at them.

She tried to think of the last thing she could remember, and started to wiggle the fingers of her left hand. Thank god, Kate thought, then she giggled, thinking about everything she liked to do with that hand.

"Hey! You're awake! What's so funny?" Steve was peering over her, blocking the light.

"I can move my hand!"

"Yes! I see!" Steve grinned at her.

"I don't know how I'd survive without use of that hand."

"Well, you're left-handed and it's your right arm that got busted so -"

135

"So it doesn't matter?" Hanna piped in as she stood up from her chair.

"I'm left-handed?" Kate asked, looking up at Steve as she tried to wiggle the fingers on her right hand.

"Uh huh. Unless you've been lying to us all this time."

"Oh. Hm. My head hurts." Kate frowned. "What happened?"

"You don't remember?" Steve asked, moving out of the way so that the light once again blinded Kate.

"Can you help me sit up?" She tried to push herself upright, but her arm was in a sling across her chest and hurt like hell when she tried to move more than just her fingers.

Steve fiddled with the bed. "I'm a pro at this, these days." He rearranged Kate's pillow and blanket.

"Where are my clothes? Was there a puppy?" Kate asked as she looked at Hanna and Steve. "And Cass was there?"

Steve shook his head. "Your clothes got all muddy, so we're taking them home to wash. And, yes, there was a puppy. Trust you to remember that first. But Cass is in Amsterdam, Kate, with Jupiter." Steve laughed and explained what had happened.

"But it wasn't Cass?"

"No. Kate, that ball hit you pretty hard. You're bound to be a bit confused." Hanna poured Kate some water and handed her the tumbler.

Kate sipped, then asked again, "So, Cass definitely wasn't there? I could swear I saw her."

Steve glanced at Hanna, who frowned and said she was going to the washroom. She came back a few minutes later with a doctor who started asking Kate questions and shining a bright light in her eyes.

After he was finished assessing her, the doctor said, "Kate, we'd like to keep you in overnight, OK? Your arm looks fine. A simple dislocation, no broken bones or major tissue trauma. But, while some confusion is normal, we just want to watch you for a little while to be safe. OK? Sound good? OK?" The doctor nodded repeatedly, like a car dashboard ornament, and it made Kate feel even dizzier.

"OK." Kate didn't nod back as she was trying to quell another bout of nausea.

After the doctor had gone, Kate asked which hospital they were in. "Can I go see Em? Which floor am I on?"

Steve laughed. "Maybe in the morning, when you're discharged, we can all go up and see her. Right now, you're under strict orders not to move. And anyway, Em will most likely be asleep already. It's a pretty sleepy ward now that Sonia's gone."

"Are you leaving now?" Kate asked, suddenly realising that she would be alone among strangers all night, with only a thin curtain to separate them. How had Em survived this for so long? Kate felt like crying again, and she wished she could be upstairs with Em.

"You'll be fine. You'll fall asleep in no time and when you wake up, there'll be delicious magic jello for breakfast."

"But... vegan jello?"

Steve and Hanna exchanged a glance and then looked back at Kate, who was laughing at them. "Just kidding. I wish they had magic vegan jello though. That'd be amazing."

Hanna said, "It's a good job you're only in here overnight. I'm pretty sure you'd be overhauling their menu if you had to stay any longer."

"No artisanal vegan almond cheese round these here parts, that's for sure." Steve smiled and then kissed Kate's forehead. "Get some rest, and we'll see you in the morning with clean clothes. Then we'll see about taking you up to see Em if you're feeling better."

Steve and Hanna pulled the curtain aside and then shut it again to give Kate privacy. As they walked down the ward towards the nurses' station they spotted Alice and stopped to say thanks.

"No problem! I'm glad I was there and could help. Such a weird freak accident." Alice smiled and turned back to the person she had been talking to, handing her Drew's car keys and then saying, "Scout, this is Steve and his girlfriend, Hanna."

Scout turned to say hi, putting out her hand to Hanna first. Scout's hand hung in the air for half a second as Hanna did a double take. She took Scout's hand and shook it, as did Steve, but neither of them said anything. Then they looked at each other and back at Scout.

Finally, Steve cleared his throat and said, "Sorry, it's just, you totally look like Kate's girlfriend. It's really weird."

"Yeah, like, you could be twins." Hanna peered at Scout and then shook herself and apologised. "I'm sorry. It's just... well." She turned to Steve and asked, "Cass doesn't have a sister, right?"

"Yeah, but she's a lot older," Steve said, then turned to Scout and laughed, saying, "Maybe you have a long-lost twin or something."

Scout laughed. "Maybe. I was a foster kid, so anything's possible!"

"You were in foster care?" Alice asked, looking curiously at Scout. "I didn't know that."

Scout felt her face flush as the three of them stared at her. She smiled widely at Alice, and shrugged, saying, "It's true, but I'm totally normally. Honest." She mock-saluted and smiled, causing Hanna, Steve and Alice to laugh awkwardly.

Hanna and Steve thanked Alice again for the help and said goodbye to her and Scout.

When they reached the stairwell, Hanna touched Steve's arm and said, "Do you think Kate thought that Scout was Cass? Maybe that's why she was confused."

"Maybe. She was acting a little weird." Steve nodded and held the door open for Hanna. They walked down to the ground floor and were about to walk out of the hospital when Steve stopped. "I kind of want to go and see Em. She'd want to know that Kate was OK."

Hanna smiled and slipped her arm into his. "Steve-O,

Em has no idea that Kate is even in the hospital. Waking her up to tell her that Kate's three floors below would only make her anxious. Let her sleep. You'll see them both in the morning."

Steve put his arm around her shoulder and kissed the top of her head. "I love you," Steve said, "and I am super tired. Let's get home."

"Yes please. I'm beat."

"You have work tomorrow, right?"

Hanna nodded, "At noon. Then we're on at Fortune Sound Club at 8. I'll swing by the hospital at 11 on my way to work, but I can't take Kate to Janice's."

They both stopped walking and looked at each other.

"Shit," Steve said. "I'll call Janice and let her know what happened."

"Someone should probably tell Cass too. Do you have a way of contacting her?"

"Em will. I don't. I'll figure it out tomorrow. It'll be super early in the morning there now anyway." Steve scrolled through his contacts for Janice and was about to call when he realised how late it was. "Maybe I should just text," he said, and Hanna guided him around street obstacles as he tapped out a message on their way to the bus stop.

TWENTY-TWO

"Goddamnit, hospitals are horrible," Kate muttered to herself as she made her way back from the bathroom, trying to avoid having her flimsy gown come loose.

Why was she in a gown anyway? Where had her clothes gone? She hadn't even been able to find her shoes when she was woken up by her bladder screaming at her, so she was cold, bare foot and cranky. She was also still quite dizzy and wondered if she should even be out of bed. The thought of waiting for a nurse to come and help her to the bathroom had made her bladder do somersaults though, so she had scurried as fast as she could, keeping a watchful eye on things she could grab for support if necessary.

Having safely returned to her bed, Kate awkwardly wrapped the blanket around her shoulders using her left hand, trying not to knock her right arm which was still sore. She looked around for her things and checked the time on her phone. It was only six-thirty and her battery was about to die. Unless she was discharged, she would have to wait for almost five hours before Steve or Hanna came to visit, hopefully with some clothing. She wondered if Em would be awake, and if she could sneak up to see her.

Kate spotted her muddy sneakers under the bed and slipped them on. They were better than nothing, she thought, despite being damp and cold. She picked up her phone and wallet and looked down the ward to see what the nurses were doing. They were engaged in a whispered argument with a doctor, hands on hips and faces wrinkled with consternation. Kate took off in the other direction down the hallway to find an elevator. She was glad she wasn't dragging an IV stand.

The hospital was quiet, with just a few patients waking up and reading in bed or watching TV with headphones. Most were still asleep, snoring softly, with a few notable exceptions. Kate was glad she had managed to get some sleep herself, despite being woken up every two hours by a nurse who wanted to check that her brain hadn't imploded from the shock of being struck by a very fast softball.

Kate was hit by a wave of tiredness and so she leaned against the elevator wall and indulged in a little daydream about her bed back in Amsterdam, with Cass's arms around her. Cass would be finishing her class right about now and cycling home to Jupiter, ready to take him for his afternoon walk. Kate had anticipated staying in Vancouver for a week as that was all the time she could reasonably take off from work. Getting a serious concussion and a dislocated shoulder four days into her visit had not been part of the plan, and she wondered if this meant she couldn't fly. Jupiter would be thankful at least that her Frisbee-throwing arm hadn't been injured.

The elevator came to a halt and the doors opened, revealing an empty hallway leading to Em's ward. Kate held the blanket tight at her neck and walked quickly and quietly towards Em's room. As she was about to pass by the washrooms, a nurse rushed out and narrowly avoiding slamming into Kate. The man jumped back in surprise and then looked at her with narrowed eyes.

"Do I know you? Are you meant to be on this ward?"

He smiled at her, having a hard time figuring out that he had met her yesterday, when she had been wearing civvies and visiting Em.

Kate explained in a hushed voice and asked if Em was awake and if she could sneak in. "I'll be quiet. I promise." She smiled and the nurse rolled his eyes.

"The problem is, I don't know if you should be out of bed. So if I don't send you back downstairs, it's my neck on the line, see."

"I'm fine. I feel great!" Kate lied. "They were just keeping me in for observation overnight, and now it's morning, so..." she smiled again and tried to shrug her shoulders, but that just made her wince, somewhat ruining the effect.

"Which floor were you on? Which ward? I can call down and see if it's OK for you to be running around the hospital unattended." The man shook his head, laughing softly. "It's patients like you that make our lives hell. No one ever wants to follow the rules. Rules that are in place to help you get better faster!"

Kate grinned again and apologised. "I just want to see Em. And maybe steal some of her clothes." Kate looked down at her sad attire and raised her eyebrows.

"Fine. But be quiet. OK?" The nurse went to make his calls and Kate slipped into Em's room and quietly pulled aside the curtain.

"I thought I heard your voice," Em said quietly as she put down her copy of *Harry Potter, A L'Ecole des Sorciers*. "What happened?!"

Kate clumsily manoeuvered her body to sit on the bed, finding it hard to get the necessary leverage with just one functional arm. She explained in whispers, at least as much as she could remember, while trying to keep Em from laughing.

"A puppy!"
"Shh!"
"Wait, what? Your head?"

"Shh!"

"Sorry." Em put her hand over her mouth and laughed as quietly as she could. "Oh, Kate. You know there are easier ways to spend time with me while I'm in hospital."

Kate grimaced, "I honestly don't know how you can stand it in here. I've just been in for one night, but they've already stolen my clothes and my dignity!"

Em bit her hand to stop herself from guffawing, widened her eyes and used her other hand to motion at Kate to stop talking. When she recovered, Em reached over to the cabinet beside her bed.

"Have a rummage in there. Now I've wasted away and have no chest, we're about the same size, so something should fit." Em grinned. "Luckily for you!"

"Um, thanks. I guess," Kate said as she crouched to see if she could find a cardigan that she could easily slip over her shoulder. She pulled a grey sweater dress out of the cupboard and held it up to show Em. "Is this...?"

Em laughed. "Yeah, sorry."

"When did you...?"

"You left it one night when you stayed over, and I only found it once you were away. It was pretty nice having something of yours around." Em smiled and Kate stood up to hug her but lost her balance and had to grab onto Em's outstretched arm to stop herself from falling. Em held Kate still until the dizzy spell passed.

Opening her eyes and smiling thinly at Em, Kate said, "Well, now that I'm horribly injured, maybe I'll be in Amsterdam for a little longer."

"Vancouver, you mean?" Em said.

"Yeah, Vancouver, like I said," Kate shook her head at Em and then winced and put her hand up to the hard lump where the ball had hit her.

"You said Amsterdam."

"No. I said Vancouver. I know where I am, Em." Kate shot Em a look and Em held up her hands in mock defence.

"OK. Sorry. Well, for your sake, I hope you don't have to cancel your flight. But it would be nice if you came back home." Em helped Kate pull a cardigan over her good arm and buttoned the top button to keep it closed. Kate found some lounge pants and Em helped her on with those as well, pulling them up just as the curtain was whisked aside by the nurse Kate had run into in the hallway.

"Oh!" The man turned around and said, "Are you decent?"

Kate smiled, "Always."

The nurse turned and said good morning to Em.

"Good morning Kamran, great security you've got in this hospital." Em laughed.

"Insistent friends you've got, Emilie," Kamran countered, pursing his lips.

He looked at Kate and smiled, letting her know that she was needed back in her bed right away. "Morning rounds. If it's just a minor concussion you'll most likely be discharged, but they'll want to check a couple of things first."

"Like if she's having dizzy spells or forgetting where she is?" Em asked Kamran, without looking at Kate.

"Em!" Kate cried, punching her lightly on the shoulder. Em didn't laugh, she just maintained eye contact with Kamran, who had crossed his arms and was now peering at Kate.

"I'm fine," Kate said. "I just stood up too quickly when I was trying to get the, the," Kate waved her arm in the direction of the sweater dress. "The thing," she said quietly, dropping her gaze to her sneakers.

"How about I help you get back downstairs, to your bed, where you'll stay until your doctor checks on you?" Kamran said, offering Kate his arm. "Emilie, Doctor Chan is coming in to see you at eleven. Steve will be here by then, yes?"

Em nodded and said, "Yes. Why? What's going on?"

"Who's Dr. Chan?" Kate asked, holding gratefully onto Kamran's elbow as he steered her around the bed, which

144

suddenly seemed like a very confusing object to navigate.

"She's my oncologist," Em said flatly, her face turning pale.

"It's just routine though, right?" Kate asked, looking up at Kamran and then back at Em.

"Oh, yeah," Kamran nodded and smiled. "Now, let's get you downstairs and let Emilie eat her breakfast in peace."

TWENTY-THREE

Once Kate was safely back in her bed, she was hit by a wave of extreme tiredness, coupled with nausea. She pressed her eyelids closed and swallowed.

Kate realised that she had forgotten to let Cass know what had happened. She reached for her phone, hoping it still had battery power. As she moved, the room started spinning, forcing Kate to lean back into the pillows. She could text Cass later, she thought and closed her eyes again, letting the darkness blanket her mind.

"Kate? You're Kate, right?"

She tried to open her eyes to see who was saying her name, but her body hadn't quite woken up and she began to panic that she was paralysed.

"Kate?"

This time Kate managed to open one eye and saw a vaguely familiar person standing in front of her.

The tall black woman peered at Kate and said, "Sorry.

You were mumbling something, so I assumed you were awake. I didn't mean to startle you."

She held out a jacket and placed it gently on the foot of Kate's bed. "You left this in my car last night, so I thought I'd drop by on my way to work, on the off chance you were still here."

Kate smiled and said, "Thanks, um, Da-, Dor-, Dee?" She frowned.

"Drew. We met last season, when you came to some games with Cass." Drew smiled and held out her hand to Kate, then switched hands as she noted the shoulder sling.

"Drew, right. Of course. Sorry, I seem to be having some issues remembering stuff."

"That'll happen when you take a whack like you did. Concussion's no joke." Drew shook her head. "Anyway, I hope you feel better soon. Take it easy, alright? Don't go chasing any more giant dogs around on sports fields."

Kate laughed, "I'll try. And thanks for dropping off my jacket. Oh, and for driving me to the hospital last night."

Drew frowned. "Your friends drove you, but you're welcome for the loan of the car."

A nurse peered around the curtain and asked, "You found her? Everything OK?"

Drew nodded. "Yes, thanks. Jacket returned safely. Take care Kate."

"Thank you," Kate said as Drew turned to leave.

The nurse pulled the curtain aside and told Kate that the doctor was about to come and see her. As she moved away, Kate saw Drew slip her arm around the waist of a person standing by the hand-wash station.

"Cass?" Kate whispered, her eyes suddenly filling with tears. "Cass, what are you doing?" Her voice grew louder and the nurse looked at her, puzzled. Kate started to cry and called out again, "Cass, you promised! You promised me!" She started to climb out of bed, but the nurse held her back and turned to look at Drew and Scout, who were now staring at

Kate.

The nurse asked Kate what was upsetting her.

"My girlfriend is cheating on me! With the coach!" Kate yelled, and Drew let go of Scout's hand and took a step towards Kate.

"Kate, it's OK," Drew said, holding out her hands and gesturing for Kate to relax. Kate glared at her and the nurse turned to look at Drew.

"It might be best if you just leave. You and your, um, friend seem to be upsetting my patient." The nurse started shooing Drew and Scout away, but Drew stood her ground and called Scout over.

"Kate, this is Scout. She's on the softball team." Drew took Scout's hand and pulled her closer.

Kate blinked and wiped her eyes.

"Hey," Scout said, holding out her hand to Kate.

"You're not Cass?" Kate said, gingerly reaching out her hand. "I don't understand. Who are you?"

Scout smiled. "I'm Scout. I don't know who this Cass person is, but she's starting to cause me a whole lot of trouble, that's for sure."

"You have a prairie accent, right? You don't sound like Cass." Kate said, still frowning and peering at Scout.

"No ma'am. I sound like me. And I'm Scout."

Drew put her arm around Scout's shoulders and said to Kate, "Scout joined the team this year. She's from the prairies. She sure as hell looks a lot like Cass though, I know." Drew smiled and asked, "So you and Cass finally got together, huh?"

Kate nodded and sniffed. She leaned forward and the nurse watched her closely, then shrugged and got on with seeing to other patients, muttering to herself.

"What did she say?" Scout said, turning to glare at the nurse.

"Oh, she just made some small-time homophobic comment," Drew said loudly enough for the nurse to hear. "I got her name. We'll file a complaint."

148

Scout laughed and stretched up to kiss Drew's cheek.

"Your laugh, it's -." Kate smiled. "Your laugh is Cass's laugh. And you have her face. But you're... you're not her. Sorry." She shook her head and then looked Scout in the eye and said again, "Sorry. I'm just a bit confused and I thought you were my girlfriend and I thought you were cheating on me with -." Kate flapped her hand about, trying to locate the name.

"Drew."

"Right. Sorry. Drew." Kate shuffled and then looked at Scout again. "How old are you?"

"Almost twenty-five."

"Three years younger than Cass." Kate bit her lip. "Do you have cousins or, well, like estranged family or anything?" Kate asked, then blushed. "Sorry, I'm being really rude. You don't need to answer that."

Scout smiled and lifted her baseball cap to run her hand over her hair. "It's cool," she said, "but, honestly, I don't know."

Kate frowned and wondered if Cass had failed to mention having family in the prairies. "How can you not know? Sorry, I don't understand." Kate put her hand to her head, which was throbbing. She closed her eyes.

"I was put up for adoption. I lived in foster care."

Kate opened her eyes again and met Scout's gaze. "What?"

"I don't know my birth family. Never met 'em."

"Do you know your surname?" Kate asked, gripping the blanket, her knuckles turning white.

"Huh?"

"Your family name, second name," Drew said quietly. "It's Stone, right?"

Scout shook her head. "No, I changed that too. It's McAndrews. I was born Dana McAndrews."

Kate gaped at Scout. "McAndrews?"

"Yeah." Scout looked at Drew, who had narrowed her

149

eyes. "What? What's going on?"

After a second, Drew said quietly, "The person I was talking about, the one who played on the team last year. The one who looks a hell of a lot like you. Her name is Cass McAndrews."

"This is too fucking weird," Scout said. "You're both looking at me like I've got three heads."

"No, just two," Kate said. "Your own and my girlfriend's."

"Did you ever look for your birth family?" Drew asked Scout.

She shook her head. "They threw me away. Why would I have wanted to try to find them?"

"Did anyone tell you where you were born at least?"

"Hah," Scout laughed. "Kind of. I had a look at my file one time. One of the foster families wasn't so good at locking up paperwork. It was such a joke. Apparently, I was left to God's devices. I was just dumped in a church. Hope Church. Ironic, eh?"

"Hope Church, like in Hope?" Drew asked.

"No, it's a Lutheran church and school a little east of here. I looked it up, just to see," Scout shrugged.

"Is it in Port Coquitlam?" Kate said quietly, wondering what she had stumbled into.

Scout nodded.

"Cass's family lives there. Her sister, Caroline, and her parents are Lutheran." She bit her lip again and they were all quiet for a few seconds.

"Now you're freaking me out," Scout said, holding up her hands and shaking her head. She turned to Drew and tried to turn her away from Kate. "Drew, let's just go."

"But, what if -" Drew said, standing her ground.

"Let's go. You have to get to work." Scout began to walk away.

Kate called after Scout, but she didn't stop, and Drew just furrowed her brow and then smiled at Kate before

150

leaving.

Feeling suddenly cold, Kate used her good arm to pull the blanket up to her chin. She reached for her phone, wanting to talk to Cass, but she didn't know what to say. She could hardly ask Cass if there was any chance her mom had had another daughter that she'd failed to mention. But what if Scout was Cass's sister? The throbbing pain in Kate's head was getting worse, bringing tears to her eyes again. Maybe she had just imagined the whole thing. She was feeling pretty confused after all. Maybe she just needed to rest, she thought, and closed her eyes.

TWENTY-FOUR

"Kate?"

"Kate, wake up."

"Kate?"

"Can she hear us?"

"Goddamnit, why do people keep having to wake me up!" Kate opened her eyes and saw Steve and a doctor standing at the foot of her bed.

"Is she prone to angry outbursts?" the doctor asked.

"Only when people keep goddamn waking me up," Kate said.

Steve laughed and hugged her. "She seems pretty normal to me."

"Kate, I'm Doctor Ross. I'm just going to have a look at your shoulder. OK?"

"Sure," Kate said, struggling to push herself to a more upright position as the doctor approached.

While Dr. Ross examined the range of motion in Kate's arm, he said, "Now, a couple of the nurses had some concerns that you were a bit confused and upset this morning. Can you tell me what was upsetting you?"

Kate sighed. "It's going to sound crazy."

"What's new?" Steve said, smiling.

"Shut up, Steve."

The doctor paused, waiting for Kate to explain.

"Look," Kate said, "there's this doppelganger of my girlfriend running around, taking over her life, and now I think that they might actually be sisters or something, and that Cass's parents have been lying to her for almost thirty years. So I have to figure out if I should tell my girlfriend that she may have a long-lost sister, or if I should just let it go."

Dr. Ross stood up and scratched his beard. Steve frowned, and Kate rolled her eyes and then regretted it because it made her head hurt even more.

Steve spoke first, saying, "Kate, honey. Where did you see this person that looks like Cass?"

"At the softball game, and then here, this morning."

"She was in the hospital?"

"Yes. Drew, the coach, dropped off my coat, and she's dating Cass's sister. Well, this person who looks almost exactly like Cass. They even have the same laugh. It's honestly quite, um, I, quite," Kate thumped her fist down onto the bed twice and then settled on, "creepy. It's really creepy."

"What's her name?" Steve asked.

"Scout. No, Dana," Kate said. "Her birth name was Dana McAndrews." Kate raised her eyebrows at Steve and widened her eyes. "What do I do?"

"What can you do?" Steve asked, as the Doctor continued stroking his beard while watching Kate curiously.

"I mean, do I tell Cass? How does that go?" Kate shook her head. "How about I just call her now and say, 'Hey, darling, so I think I might have met your sister. Yeah, maybe your mom had a baby she forgot to tell you about? Remember any very small babies at your third birthday party?'"

"She's three years younger than Cass?" Steve asked.

"Yeah, twenty-five."

"But," Steve squinted, as if he was constipated.

"What? Spit it out," Kate said.

"I don't know. I mean, I've met Scout and, sure, she looks a lot like Cass, but I thought you'd said that Cass's parents were super old. So, how likely is it that her mom had another baby after Cass? I mean, isn't Cass's sister like a decade older than her?"

"Twelve years older, yeah."

"So... wouldn't her mom have been, I don't know -"

"Forty-five."

"OK. So Cass's mom would've been forty-five when she had this mystery daughter." Steve turned to the doctor, who appeared to be mesmerised by the whole discussion. "So, doc, what's the likelihood of someone getting pregnant at forty-five?"

"Oh, less than five percent," the doctor said, before shaking himself slightly and taking charge. "Kate, any headaches?"

"Yes. My head is killing me."

"Nausea?" Dr. Ross asked, getting out a tiny torch to shine in Kate's eyes.

Kate blinked and said, "Yes. It comes and goes."

"Dizziness?"

"Yep. That too."

"OK. So, I'd like to send you for another quick scan, just to be sure there's nothing going on in there that we don't want to be going on, OK."

"Nothing going on in where?" Kate asked.

"In your head, honey." Steve said, smiling. "But we all know that brain is far too busy for its own good most of the time."

Dr. Ross frowned and put the torch back in his coat pocket. "I'll get a nurse to take you to radiology. Sit tight."

"Doctor?" Kate called. "Where are my clothes?"

Dr. Ross looked back at Kate, then at Steve, who said, "Hanna and I took them home to wash them, remember? You got pretty muddy." He pulled Kate's clothes from this
154

backpack and Dr. Ross sighed and left the cubicle.

"He totally thinks I'm crazy. Thanks," Kate said.

"What did I do? You're the one talking about doppelgangers."

"You stole my clothes!" Kate said.

"And here they are nice and fresh."

Kate smiled at Steve and laughed. "Thank you. Sorry I'm grumpy. My head hurts like hell and I wish Cass was here."

"Did you let her know what happened?"

"No. I keep falling asleep. And I went up to see Em at the crack of dawn."

"Ah, so that's why you're wearing Em's cardigan," Steve said, grinning.

Kate sat up sharply and moved to get her phone, saying, "What time is it?"

"Eleven fifteen," Steve said, looking at the watch Em had bought him for Christmas. "Why? Got somewhere to be?"

"Em. Go up to Em," Kate said, shooing Steve away.

"Why? What's going on?"

"Dr. Chan is, was, seeing her at eleven."

"Dr. Chan? But -" Steve blanched and scratched his beard. "Do you know why?"

"No, but you should go see and then come and let me know."

Steve blew Kate a kiss and left, trying to get to Em's ward as fast as possible without anyone yelling at him not to run in the hospital.

TWENTY-FIVE

The stoplight turned yellow and Drew sped up to make it through, jolting Scout and causing her to spill coffee onto her shirt.

"Sorry," Drew said as Scout yelped, anticipating pain.

"No worries. All my layers of plaid saved me. Again."

Drew took a left turn onto Hastings and had to stop suddenly as a cyclist with a giant trailer full of organic smoothies for office workers swung out in front of them.

"Way to go, buddy!" Scout yelled as she put her coffee in the cup holder and gave up. "Jeez!"

"You OK?" Drew asked. "You've been a bit on edge all morning."

Scout said nothing, just turned to look out of the window as they looked for parking near the Dominion building.

Drew gave her a minute and then asked, "Nervous about the interview? Or are you still thinking about what happened at the hospital yesterday?" They hadn't talked about the encounter with Kate, and Drew didn't want to push Scout but was a little alarmed that she hadn't mentioned it at all.

"I guess I'm just anxious in general," Scout said and looked down at her attire, wishing Afra had given her more guidance on what to expect from this interview. After abruptly ending their summer of partying, Afra had landed a job as campaign manager for a Green Party candidate and had angled for Scout to join the team, just on a voluntary basis at first. Scout frowned and pulled at her shirt. "I should've worn something more, I dunno, less casual. Something green maybe?"

"You look fine," Drew said. "Well, you look more than fine." She laughed and reached across to put her hand on Scout's thigh. "You'll do great." She found a parking spot and quickly backed into it before the lights changed behind them.

"You'll have to teach me to parallel park one day. I totally would've just gone past this spot," Scout said.

"Maybe if I wasn't so fantastic at parking, I'd find it easier to stay in shape. Walking all those extra blocks." Drew laughed.

"Hey, thanks for staying over last night, and for giving me a ride today," Scout said and leaned over to kiss Drew. "Maybe I'll see you later?"

Drew nodded, "I have my appointment with the doctor later, but you could come by after if you like."

"Wait, do you want me to come with you? To see about the sperm and stuff?" Scout held Drew's hand and raised her eyebrows, and Drew smiled.

"Nope! This is my thing. It'd be nice to see you after though, if you're not busy."

"So, you might actually be pregnant next time I see you?" Scout said. She chewed on the inside of her cheek and Drew laughed at her.

"Maybe. I am ovulating, and I've got to take any chance I can at this point."

Scout made an involuntary gagging noise. "Sorry. It's just, I dunno, that word grosses me out."

"Well, stick with me kid and you'll be hearing a lot of

157

other lovely words. Sorry."

"No, no, it's fine. It's just weird. I don't think about this stuff."

Drew squeezed Scout's hand. "And you don't need to, you know? I'm happy with how things are with us, and I'm not asking you for anything else."

"I know. But it seems like I should be more involved, or something." Scout started chewing her cheek again.

"Look, if you think it's too weird, once I get pregnant, if I get pregnant, you can totally just bail, OK?"

"I don't want to bail! I'm not going to just ditch you because you have a baby!" Scout kissed Drew, but Drew pushed her away gently.

"Scout, it's cool. This is what I want, and this is the last chance I really have. I'm not looking for someone to have a baby with."

Scout interrupted Drew, but she put a finger on Scout's lips and said, "I want to be with you, but I know you don't want kids of your own: not now, maybe not ever. And I don't have any expectations from you except being honest with me." She kissed Scout, who smiled.

"OK. That I can do. It still feels weird though, not to be involved."

"Why?" Drew asked quietly.

"I guess just because it's, like, the right thing to do. Like, no one should have to go through being a single parent or whatever. That's hard stuff, and I just -"

"You can't see why I'm choosing to do this," Drew said, "and I get that. It's OK. Your life experience is different to mine, and I can see why you might think it's foolish and that I'm just making life hard on myself. But I've wanted to have a baby for a long time, and I've got a huge support network, so I won't be doing this alone."

"I don't think it's foolish. I just -" Scout looked away from Drew. "I guess I just think about what might happen to the kid, you know? If you can't -. If you change your mind."

158

Drew shivered and then took a deep breath. She wiped at her eyes and then leaned over to cup Scout's chin. She turned Scout's face so that they were looking at each other, and Drew said, "If this works, if I have a baby, this kid will be loved and have a great life, full of family and friends. I am choosing this. And that puts me so far from being some frightened woman who is stuck with a baby she can't care for or maybe doesn't want to care for."

"I know," Scout said. "I guess I'm just wondering about stuff, you know?" She looked at Drew and then lowered her eyes.

"About your birth parents? I get it. But if it was a closed adoption, you might need to try to reconcile yourself to the idea that you'll never know, despite what was said at the hospital."

Scout used her shirt sleeve to wipe her eyes. She took a big gulp of air and swallowed, then shook herself and sniffed. "Anyway, I gotta go ace this interview."

"Yeah you do," Drew said, putting out her hand, palm down. Scout placed her hand on top of Drew's and smiled while shaking her head.

"Go team!" Drew cried, bouncing their hands and then lifting hers like she always did at the start of a game.

"You doofus," Scout said, and then kissed Drew one last time. She got out of the car and called over her shoulder, "Good luck later."

"Good luck now!" Drew yelled as she turned the key in the ignition and waved at Scout.

TWENTY-SIX

There was no cell reception at the terminal as Cass made her way to the luggage carousel, and she narrowly missed bumping into several people as she tried to find a Wi-Fi network to join. She had been out of touch with Kate, her school, and Sami, their dog sitter, for almost twenty hours and was convinced that something terrible had happened to everyone while she'd been on a rerouted plane with an emergency stop in Halifax, where there had been a cellphone coverage blackout.

She felt a hand on her shoulder and stopped, spinning around with her fist raised. Cass saw that the hand belonged to Guy, the nurse from the plane.

"Oh man, I nearly punched you," Cass said, dropping her fist. "Don't do that!"

"What? Stop you from falling down an escalator?" Guy looked ahead of Cass, who was inches away from walking onto an elevator full of people heading towards her.

"Ah. Thanks."

"That's right," Guy said, laughing. "Luggage is this way. I assume they didn't lose it in all that rerouting chaos."

"I'll be claiming for some pretty expensive wine if they did," Cass said, scowling.

"Oh yeah? You don't strike me as a connoisseur of fine wine," Guy said, raising his eyebrows.

"Oh, I'm not. But I'll be claiming for it anyway." Cass shrugged. "And didn't you mention you had a pricy tapestry in your case?"

"Oh yeah, that old thing. I forgot about that. Thanks!"

"No problem, buddy."

"So, did you get in touch with your girlfriend yet? She know you're on your way?"

"No. Still no reception, weirdly," Cass checked her phone again and saw the screen freeze as a barrage of texts started flooding in.

"Shit. Looks like you were missed. High maintenance lady, huh?"

Cass stared at her phone, trying to click on messages to read them, but the onslaught continued and every time she hit a message it jumped and was replaced by another. She kept getting glimpses of words: 'hospital', 'head injury', 'puppy', 'delayed'. Finally, she managed to open a message from an unknown number, which turned out to be Janice, Kate's ex.

"Oh shit."

"What?" Guy asked, "Everything OK?"

Cass held out a hand to silence him, "Wait, just, what? No. Oh shit."

"Cass?" Guy waited.

"Kate's in the hospital."

"Visiting her friend, right?"

"No, like she's in the hospital, for real. She was chasing a puppy."

Guy laughed, causing Cass to glare at him. "Sorry," he said, "but, c'mon. It sounds pretty funny. I mean, who chases puppies?"

"Dude. It's not funny. My girlfriend is in hospital and you're laughing. You're a shitty nurse." Cass punched him in

161

the shoulder and scrolled through more messages. "She has a dislocated shoulder, and she hit her head, at a softball game." Cass frowned. "Why was she at a softball game?"

"Maybe her friend made a miraculous recovery and hit a home run," Guy offered and Cass looked up at him, narrowing her eyes. She spotted her backpack on the carousel behind Guy and yelled, "Mine!" She lunged forward but an old man blocked her way, followed by an old lady, two giggling children and one very harried looking middle-aged guy pushing a luggage trolley that was perilously over-stacked.

"I'll get it," Guy called as he ran around the family and jogged along with the carousel. He pointed at Cass's backpack, "This one?" Cass nodded and Guy hauled her pack onto his shoulder and brought it over.

"Which way are you headed?" Guy asked. "I have a ride and we could give you a lift if you're going downtown."

"That'd be amazing, thanks," Cass said, "I think I'll head straight to the hospital."

"Which one?"

"Um, I don't know."

"Your girlfriend didn't mention that?"

"She hasn't been in touch. It's her ex who's texting."

"Oh," Guy said, biting his lip. "Yikes."

"No, it's cool. They're friends I guess."

"Sure." Guy grinned and went to grab his suitcase.

Cass checked the rest of her messages and saw one from Em, saying she was with Kate, who was being kept in for more tests. Wasn't Em in ICU, Cass thought? What the hell was going on?

"You all set? Just that one bag?" Guy asked when he returned with his case.

"Um, yeah. Just that." Cass was scrolling through messages trying to figure out where Kate was.

"Come on, let's go find my friend and head into the city. Your girlfriend might be at VGH." Guy grabbed Cass's backpack and picked up his case.

162

"Hey, you don't have to -"

"It's cool. I've been sitting around on planes and in airports for so long, my body needs to exert some energy," Guy said, and led them to the passenger pick-up area.

TWENTY-SEVEN

Following a flurry of anxious texts to Em, Cass learned that Kate was at Vancouver General Hospital. Em and Steve were there, waiting to find out what was going on with Kate. Cass tried calling her, but the call went straight to voicemail.

"Goddamnit!" Cass said, throwing her phone onto the seat next to her.

"Hey, chill, champ, OK?" Guy said from the front of the car. "You find out where we're taking you?"

"Sorry. Yeah. VGH? You know where that is, right?"

Guy and his friend laughed. "Yeah, Dave works there. So I think we can find our way."

Dave smiled at Cass in the rear view mirror and said to Guy, "You really pick up some charmers on these transatlantic trips of yours. Maybe try for a demure hostess next time around, eh?"

Guy laughed and said, "I think our hostess was a little more interested in Cass than in me." He turned to Cass and cocked an eyebrow. She scowled at him. "Oh, I noticed. I definitely noticed. She was hot."

"Yeah, well, I'm trying this whole monogamy thing these

days. I hear it works out well for some people," Cass said.

"Not for me. Or poor Guy here," Dave said, hitting Guy on the shoulder with the back of his hand. "Hey, did you hear from Sarah while you were away?"

"Nah. I don't think she gives a shit," Guy said, looking out of his window.

"Sorry, dude. That's too bad."

"It is what it is."

Cass leaned forward and asked, "So, what, so you cheated on this Sarah girl and she found out and won't talk to you?"

Guy turned to look at Cass and shook his head. "Nope. I'm the cheatee here, I guess, or what's that word?"

"Cuckold," Cass offered.

"Yeah. That. Sarah sort of started seeing someone else and didn't bother telling me about it until I spotted her making out with him on the street, which was nice."

"That sucks. Sorry."

"Yep. Three years in and then that happens."

"You still got the ring?" Dave asked quietly.

"Woah!" Cass yelled, "You were going to marry this broad? Harsh."

Everyone was quiet for a second, and then Guy said, "Yeah. Pretty glad I dodged that bullet."

"Monogamy man, it's a tough sell for some," Dave said as they waited in traffic after getting onto Oak Street.

"It's more fidelity than monogamy that's the issue, though, right? I mean, my girlfriend's ex is now seeing her best friend and her boyfriend. That seems to be working out pretty well," Cass said.

Both Guy and Dave turned to look at her. "What?"

Cass explained.

"So, like a threesome?" Guy asked.

"I guess."

"Every night?" Dave asked.

"Well, I guess."

Guy whistled through his teeth and Dave shook his head.

"Lucky dude," Dave said.

"No way!" Guy stared at Dave. "Your friend, Steve, right?" Cass nodded and Guy went on, "Steve must be fucking exhausted. Literally. Two women? All the time? I'm tired just thinking about it."

Dave laughed, saying, "That's just because Sarah was a nightmare, and you haven't had a threesome man. It's a fucking delight is what it is."

"Nope. Not for me." Guy shook his head.

"Your buddy's right," Cass said. "It can be a real fucking delight."

"So, er, you and Kate? You ever, you know?" Dave said, wiggling his eyebrows at Cass in the mirror.

Guy slapped his shoulder, "Hey! You can't just -"

"No. Not with Kate. And not with a dude. Sorry, man. You're barking up the wrong dyke."

"And you're monogamous anyway, right?" Guy asked Cass.

"Yeah. But a threesome is different," Dave said.

"Oh yeah? How is it different?" Guy asked, laughing.

"Well, you're both kind of cheating at once, with the same person, so it doesn't count."

Cass grinned and said, "Yeah, and that always ends well."

"No, I'm serious. My ex and I had a whole thing where we would hook up with some woman online and they would both come over to my place."

"And your ex now dates women, right?" Cass said, trying to keep a straight face.

Dave laughed and said, "Nice try on the recruiting. No, she became a nun."

Cass bit her lip. "Shut up. No she didn't. Your ex is totally queer now, I know how this goes."

Guy turned around and looked at Cass. "No, Dave's serious. Lynne is actually a full on nun. She moved to

California and lives in a convent and works with orphaned kids."

Cass stared at him, open mouthed. "No. You serious?"

Guy nodded.

Cass met Dave's eye in the mirror and said in a serious voice, "Wow, those must've been some pretty terrible threesomes." She paused and followed with, "and I never thought I'd have cause to say that in my life."

"So, VGH, right?" Dave said, after they had all enjoyed a minute of silent contemplation.

"Yeah. If that's cool. Or just drop me off at a transit stop."

"No, you're good. We'll be going right by there on the way downtown, so it's no trouble."

Guy turned around to hold out a piece of paper to Cass. "It's my number and email. Get in touch if you were serious about what we talked about before and want to set something up."

Dave glanced at Guy and furrowed his brow. "She just said no dudes, dude."

"Not that," Guy said, "I mean about the documentary."

TWENTY-EIGHT

When Cass arrived at the hospital she realised that she was absolutely ravenous and desperately in need of coffee. She also realised that she had no real idea of where Kate would be. Em's messages and Janice's messages were all mixed up because they had arrived in a sudden flurry rather than in real time.

She switched some Canadian money from a Ziploc bag to her wallet and found a couple of loonies to throw into a vending machine, thereby acquiring a lacklustre granola bar. The coffee machine was out of order, which seemed dangerous in a hospital, Cass thought.

A nurse hurried by carrying bags of blood and Cass tried to ask for help, but the nurse just turned and walked quickly backwards while nodding up at the board behind Cass. It was covered in numbers and department names, but that didn't help as Cass still didn't know where Kate was.

She quickly ate the granola bar and rubbed sanitizer over her hands before walking down the corridor to find someone to help her navigate the place. After talking to a couple of people, Cass headed over to the neurosurgery ward and almost ran into Hanna who was carrying a tray of coffee.

"Hey!" Hanna cried, "How the hell did you get here so fast?" She hugged Cass with one arm and then stood and stared at Cass. "Em only just texted you, right? Did you teleport?"

"What's going on? Where's Kate?" Cass asked as they walked through the automatic doors.

"Oh, yeah. So she just got moved to neurosurgery as they're a little worried that there's some bleeding in her brain that they can't see," Hanna smiled.

"What the hell? Why are you so calm about this?" Cass gaped at her.

"Oh, sorry. Yeah. I guess I'm just sort of used to being in hospitals these days. Not much phases me any more." Hanna scrunched up her face and offered Cass the tray of coffee. "You might need this more than me."

Cass took one of the cups and thanked Hanna as they walked into the elevator.

"So, seriously, how did you get here so fast?"

"I was already on a plane. I wanted to come and be with Kate while she was here to see Em. She didn't really leave on the best of terms and I felt like an ass. As usual. And I just, I don't know. I guess I just wanted her to see that I'm sincere."

Hanna grinned and tried not to laugh. "Europe changed you, huh?"

"Shut up." Cass rolled her eyes at Hanna.

"It's cute. It suits you. You should have been less of an ass a while back."

"Hey!" Cass glared at Hanna. "My girlfriend has a bleeding brain and you're teasing me. Not fair."

"Sorry, you're right." Hanna grabbed the coffee cup from Cass and took a sip before handing it back. "I just sort of feel weirdly celebratory today because Em is coming home."

"That's great! Wait, what? How come?"

"Well, the infection that landed her in ICU looks like it's

169

clearing up nicely, and her oncologist says that everything is looking good. So she's probably better off recovering at home with us rather than being in hospital with all these sick people and their bugs." Hanna grinned and said, "I'm pretty fucking happy. Sorry!"

"No, that's awesome news. It just sucks that they're trading places. Kate and Em." Cass frowned. "Well, I don't mean I'd rather Em had a bleeding brain. Just -."

"I know what you mean, and it does suck. I'm sure Kate will be fine. I mean, they haven't actually found any bleeding, they're just being cautious as she's got some symptoms of major concussion. She's in the right place though, that's for sure, and we're all old hands at this now." Hanna smiled. "I mean, I know where to get the best coffee round here, and that's key to any recovery."

The elevator doors opened and Cass and Hanna stepped out into the corridor. Cass spotted Steve leaning against a wall a few metres away and he looked puzzled as Hanna called, "Look who I found!"

"How did you -?" Steve asked as Hanna handed him coffee.

"Where's Em?" Hanna interrupted him as she looked around.

"Washroom."

"On her own?" Hanna asked.

"Yep. She insisted. She figured she needs to be independent now she's coming home." Steve held out his hand and shrugged. "I wasn't going to tackle her. I mean, the woman has no hair right now. I'd just look mean."

Cass stared at Steve, then looked at Hanna with narrowed eyes. "You two have clearly spent way too much time in this place. You're full of darkness."

Hanna laughed. "Waaaay too much time. Yes."

Em emerged from a door just down the corridor and Steve rushed to help her.

"I'm fine, I'm fine," Em said, but she took his arm and

let him help her to the seats by Cass and Hanna.

"Woah!" Em said as she spotted Cass. "That was fast!"

Cass bent down to hug her and smiled. "I was already on my way. I only got your texts after I'd landed at YVR. Not quite the welcome I had anticipated." She held out her arms and said, "So where is she?"

"Radiology again. They're doing some more tests to see if they need to do surgery." Em looked up at Hanna and asked, "Is that coffee for me?"

Hanna sat beside Em and handed her the coffee. Em kissed her and said, "You're the best," prompting Steve to pout.

"I was the best first," he said, and Em reached out to grab the bottom of his shirt and pull him down to kiss her.

"You're both the best," she said, and held Hanna's hand.

"Oh man, now I'm feeling nauseous," Cass said. "Maybe I'm sick too." She took a sip of coffee, feeling overwhelmingly grateful to have something to help her stay awake, then asked, "So, Kate needs surgery? Like, brain surgery?"

"Maybe," Em said. "They think she might have some bleeding that is putting pressure on her brain. So they're just running tests and they might need to drill a hole and relieve the pressure."

Cass blinked and Steve reached out to grab her elbow in case her knees buckled. Hanna stood up so Cass could sit down.

"I'm fine, thanks. But, brain surgery?" Cass said, then sat down beside Em and shook her head. "Woah."

"It's not as bad as it sounds," Em said, patting Cass's arm. "She's a trooper. She'll be fine."

Cass looked at Em, wide-eyed. "They're going to drill into Kate's brain. That's not cool, man. That's really not cool. We were just, like, figuring stuff out and -. Oh."

Em put her arm around Cass's shoulders and squeezed. "Ah, she'll be OK. And she'll be so stoked you're here!"

"Well, she'll be a bit confused too," Steve said, glancing

171

at Em. "I mean, what with the whole Scout thing."

"Huh?" Cass looked up at him. "Which scout?"

"No, Scout's a person. A person who -" Steve started, but Em interrupted him.

"Now's not really the time, Steve-O, yeah?" Em looked at Cass and said, "You should know though, that Kate does have a pretty bad concussion, so she is a bit confused. She's forgetting some words and she can't really focus on anything, and she might just start crying for seemingly no reason or get really angry at nothing much, and the doctor said that people sometimes start saying really inappropriate things, so we should watch out for that."

Cass swallowed. "Wow. OK. I mean, that kind of just sounds like a normal day to me, but I guess not for Kate."

Em laughed. "Yeah, not for Kate. So we have to keep an eye on her and let them know if anything weird starts happening. Like if she starts slurring her words really badly or anything, or if her headache gets any worse. It's already pretty bad though, so I don't really know how they could tell."

Cass's shoulders started to shake and she covered her eyes with her hands. Hanna crouched down in front of her and put her hands on Cass's knees. "Hey, she's going to be OK."

Cass wiped her eyes and nodded. She blinked at Hanna, thinking about how she had cried twice in the last twenty-four hours: she must be getting soft, she thought.

The elevator dinged and they all turned to look as a gurney was pushed into the corridor. Cass stood up and Hanna moved aside as the nurses wheeled the gurney past them.

Cass saw Kate, who saw Cass, who reached out to grab her hand. "Hey!" Kate said.

"Hey yourself!" Cass said, feeling the tears burning her eyes again as she took in the shoulder sling and Kate's tired, pale face.

"Wait, who are you? Cass?" Kate said, blinking at Cass

and pulling her hand away.

The nurse carried on pushing the gurney, and said, "Let's get you back to your room, Kate. OK?" said the nurse.

Cass and Hanna followed them, while Steve helped Em up and picked up Cass's backpack, which she had left leaning against the wall.

In the room, the nurse was fiddling with various controls on Kate's bed, helping her to sit up. He turned to look at Kate's visitors and said, "Who's the next of kin?"

Em, Steve and Hanna all looked at Cass, who put up her hand. "Um, I guess that's me now?"

The nurse spoke to Cass, explaining that it looked like they didn't need to do surgery, but that they wanted to keep Kate under observation for another night. "I understand that she's supposed to be flying home in a couple of days?"

"To Amsterdam, yeah. Yes."

"You might want to delay that flight."

"Seriously?" Cass asked, looking at Kate, who was struggling to keep her eyes open.

"Yes. At this point we just don't know what might happen, but it's not usually a good idea for someone with such a serious concussion to fly. Especially not a long haul flight."

"Sure, yeah," Cass said. "But she's going to be OK, right?"

"We'll be keeping a close eye on her. Don't worry." The nurse smiled at Cass and nodded, then began to walk out of the room.

"Hey!" Cass called, and the nurse turned. "So, what do I do now?"

"Well, she should get some rest, and we'll keep checking on her. You can stay if you like, but let her rest."

The nurse left and Cass turned to Kate, but she had her eyes closed.

"Why don't we take you back to ours and feed you, and you can get some sleep too," Em said, putting an arm around

Cass's shoulders.

"Thanks, but now I'm here, I just want to stay, you know?" Cass gave Em a lopsided smile.

"Of course."

"But, you go home. I mean, you just got let out of this place, right? You should go celebrate or something!" Cass sat down in the chair next to Kate's bed and shooed Em, Steve and Hanna away. "Go home," she whispered.

"Let us know if anything happens?" Em said.

"Of course."

Em glanced at Kate one last time and smiled. "We'll be back in the morning." She took Steve's hand, "Right? We can come visit tomorrow?"

Steve nodded. "Absolutely. I mean, where else would we be? We all practically live here now." He grinned and put his arm around Hanna.

"I can stay with you if you like," Hanna said to Cass.

"No, no, thanks. Go home and be with your little adorable-as-fuck family," Cass smiled and looked over at Kate, whose hand was twitching as she fell deeper into sleep.

Alone with Kate, Cass reached over to slip her hand under Kate's hand. "You idiot," she said. "Look what you get when you chase tail." Kate snorted in her sleep and Cass laughed. "Yeah, I love you too."

TWENTY-NINE

When the doctor came in to check on Kate before going home, he had to stop himself from laughing as he found Cass sprawled in the chair, her head tilted back as she snored, one hand holding Kate's hand and the other clutching her coffee cup as if desperately trying to hold off sleep. He felt bad for having to wake up Kate to do more tests, and he tried to be quiet, so as to let Cass sleep, but Kate immediately wrenched her hand away when she woke and saw Cass beside her.

"Why is she here?" Kate cried, "Get her away from me!"

"Kate, isn't this your partner? The nurses said she was." The doctor looked at Cass, who had been startled awake and was now staring at Kate.

"Yeah. Kate. Hey, it's me. It's Cass." She reached out to take Kate's hand again, but Kate clutched it to her chest and looked at the doctor, wide-eyed.

"No. That's Scout, and I don't know her. But she's screwing the coach, and she's Cass's sister. Where's Em? I want Em."

The doctor frowned at Cass and asked who Em was.

"Kate's best friend. She was just discharged. She has

175

cancer. Well, had, I guess. I don't know. Is that how that works?"

The doctor, struggling to keep up, called for the nurse.

"Oh, hey, Kate, you're awake. And look who turned up while you were asleep?" the nurse looked at Cass and said, "She flew all the way in from Amsterdam just to see you!"

Kate looked again at Cass and squinted, then looked back at the nurse. "Cass?"

"Yes," the nurse said.

"Not Scout?"

"No. This is Cass, your girlfriend. Right?" The nurse was starting to look worried, wondering who he had let into his patient's room.

Kate looked at Cass again and her face softened and she started to cry. "Cass? But, I didn't even tell you what had happened. Did I?" She reached out her hand and Cass grinned and took it and kissed Kate's fingers.

"I was already on my way here. I wanted to be here while you were visiting Em, but then I got word you'd been hurt. I came straight here from the airport." Cass gestured at her backpack and Kate pulled her in to kiss her.

"I can't believe you're here!" Kate said, kissing Cass's face and crying.

"Clearly!" Cass said, marvelling at Kate's sudden affection. She pulled away and looked at the doctor. "Is this normal? Is she OK?"

"Well, I'd say it's pretty normal for a patient to be happy when their partner comes to visit, yeah. But the emotional lability can be a symptom of concussion. It may last a little while, or it may become permanent."

"Does it mean the bleeding is worse?" Cass asked, holding Kate's hand.

"What bleeding?" Kate asked.

Cass looked at the doctor, who stepped a little closer. "Kate, we thought the blow to your head may have caused some bleeding in your brain, which could explain why you're experiencing these episodes of confusion. The tests we've done so far don't show any bleeding though, but we're keeping an eye on it. It's possible that we'll need to operate, so you should be prepared for that, but for now just rest up."

"Wait, so I might need, like, brain surgery? I need brain surgery?" Kate said, her eyes wide.

Cass squeezed her hand. "Exciting, huh? And all from chasing puppies."

Kate laughed, "Oh yeah! The puppy!" Then she frowned again as the doctor started towards her with his little torch to check her pupil responses.

After the doctor and nurse had left, Cass turned to Kate and asked if she could ask her something.

Kate raised her eyebrows and Cass laughed and said, "Not that. Don't worry."

"What then?"

"Who's Scout?"

Kate patted the side of her bed, motioning for Cass to scooch in next to her. "I'm all stinky from the flight," Cass said, sniffing her armpit and longing for a shower.

"I love your stink," Kate said, nuzzling in. "I missed your stink."

"That's delightful, thanks."

"You're welcome."

"So...."

"Yeah. OK. So there's this person on the softball team."

"The one who hit you with the ball?"

"No. No. I don't think so anyway." Kate tried to remember. "No, Scout was at third base."

"In the game?"

Kate laughed, "Yes. In the game." Cass kissed the top of Kate's head.

"So Scout is on the softball team, and?"

"Well, she totally looks like you. And she was here earlier. Which is why I thought you were her. And Steve saw her too. And she's dating Drew, I think."

"Drew, like the coach, Drew?"

"Yeah."

"Oh. That's weird. I thought Drew was married."

"Oh. I don't know. Maybe she's poly?" Kate said. "Anyway, that doesn't matter."

Cass sat up and looked at Kate. "So why is this Scout person so important all of a sudden?"

Kate took a moment and then said, "Did your mom ever have any other kids. You know, aside from Caroline?"

"Woah." Cass held her hands up and laughed. "What kind of a question is that!?"

Kate shrugged and blew out her cheeks.

"You know what my mom is like. God-fearing and all that jazz. If there was another kid, I'd have known about it."

"But what if you didn't? What if your mom had another baby and gave her up for adoption?"

"Like, before Caroline was born?" Cass asked.

"No, after you were born. You would've been three."

"Why? Wait, what?"

"Scout is twenty-five. She was born and put up for adoption when you were three. She was left at a church in PoCo. And -"

"No. This is ridiculous. I would've known about this."

"You were three, Cass. How could you have known?" Kate said gently.

"OK, OK, so this Scout person looks like me?" Cass said, and Kate nodded. "So what? There are plenty of people who look like other people, it doesn't mean they're related, or that there's some weird family secret."

Kate nodded again, and winced, the pain in her head growing stronger. She remembered that her brain might be bleeding and suddenly didn't want to move ever again, thinking that the blood might be sloshing around in there, and wasn't that a bad thing? She realised she had started to cry, but couldn't stop.

178

"Hey, hey, what's wrong?" Cass wiped at Kate's eyes and kissed her.

"Sorry. I just, I can't help it."

"Should I call the doctor? I don't know what I'm supposed to do."

"No. No. I'll be fine." Kate sniffed and leaned back onto the pillow. "She has your name," Kate said.

"Who? What?"

"Scout. Her real name is McAndrews. Dana McAndrews." Kate looked at Cass, whose mouth was now hanging open.

"You're sure?"

"Yeah. It can't be a coincidence -"

Cass interrupted Kate. "No, it can't be, because Dana is my mom's middle name."

THIRTY

Two Canada geese waddled past Scout as she leaned on her bike outside Cartems Donuterie, waiting for Drew. Scout watched the birds go by and laughed. They looked like two office workers just taking a stroll to go and get lunch, but their nonchalance was bizarre, considering they were geese on a busy street in downtown Vancouver.

Drew came out from the store and held out a box of doughnuts to Scout.

"What's funny?" she asked, and Scout nodded her head in the direction of the geese, who had reached an intersection and were now holding up traffic. Drew smiled and took a bite out of a banana stuffed doughnut, causing coconut cream to ooze down her chin. "Damn," she said, having no free hand to wipe her face with a napkin.

Scout took out a clean hankie and mopped up the cream on Drew's chin.

"Fanks," Drew mumbled, her mouth full of dough.

"Craving satisfied?" Scout asked, taking the box of doughnuts to rest on the handlebars of her bike. "Back to the office?"

Drew nodded, "Yep, I have a meeting in twenty minutes, and you," she looked at her watch, "You start work in ten minutes, right?"

"Yeah. I think I'll be late tonight. There's a strategy meeting for the new candidate and I have to take minutes." Scout grinned.

"You're loving this, aren't you?" Drew smiled and jostled Scout's arm.

"Hey! Mind the doughnuts!" Scout laughed and said, "It's great. I mean, I know it's awful pay, but I think I could really get into this whole politics thing. It's great working with Afra. They really know their shit and are actually fun to live with now they've got a proper job. Joanna even said that I'd make a good campaign manager in a few years, when there's another local election. Apparently I have a good head for small details."

Drew glanced over at Scout and ran her hand over the short, shaved side of Scout's head. "You do have a pretty great head, it's true."

"Don't be getting doughnut crumbs in my perfectly styled hair now," Scout said, and Drew smiled.

"You want to take doughnuts for the office?"

Scout shook her head. "The vegans are in today, so turning up with doughnuts would just be cruel."

Drew frowned and said, "But these are all vegan."

Scout raised an eyebrow and Drew nodded, saying, "It's true! I was pretty tempted by the maple bacon doughnut, but then I figured I'd at least try to be healthy in my dessert choices, so I went with a dozen vegan doughnuts instead." She opened up the box and pointed at a doughnut with green frosting. "See, this one even has lime zest in it. Lots of vitamin C."

Scout laughed and said, "So healthy. What a balanced diet you have."

"Totally. I mean, this one has walnuts, so I'm even getting protein." Drew looked down and patted her belly,

181

"Lucky kid, they're gonna have a great mom who knows all about nutrition."

Scout shook her head. "Poor bastard."

"Hey!"

"Not like, a *bastard* bastard," Scout said, laughing.

"Well, you could make an honest woman out of me," Drew said, batting her eyelids at Scout as she leaned in to kiss her goodbye.

"Yeah, yeah. You'd love that," Scout said, kissing Drew and handing her the box of doughnuts before lifting her bike up the steps of the Dominion building. "See you tomorrow?"

"You don't want to come over tonight?" Drew asked.

"I want a night at home. Is that cool?" Scout said, turning to look down at Drew.

"Of course. Tomorrow I have a board meeting at seven though, so let yourself in if you like and I'll be home around nine, all being well." Drew took a key out of her pocket and tossed it to Scout. "I had a spare made, just in case."

"You're giving me a key?" Scout said, catching it and then staring at it in her palm.

"You want it?"

"I guess."

"It's not a proposal, Scout. I just figure it makes things a little easier, you know, if you get to mine when I'm not there. Save you waiting around in the cold." Drew smiled and added, "You can always give it back."

Scout grinned, "Nah, I think I'll keep it and then break in to rifle through your porn stash."

"I'm not giving you the combination to my safe," Drew countered.

"Well, damn." Scout shook the key in her fist and said, "I bet it's your birthday, right?"

"Nice try." Drew rolled her eyes.

"OK, well, thanks for the key. I should get in," Scout said quickly, realising she was almost late, "Love you," she said.

182

Drew's eyebrows shot up and Scout blushed.

"Um, yeah, so I just said that."

"Yeah you did."

"Shut up," Scout said, closing her eyes and taking a breath.

Drew smiled. "See you tomorrow," she said, her face frozen in amusement. Scout grinned and turned, before hoisting her bike up onto her shoulder to walk up the stairs to the Green Party office.

THIRTY-ONE

Kate and Cass sat in silence, staring at the road ahead, coffee cups in hand. As they passed over Boundary Road, Kate shuffled in her seat and turned on the radio.

"Please don't," Cass said, moving her hand from the steering wheel to cover Kate's and gently press the radio back to silence. "I need some time to think."

Kate nodded and sat back, looking out at the signs for Deer Lake, and remembering an open air concert she had gone to there with Janice. It had started raining just as Sigur Ros came on stage, and when Janice and Kate had returned to their car after the concert, the windows had steamed up. Kate remembered wanting to laugh, to make some joke about things getting all steamy, but her and Janice had not had sex in such a long time at that point that there would have been no humour in the comment, just sadness and longing. Cass would have made a joke about it, Kate thought, but Janice had just waited quietly for the condensation to dissipate before driving them home. Now Kate was in Janice's new car, that she and Cass had borrowed for the day, and she was in a new relationship, but still sitting silently, wondering what her

184

girlfriend was thinking and what she could do to help. She knew better than to ask this time, and let Cass drive, giving her space for her thoughts.

They were heading to Port Coquitlam under the pretext of Cass visiting Hobbes, her pup, who was living with Caroline while Cass and Kate were in Amsterdam. Cass had emailed her sister to say that they were in town, not mentioning anything about Kate's head injury, or Scout. Cass had tried to stop Kate from coming with her, saying that it would likely be stressful and that Kate should rest, but Kate had insisted. If Cass didn't want her to come because she needed to do this alone, then that was one thing, but if it was just that Cass was concerned about Kate's concussion, then Kate was coming with her as support.

Cass glanced over at Kate and was glad not to have to do this alone, although she was wary of things turning ugly. Since the accident, Kate's threshold for tears and emotional exhaustion had plummeted and Cass had quickly realised that she would need to learn to manage her own mood better so as not to get Kate too excited or upset.

There was probably no way of handling the current situation without someone getting upset though, Cass thought before turning over questions in her mind, trying to find a way to go from, "Hey sis, how's life?" to "So, about that other kid mom had when I was three." She had considered calling her mom and visiting, but things were tempestuous with her parents at the best of times, and they had never met Kate, or any girlfriend. Introducing Kate to her parents now, especially while Kate was concussed, wasn't the greatest idea, Cass figured. She would talk to Caroline and see what she knew before confronting her mom and dad. They had some time, having delayed their return flights until the following weekend, so Kate had a little longer to heal before heading back to work.

Cass was relieved that Sami was having a fantastic time with Jupiter and was more than happy to carry on looking

185

after him. Her professor was less overjoyed that Cass would be missing almost two weeks of class, but Cass suspected she could still pass the course by putting in some extra media lab hours when she got back. She was excited to get back in the lab anyway, so she could rework some footage in light of Guy's advice.

When they pulled up to Caroline's house, Kate noted the neat patch of lawn, gravel driveway and bright blue mailbox. The flag was raised, and Cass flipped down the front of the mailbox and took out a pile of mail on her way up to the front door.

"Let's do this," Cass said as Kate ran to catch her up and slipped her hand into Cass's hand.

"Go team," Kate said quietly as Cass pressed the doorbell, unleashing a volley of barks and yips from inside the house.

A tall, thin woman with long blonde hair opened the door, releasing Hobbes. The little dog leapt at Cass, frantically trying to climb her legs. Cass reached down and picked him up so he could kiss her face. She growled as she nuzzled him, and Kate laughed and reached over to scratch the dog's belly, causing his back leg to twitch.

"So you must be Kate?" Caroline said, holding out her hand. "Good to meet you, finally." She smiled and Kate shook her hand, which was cool and bedecked with rings.

Caroline stood aside to let Kate and Cass into the house, and Cass put Hobbes down so she could take off her Blundstones.

"Oh, can you put your shoes in the closet? There should be space for your coats too," Caroline said, opening the closet door to reveal two shoe racks full of perfectly neat diamante-covered ballet flats and high heels in a variety of colours. Cass's large Blundstones just fit on the end of one of the shoe racks, and Kate carefully balanced her sneakers on top of

186

Cass's boots, feeling embarrassed about how muddy they were in contrast to the shiny, pointed toes of Caroline's vast shoe collection.

"Still pouring all of Alan's money into designer goods, hey sis?" Cass said, winking at Kate behind Caroline's back.

"Not Alan's money, no. My money these days," Caroline said.

"Oh?"

"Alan got laid off a couple of months ago. But I got promoted."

Cass laughed, "So he's a kept man now? Must be nice."

Caroline rolled her eyes and led them to the kitchen. She set about making coffee, and Kate offered a "Congratulations," as she took a seat at Caroline's table.

Kate looked around at the bright kitchen, painted a cheery yellow and tiled with a subtle floral pattern. The curtains were a white and yellow check pattern, with yellow tie-backs, and Kate felt like she was sitting in a Sears catalogue. She shuffled and asked Caroline what her new job was.

"Operations Manager. I keep all the guys in line."

"I bet you do," Cass said, and Caroline turned to scowl at her, giving Kate her first glimpse of the familial connection.

Cass sat down beside Kate and Caroline handed them both a cup of coffee before opening the back door to let Hobbes out into the garden.

"I think he likes it here," Cass said. "Has he been OK?"

"Oh yeah, he loves it. He's been digging up my yard and dragging mud into the house and onto the couches. And he's decided that the guest room is his, so he likes to make a blanket fort in there, just like you used to when you'd stay."

"God, that was a while ago," Cass said. She took a sip of her coffee.

"Some things don't change," Kate said, thinking about Cass's ongoing love of blanket forts.

Caroline narrowed her eyes and Kate wondered if she

187

should have avoided drawing attention to the fact that she and Cass shared a bed.

"So how come you're in town? I thought you were both settled in Amsterdam now." Caroline looked at Cass and slowly turned her coffee cup around in her hands.

Cass didn't say anything, and so Kate said, "I came back to visit a friend who's sick."

"Then Kate got hit in the head with a softball and almost had to have brain surgery," Cass said hurriedly.

Caroline stared at Kate, wide-eyed.

"I'm fine," Kate said, smiling.

"Wow. OK." Caroline blinked and shook her head. "Good."

Kate could feel Cass's leg bouncing up and down under the table, and so she dropped her hand to place it gently on Cass's thigh.

Cass looked up at Kate and nodded her head slowly, her lips pursed. She held her leg still and slurped her coffee, the heat making her eyes water. She looked out the back door but couldn't see Hobbes.

"So, where's Alan?" Cass asked, turning back to Caroline.

"He went to the store. He'll be back in a bit. We didn't know if you and Kate were staying for dinner, so he went out to get steaks."

Cass laughed and Kate smiled and said, "Thanks, that's sweet. I think we have dinner plans in the city with friends though, right Cass?"

Cass grinned and said, "Yeah, that, and Kate's vegan, so...."

"Oh, sorry. Well, I have salmon. Is that OK?" Caroline smiled at Kate, who smiled back and was about to explain when Cass jumped in.

"So, did mom have another kid?"

Caroline looked from Cass to Kate and then back again. "Uh, excuse me?"

188

"Mom. Did she have another kid?" Cass said as she stood up and began pacing back and forth behind Kate.

"What's going on, Cass?" Caroline said, one eyebrow raised.

"Can you just answer the question?" Cass said, her voice growing louder.

Kate bit her lip and Caroline opened and closed her mouth several times, then took a deep breath and said, "What do you think you know, Cass?"

Cass pulled her head back into her chest and frowned at her sister. "What do I think I know? What do I think I know? Ha! What do you know?"

Caroline folded her arms over her chest, moving one hand up to fiddle with the top button of her pale blue cardigan. She looked up at Cass and then glanced at Kate, but said nothing.

"C'mon Caroline. You obviously know something. What aren't you telling me?" Cass yelled, and Kate reached out a hand to try to get Cass to sit back down.

Cass took a step back and leaned against the refrigerator, folding her arms and glaring at her sister.

"When I was three, did mom have another kid?" Cass said. "I don't remember, but you would have. You were old enough then."

"I -" Caroline looked up and then put out her hands to grasp her coffee cup. Kate saw that Caroline's hands were shaking, her rings catching the light that was now streaming in through the back door as the spring sun dipped. She fiddled with the bracelets on her wrist and then moved her hand back up to her throat again, twisting the button until Kate thought it would snap off.

Cass started to speak again, but Kate held up her hand to calm her, seeing that Caroline was working up to saying something.

"Not mom," Caroline said. "It wasn't mom."

Cass dropped her hands to rest her thumbs on the

pockets of her jeans. She looked at Kate, and then back at Caroline. The three of them were silent for a few seconds, then Caroline looked up at Kate, her eyes wet with tears, and said quietly, "I never told anyone."

Cass moved forward slowly, pulling out the seat beside Caroline and sitting down. "Never told anyone what, Caroline?" Cass whispered. She covered her sister's hand with hers and Caroline sniffled.

"When I was fourteen, I got into some stupid stuff, eh? There was this group of us who would hang out and drink sometimes." She pulled her hand out from Cass's and went on, "So... well, there was this guy, and he was a bit older than we were and so he'd get us some booze and we'd go back to his place. But you know what mom and dad were like, and they weren't even all that strict with you."

Cass snorted, "Yeah, right. They were pretty full on."

"It was worse for me. I had to be home straight after school, and we were at the church all the time, and once, when mom caught me making out with Ethan in the vestry, she dragged me by the ear, like, literally by the ear in front of dad and the whole congregation and called me a whore. And Ethan's dad gave him a beating right there in the Sunday school room."

"Jeez," Kate said under her breath and Caroline looked up at her, holding her gaze for a second.

"I remember Ethan, Ethan Toews, right? Didn't he move to New York to go to school or something?"

Caroline nodded. "Yeah, he got as far away as possible once he turned eighteen."

"So, you and Ethan hooked up?" Cass asked.

Caroline turned to look at Cass. "No, not like that. It wasn't Ethan that, you know? We were just making out. He was a nice kid."

"So this other guy, what about him?" Cass asked, figuring she already knew, but wanting to hear Caroline get the words out.

190

"So, I snuck out, eh? Just a few times, after everyone was in bed. I could climb out the window and drop down onto the shed roof, and then over the fence and out the gate next door. And I'd go to his place and he always had beer, and he had started dealing a little weed and E, and I was so sick of dad's preaching and mom being so holier than thou, and so I figured why not live a little. But it got pretty bad for a while. I skipped school and just went to his, and I was out of it most of the time. And then I realised -" Caroline stopped and swallowed. She took a breath and went on, "When I realised I was pregnant, it was already too late to do anything about it."

Cass put her arm around her sister, who resisted at first, but then fell into Cass and sobbed.

After a minute, Caroline sat back up and Cass offered her a hankie to wipe her face. "I've tried so hard not to think about this, for such a long time," Caroline said. "I just couldn't do it, I couldn't tell anyone."

"But when did mom and dad find out?" Cass asked.

"They didn't! They've no idea. I barely looked pregnant. I mean, I'd lost a bunch of weight, and it was a whole grunge scene, so I basically lived in baggy sweaters that whole winter." Caroline shuddered, and pulled at the three-quarter length sleeves of her pastel blue cardigan.

"So who knew?" Cass asked. "I mean, you can't have just, like, what," she looked at Kate. "No one just gives birth without telling someone, right?"

"My friend Abby helped. Her sister was a nurse and she promised not to tell anyone. So when my water broke, Abby drove me to her sister's place and I had the baby there," Caroline said.

"You didn't even go to the hospital?" Kate asked.

"How could I? Mom and dad would've found out," Caroline said.

"So what did you do with the baby?" Cass asked, but Caroline said nothing and just looked down at her hands as

191

she dug her perfectly painted fingernails into the skin of her palm.

Kate remembered something Scout had said, and reached out a hand to stop Caroline from leaving more red welts on her palm. "You took her to the church, didn't you?"

Caroline gasped and looked up at Kate. "Her?"

"Your baby was a girl," Kate said, holding Caroline's gaze.

"A girl?" Caroline said in a whisper. "I didn't want to know. I couldn't let myself know. Abby promised to take the baby - to take her - somewhere safe."

"Your friend took her to the church," Kate said.

"Which church?" Cass asked Kate.

"To Hope Lutheran."

"How do you know that?" Caroline asked, but Cass waved her hand to stop Kate from replying.

"That was the church where my mom taught Sunday school."

"So, what, your mom found the baby?" Kate asked Cass.

"How would I know?" Cass said.

"But, her name, I mean, she must have known," Kate said.

Caroline looked back and forth at Kate and Cass, her face pale. "What do you mean? How do you know any of this?"

Cass took Caroline's hand this time and said gently, "Kate met this woman. She's twenty-five - the right age - and she could be my twin. It's unreal," Cass said.

"And she was found at Hope Lutheran and put up for adoption," Kate said softly.

"Her birth name was Dana McAndrews," Cass said. Caroline's body shook, rattling the thin silver bracelets on her wrists. She wrapped her arms around herself as Cass said, "Abby must have told mom."

Caroline stood up. "I can't talk about this any more," she said. "I want you to leave. You should leave."

192

"Caroline!" Cass said, standing up and moving towards her sister.'

"No, you should go. Please go."

They all turned at the sound of a car pulling onto the gravel. "Go!" Caroline yelled, pointing at the back door.

Kate stood up and tugged at Cass's hand. "Come on, Cass."

"But -"

"GO!" Caroline screamed at them, and they scurried into the hallway to get their shoes, then fled through the back door, past Caroline, who, having wiped her eyes and smoothed down her hair, was now clearing the three coffee cups away to make the kitchen look as untouched as it had been when Cass and Kate arrived.

THIRTY-TWO

On their way back to the city, Cass suddenly swerved the car onto the shoulder and threw on the hazard lights.

"Goddamnit!" she yelled, pounding the wheel with her fists.

Kate said nothing as Cass pummelled the car, and she stayed in her seat when Cass opened her door to step out and scream at the sky.

Cass walked around the front of the car and sat down on the concrete barrier by the side of the road. She put her head in her hands and then looked up at Kate, her brow wrinkled. Kate undid her seatbelt and got out to sit beside Cass.

"My goddamn fucking piece of shit parents," Cass said, shaking her head. "And what the fuck was Caroline thinking?"

"She must have been terrified, Cass. C'mon," Kate said gently. "I mean, you've never been in a situation where you think you're pregnant and you don't want to be."

"Too fucking right," Cass said, then looked at Kate and frowned, asking, "Wait, have you?"

Kate shook her head, "No, but I remember hiding in the bathrooms at school and holding my friends' hands when they were waiting for that line to appear on the pee stick." Kate sighed, "And they didn't have a preacher for a dad, and a Sunday school teacher for a mom."

Cass stood up and held out her arms as she raised her head to the sky. She screamed again and then turned back to Kate.

"How could they do that? You know? Their own grandkid, and they just, what, like bundled this baby up and handed her in to the government. How is that the Christian thing to do? They're such hypocrites." Cass started laughing, "But they had to fucking name the kid after themselves. Make her a McAndrews."

Kate laughed, "And Dana? I mean, like, did they think about the Greek thing?"

"What Greek thing?" Cass asked.

"'Beware of Danaos bearing gifts.' It's a thing Cassandra says. Like, Dana is the Trojan horse that destroys civilisation."

Cass stared at Kate and then doubled over, laughing and clutching at her belly.

She straightened up after a minute and looked at Kate, saying, "Seriously?"

Cass walked over to Kate and put her hands on either side of Kate's head. She gently kissed the top of Kate's head and said, "I'm glad that softball didn't knock Greek Mythology 101 out of your brain. I mean, it's coming in damn handy right now."

Kate smiled and stood up to kiss Cass. "Let's get back on the road, it'll be dark soon and I'm getting hungry." Cass nodded and Kate said, "I can drive if you like."

"Nope. You can't. Remember? Doctor's orders." Kate rolled her eyes and got into the passenger seat.

Cass got in beside her, and waited for Kate to put on her seatbelt. Kate had been absent-minded since the accident, and every moment of forgetfulness, every slurred word terrified

Cass, but she didn't say anything, she just waited and watched and made sure Kate was OK.

All buckled-up, Kate turned to Cass and put her hand on Cass's thigh, saying, "So do you think you'll talk to your mom and dad?"

Cass shrugged. "I'm not really sure I ever want to talk to them."

"What about Scout?" Kate asked. "I mean, do you think she'd want to know?"

Cass turned back onto the highway and Kate waited for her to answer. "I don't know. I guess there's only one way to find out."

"What do you mean?"

"Well, I guess I should meet this mystery niece of mine."

Part Four

THIRTY-THREE

"Soy London fog!" the barista yelled, pushing a cup to the edge of the counter.

"I'll take that over," Hanna said, smiling at the new guy.

"We do that?" he said, puzzled.

"When it's for your girlfriend, yeah." Hanna grinned and walked out from behind the counter to take Em her tea.

"Thanks, love," Em said, and Hanna sat down and kissed her. "You on a break?"

"Yep. Just fifteen minutes, so you timed it perfectly."

Em leaned against Hanna's shoulder and Hanna wriggled so as to put her arm around Em, causing Em's toque to ride up her head. Hanna reached up to pull the hat down to cover the tops of Em's ears again.

"Got to keep you cozy," she said, "that fluffy hair of yours isn't the best insulation yet." Em laughed and then coughed. "How are you feeling today?" Hanna asked, trying to sound nonchalant.

"Good. A bit tired, but I actually managed to get through some emails this morning before Steve dropped me off here. You were up early. I didn't see you."

Hanna nodded. "Yeah, I had an early shift."

"And a late night?" Em said. "I didn't even hear you come home last night."

"Oh? I was pretty noisy! I felt bad. I crashed into your guitar in the hallway when I got home from practice, and definitely woke Steve up. Probably the neighbours too." Hanna laughed. "You must've been conked out. Even Thunderpuss came to see what was happening."

"Ah, Thunderpuss. There's nothing quite like a giant cat running at you in the dark."

"He's such a monster. I'd hate to be a robber."

"A burglar, you mean?" Em said.

"Do I?"

"Yeah. I think a burglar is someone who breaks into your house. A robber just, well, maybe a robber just mugs you on the street."

"What a thing to know," Hanna said, smiling.

"I'm so full of useful information."

"So, then, riddle me this," Hanna said, sitting up. "Why did I find a letter addressed to you from some lawyer in the Netherlands?" She wiggled her eyebrows at Em.

"Um."

"Yes?"

"Um."

Em took a sip of her tea and got foam on her nose. She tried to reach up to lick it with her tongue, but Hanna grabbed a napkin and wiped it instead.

"Stop being cute, you. Tell me what you're scheming?"

"Can we talk about it later?" Em asked, giving Hanna a wide grin.

"Talk about what?"

"It. With Steve. At home," Em said.

"We can talk about It now, if you like."

Em and Hanna looked up in surprise as Steve loomed over them.

"Budge up," he said, and sat on the other side of Em as

199

she shuffled to make some room.

"Aren't you supposed to be at the office all day?" Hanna asked.

"Not any more. Someone just asked to go to an open house at the development around the corner in twenty minutes, so I figured I'd swing by to see my two favourite people on the way." Steve tapped the top of his Our Town travel mug and winked at Hanna. "And I couldn't resist a top-up." Steve turned to look at Em and said, "So what's up? What did you want to talk to me about?"

Em looked back and forth between Steve and Hanna and scrunched up her face.

"Em?" Hanna said, "You're starting to worry me."

Em laughed and clapped her hands together. "OK, OK, so this isn't really how I envisaged this happening, but I guess we're just not meant to do things traditionally, so here goes." She took Steve's hand and Hanna's hand and bit her lower lip, then laughed again. "Actually, it's pretty perfect to do this here." Em looked around the coffee shop and remembered when she first saw Hanna behind the counter, focusing intently on crafting the perfect foam heart on someone's decaf latte.

Em brought their hands together and said, "Steve, Hanna, I love you both, and this last year has only been manageable because I've had you both with me. I can't imagine not having both of you in my life forever, and so I wanted to, I -" Em's voice caught in her throat, and she swallowed and said, "Will you both marry me?"

Hanna and Steve looked at each other and then at Em and then back at each other, open mouthed. Then Steve swooped in to kiss Em on one cheek and Hanna kissed her on the other cheek and Steve wrapped his arms around both Em and Hanna and whooped with joy.

"Hell yeah!" Hanna said, kissing Steve and knocking Em's hat askew again.

Em laughed, tears running down her cheeks, and Steve

said quietly, "Holy crow," and gave Em a long kiss before asking, "So, how's this going to work exactly?"

"Yeah, that's the puzzle," Em said, dipping her finger in the foam of her London fog and then licking the foam and making a popping noise with her mouth. "So, there's this lawyer I've been talking to... and there are a few issues, but I did hear about this officiant who's a bit unorthodox."

THIRTY-FOUR

The cursor blinked at Cass, and she blinked back, tapping the keys of her laptop so lightly that the screen stayed blank.

"Urrrrgh!" she groaned loudly and slammed the laptop shut. "I can't do this," she said, dropping her head into her hands.

Kate stood up and walked over from the couch. She rested her hands on Cass's shoulders and kissed the back of Cass's neck.

"I can't just send her an email. That's so ridiculous," Cass said. "I mean, why not just friend her on Facebook or tag her as family? What the fuck."

Kate kneaded Cass's tense muscles and said, "We could just wait, you know, until we're back. Then you could set up a meeting with her."

Cass reached up to put a hand on Kate's and signal for her to stop. She turned around and looked up at Kate. "Should I just let it go? Caroline doesn't want to know. Clearly my parents have never cared. And you said yourself that Scout didn't seem to want anything to do with us. Why am I pushing this?"

Kate smiled down at Cass and said, "Maybe because there's a chance you'd actually have a member of your family who you like."

Cass laughed and stood up. She wrapped her arms around Kate and kissed her. "Maybe I'm just such a narcissist that I really want to see this doppelganger for myself."

"Well, we both know you're pretty obsessed with yourself," Kate said, grinning and pecking at Cass's lips. "And quite right too," she murmured. "Why not leave this for a bit though? You've been sitting staring at your screen for almost an hour. Let's go for a walk or a ride or something," Kate said. "We could cycle down to that comic shop on Nieuwendijk and see if they have the latest issue of *Clouds*."

Cass pointed at a comic sitting on the kitchen island. "I picked it up for you yesterday, on my way home from class." Cass puckered her lips and pointed at them, closing her eyes.

"Thank you!" Kate said, after planting a kiss on Cass's proffered mouth.

"We can still go for a ride or a walk or something though," Cass said. "It would be good to do something physical and release some of this tension."

Kate laughed and slipped her hands around Cass's waist, wiggling her fingers underneath her shirt. Cass leaned back against the desk and pulled Kate closer. "I picked up something else yesterday too that you might like," she whispered into Kate's neck before biting her gently.

"Oh yeah?" Kate said, tilting her head back as Cass worked her way across Kate's collarbone with small, soft nibbles.

"At that little store by the Torensluis bridge. I saw Esther," Cass said, waiting for Kate to catch on.

Kate laughed and pulled away. "Naughty. What did Esther convince you to buy this time? Not another ornate glass butt plug to use as a paperweight?"

Cass gasped and clutched at her imaginary pearls. "What a suggestion!" She laughed and took Kate by the shoulders, spinning her around and walking her to the bedroom. "Take a look in the nightstand and tell me if it's to your liking."

Kate crouched down and Cass quickly pulled off her socks and unbuttoned her pants. She dropped her pants to the floor as Kate turned around holding the purple ShareVibe. Kate looked at Cass, whose pants were around her ankles, and moved to unzip her jeans. They raced each other to get completely naked, Cass winning and making a grab at the double-ended vibrator.

She pressed a button and it leapt into life. Kate giggled and pulled Cass closer, so they were sitting face to face, Kate kneeling between Cass's thighs. Kate ran her hand along Cass's thigh and up her body, grazing her palm over Cass's erect nipple. The ShareVibe buzzed between them as Cass moved it down to Kate's belly and then lower.

"I want you good and wet," Cass whispered, turning off the vibrator and kissing Kate hard.

Kate kissed Cass and felt herself getting wet. She reached down to turn the vibrator back on. Cass pushed it against her labia, making Kate groan and clutch at Cass's arm.

"Softer, slower. It's too good," Kate said, arching her back and dropping her hands behind her to grip her ankles for support.

Cass leaned forward and kissed Kate's breast, using her tongue to circle Kate's nipple and make it even harder.

"Lie back," Cass said, encircling Kate with her arm and slowly dropping her down to the bed. Kate slid her legs down and apart, allowing Cass room to move between her thighs. Cass kissed Kate's belly, the soft silver-lined skin of her hips, the slight projection of hip bone and the shallow valley just above her pubis.

Still moving the dildo gently against Kate's clitoris, Cass lowered her mouth to Kate's cunt and replaced the pulsating toy with her tongue. With her top lip, Cass exposed the hot, hard flesh of Kate's clit and flicked her tongue against it. She licked around and around before using her whole mouth to

204

make Kate grip the bed sheets and curl her toes.

Cass was as wet as Kate now, so she slid the shorter end of the double dildo inside herself while continuing to pleasure Kate. The vibrating dildo made Cass's thighs tremble, but she steadied herself and moved up Kate's body so she could thrust the longer shaft inside Kate's slick cunt.

Kate clawed at Cass's back and wrapped her legs up around Cass's hips, forcing her in deeper. "Oh fuck, yes."

Cass moved back and forth, loving the feeling of her skin against Kate's as she moved inside her. She grasped Kate's hands in her own and moved them up above Kate's head, against the headboard. Cass locked her eyes onto Kate's as she thrust into her again and again, their swollen clits almost touching as they moved against each other.

Cass buried her head in Kate's hair and kissed her neck as she bucked beneath her, so close to orgasm. A thrilling wave of pleasure burned through Cass's flesh. Her skin was on fire, her hips giving out and Kate taking over to bring them both to climax. Cass's groans were muffled by the pillows and Kate's hair and body, but Kate cried out so loudly that after she came a second time the neighbour hammered on the wall.

"Should we stop," Cass said, laughing but not making any move to pull away from Kate.

"No, no, I want it again," Kate said, licking her lips and then rolling Cass onto her back to straddle her. Kate lifted one hand up to gather the hair that had fallen across her face, thrusting it onto the top of her head while riding Cass. She moved her other hand down to Cass's mouth and Cass sucked her fingers, getting them good and slick so Kate could tease her clit until she came one last time, hard and fast and in such a flood that Cass couldn't help but laugh.

As Kate freed herself from Cass's body, she lowered her hand to the dildo and looked up at Cass. "Should I keep going?" she asked, and just the slightest push and the look on Kate's flushed face caused Cass to tremble again and clutch at Kate's hand to turn off the vibration so she could feel the pure, all-encompassing frenzy of pleasure as it rippled through her.

THIRTY-FIVE

Em took a giant gulp of a bright green smoothie and waved at Kate as the chat window opened.

"Good morning, lovely. Is that a kale smoothie?" Kate asked, pouring coffee from the cafetière into her cup.

"Indeed it is," Em smiled. "Steve and Hanna insist I have one every day."

"Do they have them too?" Kate grinned.

"Yep! We go through a lot of kale." Em smiled. "In fact, Hanna just built a bunch of leaning pallet garden boxes for the balcony so we can grow our own."

Kate rolled her eyes and Em laughed.

"I mean, that's grrrreat," Kate said.

"You should try it. It's almost as good as magic jello. In fact, we're all practically eating a totally vegan diet these days."

"That's awesome! Doctor's orders again?" Kate asked.

"Kind of. That whole brush with death thing can make a person pretty cautious about what they eat. And Steve has a whole family history of people dying from heart attacks."

"And Hanna?"

"She's training for the marathon," Em said, laughing.

"Didn't I tell you?"

"No, that's fantastic!" Kate gulped down her coffee and scribbled down 'kale' on her shopping list.

"She's putting up a sponsorship page in the next few days. Her and a couple of the other baristas, and the singer from Liquor Box are all training together and planning on raising a tonne of money for the Against Malaria Foundation."

Kate raised her eyebrows, "I would've assumed she would want to fundraise for a cancer charity. Malaria seems like an odd choice for a bunch of Canadians!"

Em laughed, "Aha! Yes, but if you knew about this website, Givewell.org, you would know that the AMF is one of the best charities worldwide in terms of being effective." She smiled, and added, "The way I see it, maybe one of those kids Hanna's donation helps save could grow up to be the genius who cures cancer."

"So none of you are being entirely selfless in all this do-gooding?" Kate said, rolling her eyes and laughing.

"It's like you don't even know me," Em said. She put down her smoothie and sat up straight, but before she could say anything else, Kate interrupted.

"Oh oh. What?"

"What?" Em said, holding out her hands, her eyes wide.

"You're about to say something important. I can just tell," Kate said as she smiled at Em.

Em cleared her throat dramatically and said, "Well, yes, actually, I am."

"Do you need a drumroll?" Kate asked, tapping her fingers against the edge of her desk.

Em laughed and said, "That depends. How would you feel about moving back to Vancouver and working with me on something?"

Kate stopped the drumroll and blinked at Em. "Um. I might need a bit more information, but I like the idea in general."

208

"That's the spirit!" Em said, grinning.

"So what's the deal? What plan are you concocting and what kind of trouble will it get me into?"

"No trouble. It's something I was thinking about while I was in the hospital. Remember how I said that there were so many people there who were alone and sad and how LGBTQ folks were more likely to die from cancer?"

"Yes, but I'm not really following," Kate said.

"OK. OK. Let me start again," Em rubbed her hands together and took a breath. "You remember Therese? The woman on my ward who never seemed to have any visitors or talk to anyone?"

Kate nodded.

"So, one day I dragged myself over there and got talking to her, and it turns out she is this amazingly interesting woman who was having the worst time ever. She was this big financial hotshot and everything in her life seemed perfect, but then she got this call from her sister to say that their mom died of really aggressive breast cancer."

"Yikes! So she didn't even know? She didn't get to say goodbye to her mom?" Kate asked. "How awful."

"Well, yeah, it is awful, but Therese hadn't spoken to her mom or her sister in almost twenty years. Basically since she came out in her first year at college," Em said. "Pretty intense, right?"

"I'd say. But what does all this have to do with whatever you're planning?" Kate said.

"I'm getting to that," Em said, then took a gulp of smoothie. She continued, "So Therese decides to get herself checked to see if she's carrying the gene, you know, the one that means your risk of breast cancer is way higher than average. Turns out she has it, so she books herself in for a double mastectomy, prophylactically."

"Wow. That's a bold move. But, so," Kate shakes her head and frowns at Em. "So she didn't have cancer? She looked really ill!"

"Well she was. It turned out she had thyroid cancer! They spotted it on one of her scans, and it explained a whole load of symptoms she'd been having."

"Well that seems weirdly lucky, I guess," Kate said. "Or, at least, that is, as lucky as someone can be in such circumstances."

"Right?" Em said. "So, after she has the surgery, she starts treatment for the cancer, but then she finds out that her secretary has been fiddling with finances at work and so she's under investigation for fraud."

"That's terrible!" Kate said. "I'm still not seeing what this has to do with any new job though. Are you becoming a PI or something?"

Em laughed and said, "Oooh! That's an idea. But, no. No detective work for me."

Kate waited, raising her eyebrows and leaning closer to the screen. "Em, you're killing me here. What's Therese's awful luck got to do with me?"

"OK. I'm getting there. Promise," Em said. "So, Therese's secretary has not only been screwing her over at work, she was also screwing Therese's wife, who is now divorcing her and trying to take their kids because she claims Therese has been an absent mom."

Kate gaped at Em, eventually saying, "An absent mom because she's been in hospital trying not to die?"

"Pretty much," Em said, wrinkling her nose.

"Em, that is fascinating and awful."

"Right?" Em said, shaking her head and taking another sip of smoothie. "So Therese tells me that she's basically lost her job because her secretary has been doing some pretty unscrupulous things -"

"Like screwing her wife and stealing her money?" Kate interjected.

"Like that, yeah. And now Therese is probably going to have to endure a long custody battle and divorce, this criminal investigation, and she's super sick and just had major, life

210

altering surgery." Em shakes her head and closes her eyes for a second. When she reopens her eyes, Em smiles at Kate and says, "But you know what? When I was talking to her, Therese told me that it was all a huge wake-up call and made her realise that she had been in such a bubble of denial with her wife that she'd totally turned her back on the community that supported her when she first came out. You know, like her queer family.

"That makes sense. I mean, you said no one was visiting her, right?" Kate said.

"Exactly!" Em said, "She was so alone, but then we got to talking and I told her about the cancer stats I told you about and she decided that she should do something useful with all her money, once they figure out it was her secretary who was the fraudster, not her."

"So, what, she's donating it to cancer research?" Kate asked, pouring herself more coffee.

"Not quite. She doesn't want to just throw money about. She wants to really get involved and reconnect with the community. She told me that she felt like something had to change if she survived, and I ended up feeling the same, you know?" Em started coughing and when Kate looked at her with concern, Em just waved her hands and said, "I'm just excited, don't worry."

"So what are you and Therese planning? I assume she beat the thyroid cancer?" Kate said, wondering where this conversation was heading.

"Well, not quite yet. She had chemo and radiation to shrink the tumour, and she's having surgery next week."

"It's good you're still in touch," Kate said. "You always do make friends in the oddest of places."

"People are so interesting, how can I not!?" Em said. "So here's the thing, finally." Kate laughed and waited for Em to continue. "So Therese and I decided that we should start a foundation that connects queer cancer sufferers and survivors. We'll have queer-friendly counsellors, and build a community to support cancer patients who might not have any family or financial support and who are most likely working in lower paid jobs with no benefits and no guarantee that their job will be there if – when – they beat the cancer."

"And maybe, like, a scholarship program?" Kate said, beginning to get excited at the plan that was emerging.

"Yeah! Exactly! We were thinking we could offer retraining programmes and hold workshops. But, instead of the traditional charity model of 'here is a chunk of money now go to this school' sort of a program, we would get a survivor with experience in one industry to be a mentor to someone interested in learning about that industry. The mentor gets to see their profession in a fun new way and encourage more queers to get involved in whatever industry they work in, and the mentee gets to change their career path and have an industry ally."

"OK, Em. I'll bite. How will this work? I mean, you can't just go around with a rainbow bucket asking for handouts for queers." Kate laughed at the image then said, "Oh! Maybe you can trawl cancer wards to ask if anyone is rich and queer?" Kate laughed.

Em shrugged. "Well, actually, that's not all that outrageous. There are some super lonely rich people who are closeted. Why not give them a great way to support the community? We'll just make that rainbow bucket a little more high-tech, letting people donate anonymously if they want to. And we'll start out local, matching up people desperate for a change in their career with craftsman and artisans and people with really practical skills like carpentry where there's already an apprenticeship type model." Em was grinning and bouncing in her seat, and Kate shuffled, starting to see how this might actually work.

"Would you expand it to match up people province-wide, or even across Canada and the US? Maybe even globally eventually?"

Em laughed. "Yeah, we could do that, if it works out.

212

And we could give people an opportunity to directly fund an apprenticeship, or to just give a general donation that would fund programs. People with workshop skills and community advocacy experience could train people with practical skills on how to lead their own workshops or work more effectively with community members, and everyone would get paid a fair wage, giving them some stability at a time when they might find it hard to find employment because of having been sick for so long."

"It's a great idea, Em, but a start-up? Wouldn't that cost us money? I mean, if all Therese's money is tied up until they investigate further, don't we need some initial investors? " Kate said, slurping her coffee and adjusting the screen so she could see Em better. "Honestly, Em, I don't have much to spare right now. I've just had a tough few weeks at work and I'd have to relocate, again. And I don't see how we can go from nothing to having a success story or two to show off to other investors without actually being able to pay for anything at the outset."

"I already have another investor, actually." Em said.

"Of course you do." Kate laughed and asked, "Who else did you charm during your hospital stay?"

Em grinned, "I didn't have to charm anyone. Therese did all the work for me. Justyna used to work with Therese." Em grinned and said, "Turns out Justyna is bisexual and never bothered coming out at work because she's been happily married to a man for the past fifteen years! She wants to do something to support the community, but just didn't know how to go about doing that. Therese says Justyna is on the boards for a bunch of charities and is great at grant-writing." Em paused, then looked right at Kate and said, "Now we just need you."

"Why me?" Kate asked. "I mean, you could just hire any old designer."

Em shook her head. "That's not true and you know it. And anyway, I don't want you to just be a designer. You'd be

213

my partner in this. You know how to build a brand, and how to run with an idea in an actual professional way. I'm enthusiastic, and you know I like to talk to people, but I need your brain to help tie everything together and make it look pretty and presentable and practical and realistic, but still be exciting."

"But my brain is broken, remember?" Kate grimaced.

"Nah, you've been doing so much better this month, and anyway, being your own boss means you can be more flexible and take time off when you need to."

"Start-ups are a shit ton of work, Em. C'mon."

"Well, yeah, but there'll be me and Justyna and Therese handling stuff too. It's not just you organising everything." Em's screen suddenly shook and then went black.

"Em?" Kate asked, sitting up to check that nothing untoward had happened to her computer.

"Still here!" Em cried, and the screen turned a fuzzy grey, then white, before the confused face of Thunderpuss appeared in all its glory. "He likes to sit on my laptop, which sort of crashes everything," Em said as she tried to shoo away her giant cat. "Sorry, I can't really lift him from this angle. Physio is going great and all, but my arms are still pretty weak."

"Well, I guess Thunderpuss can be our silent partner then," Kate said, laughing.

"So you're in?!" Em yelled over the increasingly noisy purring of the monster cat.

"I'm in!" Kate said, then back-tracked. "I mean, I'll have to talk things through with Cass and with work, and it'll be a big move again and everything."

"But Cass is done next semester, right?" Em said, her face re-emerging as Thunderpuss went to find somewhere a little quieter to sit.

"Yeah, she hasn't signed up for any more classes here, but there is probably more work on a new load of videos for the charity."

214

"Why don't we ask Cass to work with us?" Em said. "We'll need some kind of inspirational promotional video at some point, to show potential investors, and I'm guessing Cass is good. She's been doing it for a few years now, right?"

"She has, and she is. She's really good at it, but she's working on something right now."

"Oh yeah? What's she up to?"

"I'm not supposed to talk about it. It's kind of early days and she's not totally sure it'll work out, so I'm sort of pretending it's no big deal, in case it doesn't go anywhere. I don't want to put more pressure on her, you know? Not with this whole Scout thing hanging over her too."

"Oh right, yeah. Has anything happened with that?" Em asked.

"Not yet. We didn't really have time to track Scout down before flying back here. And Cass hasn't talked to Caroline since the grand revelation." Kate sighed and said, "I think Cass is struggling with the idea of connecting with Scout. They're so close in age, and so similar, but even though her childhood wasn't the best, Cass definitely has some serious advantages over Scout. I think she feels guilty on behalf of her parents and Caroline."

"She was three though, and had no idea, clearly," Em said.

"Well, yeah. But guilt isn't the most logical of emotions," Kate said, smiling thinly. "The thing is, even if Cass doesn't reach out to Scout, we're bound to run into her when we're back in Vancouver. I mean, the queer scene is pretty small, and anyone who meets them both will assume they're related."

"If not the same person," Em said.

"Well exactly," Kate shook her head. "I hope it doesn't make Cass reluctant to move back home."

"But you want to? Move back to Vancouver I mean?" Em asked gently.

Kate smiled. "Yeah. I miss you and the gang, and the

215

mountains and, honestly, my Dutch is abysmal."

Em laughed and asked, "Can you just resign? Would that leave everyone in Amsterdam in the lurch?"

"I'll have to talk to some people about the transition, but it should be fine. The last few months have really been about setting up a good team that can run itself. Essentially, I have organised myself out of a job."

"Picking up some handy skills on the way that will be helpful for our start-up?" Em smiled and winked at Kate.

"Oh, heck yes," Kate said, starting to think about a name for their organisation. "This is going to be so much fun! I'm so excited to work with you!"

"Why did we not do this sooner?" Em pouted.

"I guess we both needed a little dash of near-death first. Thanks, cancer! Thanks, brain trauma!" Kate laughed, then grimaced at her off-colour joke and started to apologise. "Too soon?"

Em was already grinning.

"I do think that's true though. I mean, writing copy to help people sell products that no one really needs was fun for a bit, but this feels like a more worthwhile use of my energy and skills." Em held up her glass and said cheers before draining the last of her smoothie. Kate finished her coffee and then noticed the time.

"Cass will be back from her bike ride soon, and I was supposed to be making dinner. Oops."

Em smiled. "Well at least you're full of coffee to get you moving."

"True. I should've cut myself off hours ago, but we're going to a movie premiere tonight so I need to stay awake."

"Oooh, fancy," Em said. "Well, enjoy. And have a real think about if you want to be in on my scheme."

"I will! I'm excited!" Kate said. "What do Steve and Hanna think?"

Em raised an eyebrow and said, "I've been holding off on telling them anything concrete until I spoke to you. If

216

you'd shot me down, I would've had to think of something else to do."

Kate laughed. "So go tell them you've had a brilliant idea and that we're hatching a plan-baby, OK?"

"Will do. Oh, and Kate?"

"Yes?" Kate smiled and wrinkled her brow as Em squirmed in her seat.

"Watch out for something in the mail, from me."

"What?" Kate laughed. "Why so mysterious?"

"You'll see."

"If you've sent me another glitter bomb, I won't be happy," Kate said, remembering how long it took to eradicate glitter herpes from her apartment after Em's last practical joke.

"Ha! No... but now you mention it," Em wiggled her eyebrows. "Just keep an eye out for mail. You'll see."

Kate promised to let her know when the mystery mail arrived, and they said goodbye, just as Cass turned her key in the front door.

"Hey!" Kate called, shutting her laptop and leaping up to greet Cass. "I was about to start making dinner, promise!"

Cass laughed and dropped her bag to the floor before kicking off her shoes. "Let's go out for dinner before the screening instead!" she said, and kissed Kate, lifting her off her feet. "We're celebrating!"

"Woah! A good day at school?" Kate said as Cass set her back down.

"Oh, not really, but this arrived." Cass handed Kate a pile of junk mail.

"Er?" Kate said, "You're this excited about a sale on power tools?"

Cass cocked an eyebrow and said, "Well, now you mention it." She rifled through the pile of flyers and presented a stiff green envelope to Kate.

Cass watched as Kate read the address. "Kate, Cass and Jupiter," Kate said quietly. "This is Em's writing, and this is a

217

very nice envelope."

Cass laughed.

"You opened it? You read it?" Kate said.

"It's got my name on it, so yeah," Cass grinned. "Read it already!"

Kate slipped the stiff card out of the envelope and held it up, running her fingers over the embossed tree design.

"Hanna, Em and Steve are tying the knot! Please join them for cakes and ale. October 20th. CRAB Park and the Ironworks, Vancouver."

Cass took Kate's hands and twirled her around as she whooped with joy. "Holy crow!"

"That's a bloody big knot to tie," Cass said, and then kissed Kate. "Hey, am I finally going to get it on with a bridesmaid?"

Part Five

THIRTY-SIX

"We're going to need a longer ribbon," Hanna said, her face deadpan, which sent Em into a fit of giggles. "I'm serious. Steve's enormous hands don't help," Hanna added as she tried for the third time to tie the ribbon around both Em and Steve's hands as well as her own.

Steve gave Hanna a quick kiss on the temple as she concentrated. "How are we going to jump over a broom while we're all tied together?" Steve said.

"Hmm," Em said, looking up at him and gesturing with her hands, causing Hanna to sigh and drop the ribbons, leaving only her own hands tied together.

Hanna wriggled free and said, "Some people jump over a fire instead."

"Oh, great, that sounds even safer," Steve said, grinning.

"Well, every wedding should be memorable," Em said.

"Maybe not because the groom and the two brides tied themselves together and then set themselves on fire by accident," Steve said.

"Steve has a point," Hanna said. "Maybe we should skip the fire thing, and the broom thing."

220

"I thought you both liked the whole handfasting shebang though?" Em said. "I mean, I'm easy. At least if we have both the fire and the broom there's something for our guests to use to sweep up our ashes."

Steve untied Hanna's hands and then tied himself to her and then to Em.

"Looks like we have a winner!" Steve said, shimmying his head from side to side. "But, yeah, this ribbon needs to be longer. That was tricky."

"Is there an eject button?" Hanna asked, tugging at the ribbon and feeling the knots tighten around her wrists.

"I think the point is that there's no escape," Em said.

"But, realistically, how long do we stay tied together at the ceremony?" Hanna asked, wide-eyed. "I'll be drinking champagne and it's going to get messy."

"Hells yeah it is!" Steve cried, before bending over to pull at the ribbons with his teeth. "Um, maybe we need a knife."

"Fire, knives, no escape. Yeah, our wedding will be memorable alright," Hanna laughed and wriggled her hands so she could slide one of them out of the ribbon. "Polyamory is a dangerous path indeed."

"Hey! Where's your commitment?" Em said, smiling, before slipping her own hands free, leaving Steve wrapped in ribbon.

The three of them collapsed onto the couch, displacing a disgruntled Thunderpuss.

"Do you think he could be ring bearer?" Em asked as Steve picked up Thunderpuss and placed him across his lap and Em's.

Hanna tickled the enormous cat's ears and said, "I thought Jupiter was going to be ring bearer?"

"I don't think he has time in his busy European schedule," Em said, her shoulders slumped. "We really can't fly him over just for the wedding and then send him back to Amsterdam."

"Aren't they all moving back anyway?" Hanna asked as she stood up to get her phone, which was vibrating on the kitchen counter.

"Not until after the wedding," Em said. She picked up her own phone and checked to see if the officiant had responded to her message with a draft copy of the wording for the ceremony. The three of them had met the officiant, Abigail, the day before to talk about how to do everything in triplicate and had immediately fallen in love with the tiny, but energetic woman in her seventies.

When they'd asked her if she was absolutely sure she was OK to perform a polyamorous wedding ceremony, Abigail had clapped her hands in glee and said she'd been waiting years for something a little bit different. This was certainly going to be different, Steve had said, but Em pressed the issue, worried that Abigail would back out over concerns about legality, leaving them without an officiant at the last minute. Abigail reassured them all that she was excited to officiate and pointed out that she planned on retiring pretty soon, so if anyone threatened to strip her licence, it was no skin off her nose.

Abigail had responded to Em's email, but only to say that she was heading to the Sunshine Coast for three weddings that weekend and would check over the wording as soon as she could. Just as Em was about to put down her phone, she saw an email alert saying that the broom she had ordered was about to be shipped. She started to tell Steve and Hanna but realised that Hanna had stopped listening and was bouncing on the spot, her eyes screwed shut and her mouth wide, as if she were screaming silently. "Um, care to share?" Em asked as she and Steve stared at Hanna in amusement.

"The single's been chosen as the theme song!"

Em leapt up and joined Hanna in the bouncing. "That's amazing!"

Steve, still sitting on the couch under a startled cat, looked over at them, one eyebrow raised. "Could someone put me in the loop?"

Hanna and Em, still holding onto each other, turned to Steve and both started babbling. He held up his hands in surrender and Em gestured for Hanna to explain.

"Liquor Box's new single -"

"Fist of Fury?" Steve said.

"Yep. Well, it's been selected as the theme song for this new show that'll be shot here in Vancouver." Hanna grinned and hugged Em, lifting her off her feet.

Steve picked up Thunderpuss and joined in with the hugging. "That's amazing. You're awesome." He looked at Em and said with mock concern, "We're marrying a celebrity. How ever will we keep the paparazzi away?"

Hanna scowled at him and Steve asked, "So, practically speaking, does this mean you've made it, as a band? Are you going to quit baristaing?"

Hanna snorted, "Nope. We'll probably get enough money to replace one of my broken drums and restring Claire's guitar."

"But it's a good sign, right?" Em said.

"Oh, totally. And the money is always welcome, and the exposure. Here's just hoping the show is decent and people watch it."

"What's it called?" Steve asked, cradling Thunderpuss in his arms and petting him as he squirmed and demanded to be put down.

"Give it up!" Hanna said.

"OK! OK!" Steve said, carefully dropping Thunderpuss to the floor.

"No, the show, it's called, 'Give it up'," Hanna said. "It's some kind of weird resurrection drama where the main character is dead and goes around haunting people who need to make major life changes to be happy."

"That sounds like an entirely reasonable premise," Em said, demonstrating her best poker face, which was not at all convincing.

"Yeah, maybe I'll even watch it," Hanna said, smirking. "I'll watch the credits at least."

"Isn't that your phone ringing?" Steve said as he returned from the kitchen with two bottles of beer. He handed one to Hanna as the three of them looked around to see if they could spot Em's phone before it stopped ringing.

Em made a quick dash towards the couch and looked suspiciously at Thunderpuss, who had stretched out so he had claws in one arm of the loveseat and claws in the other arm too.

"Scram!" Em said, making a move to tickle the cat's belly, which never failed to make him leap out of the way. She found her phone wedged between the cushions and saw that she had two missed calls from the building buzzer entry phone.

"Damn," Em said, but was relieved to see her phone ringing again. "Hello?"

"Herrooooooo!"

"Um, who is this?" Em said, holding up her hands to Steve and Hanna and asking them silently if they were expecting guests. They both shrugged.

"It's Kate and Cass! We have come to see that magnificent pussy of yours," Kate said, and Em gasped and buzzed them in.

Em told Steve and Hanna who was coming up and Steve went to get two more beers so he could greet Kate and Cass at the door in style. "Did you know they were coming?" he asked, and Em shook her head.

"They're a week early," Hanna said. "I thought they were arriving just before the wedding."

Em shrugged and grinned, then sprinted to the door as Kate appeared. Em wrapped her arms around Kate and said, "Best early wedding present ever! How come you're here now?"

"I figured I'd take all that holiday I stored up over summer while I was working my butt off training my

224

replacement," Kate said.

Steve hugged Cass and handed her the beer. "Oh man, yes please. That flight is killer."

Steve picked up the two suitcases Cass had been carrying and moved them out of the way so he could shut the apartment door. "How come you're not in school?" he asked, and Cass took a swig of the beer and then cocked her head to one side.

"Yeah, about that," she said and raised her eyebrows.

"You flunked out?" Steve asked quietly, stealing a glance at Kate who was busy hugging Em and Hanna again.

Cass shook her head. "No, no. I passed everything. I just didn't take any classes this semester as I was working on something else."

"Oh yeah, like a video thing?"

"Kind of. A documentary of my own actually."

"No way!" Steve said, causing Em, Kate and Hanna to stop giggling with delight and look over.

Kate walked over to Cass and put her arm around her waist. She kissed Cass on the cheek and said, "Are you going to tell them, or shall I?"

Cass laughed and lowered her head, feeling her face getting hot.

"OK, me!" Kate said. "So Cass made this short documentary and submitted it to DOXA a couple of weeks ago and one of the panel got in touch right away and asked to meet with her to see about turning it into a bigger project!"

"That's amazing!" Hanna said, and Em put up her hand to high-five Cass while winking at Kate.

"Good job!" Steve said, also going in for a high-five. "So what's it about?" He gestured to the couch and armchairs so they could all sit.

"It's called #facesofprostitution," Cass explained. "It started out as just a short piece where I interviewed three queer sex workers in Amsterdam about the particular health issues they face. But then this friend, Guy, who I met on my

225

flight here last time, suggested I interview front line health care workers in Amsterdam too. Then I ended up talking to some nurses here, including Guy. He's this rad dude who helped organize a nursing conference in Groningen, which led to a super interesting panel on diversity in health care. He got me thinking it'd be good to get the front line workers and sex workers together, you know? Like, to really highlight the impact of having diversity in health care so people feel comfortable getting help when they need it."

Em applauded and looked over at Kate, grinning. "That's wonderful! I want to see it!"

"You'll still have to wait a little while, and I might make a few more edits. I'm trying to get hold of Tilly Lawless to interview her."

"Who?" Em asked.

"The queer Australian sex worker who started the #facesofprostitution movement," Cass explained.

Em sighed and said, "I'll have to look her up. I'm out of the loop these days."

"You were in the loop?" Hanna said, looking puzzled.

"Yeah, I volunteered at Pivot Legal Society a while back, when they were working on the case for sex workers' rights in Canada."

"Wow. Cool," Hanna ruffled Em's hair, which had grown back in wispy blonde curls, surprising them all. "What else don't I know about the woman I'm marrying?" Hanna said, grinning.

"Oh, she's a dark horse, this one. Lots of underground charitable and voluntary work she's not disclosed to you yet," Steve said, one eyebrow raised.

Em laughed and put out a hand toward Cass to prompt her to continue. "So, what's the deal with DOXA? Isn't that in May or June?"

"Yeah. Submissions are still open, and the festival is in May, but this person on the judging panel, who used to be a sex worker, was already thinking of making a documentary

226

about queer sex workers worldwide and how decriminalisation, or the lack of progress in that area, is affecting them."

"So she wants to work with you, or she's stealing your footage?" Hanna said.

Cass laughed, "No, no, she's cool. We talked on Skype last week and she asked if I could meet with her and a couple of other people in person. So I figured I'd just come to town a little early for the wedding and meet with them and with Guy." Cass paused and added, "And there's something else I've got to do while I'm over here."

They were all silent for a moment, and then Kate took Cass's hand and smiled at her, saying, "Do you want to tell them?"

Hanna, Steve, and Em all held up their hands and simultaneously said, "No pressure!"

Cass laughed and said, "Is that in your vows? That was great timing." She took a swig of beer and said, "So, this other thing. It's, well.... So, so I've been emailing with Scout for a few weeks, and she said she wants to meet me."

"Woah," Em said, "That's awesome."

"And a big deal," Hanna added, patting Cass's knee. "How do you feel about it?"

Cass grinned and shook her head. "Fucking terrified."

THIRTY-SEVEN

There was a line-up at Alibi Room when Cass and Kate arrived, so they added their names to the list and headed outside to wait to be called. Cass had wanted to arrive early so she could settle before Scout turned up, but Scout had the same thought and was about to open the door to the bar as Kate walked out.

Scout stood aside, holding the door and nodding at Kate, wondering why she looked familiar. Then Cass appeared behind Kate and Scout took a step backward and let go of the door.

"Hey!" Cass said as the door hit her trailing leg and she bumped into Kate, who had stopped walking. She looked up at Kate, then followed Kate's gaze to see Scout. "Oh. Oh shit."

Scout put her hand to her mouth and said, "This is too fucking weird." She recovered herself and took a step forward to offer her hand to Cass, saying, "Sorry. Scout. You have got to be Cass, right?" She shook Cass's hand and then smiled at Kate and said, "How's the head?"

Kate laughed and shook Scout's hand. "Doing much

better than last time I saw you, that's for sure!"

Cass still hadn't said anything and Kate had to steer her away from the door as some people were trying to exit the bar.

"Um, how was your flight?" Scout asked, stuffing her hands into the pockets of her jeans.

"Good, thanks," Kate said, glancing over at Cass, who was staring at Scout while Scout stared at her. Kate realised that they were wearing the same Blundstones, but didn't know if it would be helpful or a really silly idea to point this out.

"So, this is creepy, huh?" Cass said, finally. "I mean, what the fuck?" She grinned and moved slightly forward then paused and held out her arms a little. "Are you a hugger? Can I hug you? I just -"

Scout hugged her and laughed, and the two of them stood there for a little while in a silent embrace, while Kate blinked and dabbed at her eyes with the sleeve of her coat.

"Holy hell," Cass said, releasing Scout and returning to stand next to Kate. She slipped her hand into Kate's hand and Scout laughed.

"I bet you didn't grow up saying 'holy hell' much, right?"

Cass grinned. "Definitely not. Preacher pops would've had a conniption."

"A what?" Scout asked.

"It's how these weird Brits go ape-shit," Cass said, holding Kate's hand up to her mouth to kiss her knuckles.

Kate's phone started ringing and the caller ID said Alibi Room, so they headed inside, Scout holding open the door for Kate and Cass this time.

When they were settled at the table downstairs, Kate said, "We have to order at the bar down here, so I'll go get us a pitcher." She looked at Scout and asked, "You drink, right?"

Scout laughed, "Yeah." She turned to Cass and said, "Can I blame that on my genes?"

Kate rolled her eyes and said, "Don't go giving her

excuses."

Cass smiled after Kate as she walked over to the bar, then looked back at Scout and shook her head. "I totally creeped you online, but seeing you in person is a hug headfuck, you know?"

Scout nodded and said, "Yeah, I looked you up too. It was especially weird seeing some photos of last year's Mabel League party. Like, you standing next to Kerry and Drew. So bizarre."

"How is Drew?" Cass asked. "You said you were kind of dating?"

"Yeah," Scout smiled, her cheeks colouring. "She's great."

"Oh yeah," Cass said, raising an eyebrow. "She was always such a hardass on the field. Is she like that in the bedroom too?"

Scout's eyes widened and Cass held up a hand in apology. "Sorry, too soon. I just sort of feel like I already know you."

"Because you think I'm just like a younger version of you?" Scout asked, her voice quiet and level.

"Maybe that's what it is. I don't know though. I mean, honestly, I'd usually avoid hanging out with someone like you," Cass said, shrugging her shoulders.

"Someone who looks like me? Or someone who looks like you?" Scout said, grinning.

"Well... yeah!" Cass laughed. "I mean, you're competition!"

"But you seem pretty solid with Kate, right?" Scout said quietly, after glancing over her shoulder and seeing that Kate was on her way back to the table with a pitcher and three glasses.

"We're good, yeah," Cass said, smiling up at Kate. "That's why I said 'usually'."

"How's it going over here?" Kate asked as she poured a beer and handed it to Scout. "Any hilarious similarities you've
230

uncovered? Like, your shoes maybe?"

Cass and Scout looked at Kate, who smiled and glanced down, indicating that they should both do the same.

Scout raised her leg and Cass laughed, then raised her own, and they both shook their heads.

Scout raised her glass and said, "To finally meeting my doppelganger."

They clinked glasses and took a sip of beer, then Cass locked eyes with Scout, raised her glass and said, "To family."

After the second pitcher ran dry, Cass stood up to go and buy another, but Kate put her hand on Cass's arm and said, "I think I might head back to the Airbnb. I'm pretty wiped."

"You sure?" Cass said. "You feeling OK?"

Kate smiled and stood up, gathering her coat and bag and saying, "I'm fine. It's just jet lag. And I have bridesmaidy things to do tomorrow."

Cass rolled her eyes. "Rather you than me."

"I'm helping them pick out a broom," Kate said, grinning.

"No way!" Scout interrupted. "Your friends are having a handfasting?"

Cass and Kate looked down at Scout, who said, "A couple of friends got married that way just after I moved out here, and I was pissed that I didn't get to see it. They sort of sprung it on everyone on short notice and I'd just moved and had no money to go back."

"Go back where?" Kate asked. "I'm not sure Cass told me where you were living before you moved to Vancouver." She looked at Cass, who shrugged.

"I moved around. I was in Regina for a while, then Moose Jaw with one family for a few years. The friends were in Swift Current, they moved there after ageing out."

"What's ageing out?" Kate asked. "Sorry, am I... should I not ask that? Should I know that?"

Scout smiled. "Nah, that's cool. It's just when a kid gets

231

to eighteen and doesn't have to be in foster care any more, so they age out and can decide where to live."

"So you left the family you were with, in Moose Jaw?" Kate asked, sitting back down and leaving Cass standing awkwardly, not wanting to leave the conversation to get beer, but not wanting to leave them without beer.

Scout looked at Cass and said, "We've got lots of time to talk about this, but, yeah, I moved out as soon as I could and got my own place in Medicine Hat, where there were more jobs, and it was out of province."

"So why Vancouver?" Kate asked.

Scout laughed. "You've clearly never been to Medicine Hat."

Kate smiled and shook her head. "It sounds like it should be an amazing place, like it's full of magical doctors or something."

"Or something is about right," Scout said. "It was OK. I mean, it was my first real big city as an adult, but nothing to what I figured Vancouver would be like."

"And Vancouver's living up to expectations?" Cass asked.

"Well, there are enough queers for a softball league, so that's pretty incredible, yeah." Scout laughed.

"So are you a jock, like Cass?" Kate asked Scout, flashing Cass a smile.

"God, no. Not a jock. I mean, I played sports, but I was never really in a school long enough to get on any teams or anything."

"You play pool?" Cass asked, raising an eyebrow.

"Oh yeah. Do I ever?!" Scout said, grinning.

"Oh dear. Here we go," Kate said, standing up. "That's my cue to leave."

"Your what?" Cass said, shimmying her head and grinning. Scout laughed, but Kate looked puzzled. "Cue? You know, like a pool cue."

Kate groaned. "Nice. Very nice."

232

"So you're good?" Cass asked Scout.

"I'm alright, yeah. Just forming a team, actually. You want in? We need another player. Monday nights."

Cass laughed and asked, "It all depends on your team name. You've gotta have a good name."

Scout smirked and said, "We're The East Van Ladyfingers."

"Ha!" Cass clapped her hand to her mouth and guffawed. "That's an awesome name. Sure, I'm in."

Kate tapped Cass on the top of her head and said, "I think you're forgetting that we live in Europe. It might be a little bit of a commute on a Monday night."

Cass wrinkled her nose. "Not for much longer though."

"Oh yeah?" Scout asked. "Should I hold a spot for you?"

Kate and Cass looked at each other and smiled. "We need to talk about that, so how about I let you know?" Cass said. She stood up to kiss Kate goodbye and then asked Scout if she wanted to head somewhere with a pool table.

"It's a Friday night. I don't think we'll have much luck. Maybe we can meet up again Tuesday night, if you're still in town?"

"At Guy's and Dolls?" Cass asked.

Scout grinned, "Yeah. I love confusing them on 'Ladies Night'."

It was two in the morning when Cass crept into bed beside Kate, trying not to wake her.

"Ooof, your feet are freezing," Kate said, and then gasped as Cass wrapped her cold hands around Kate's body. "Get off!" she said, laughing sleepily while putting her hands over Cass's to warm them up faster. "Did you have fun?"

Cass murmured an affirmative into Kate's shoulders, then said, "We're playing pool on Tuesday."

"Yeah? That's great."

"She's really cool. It's so -" Cass's voice broke and Kate twisted around to face her.

In the dim light from the street lamp outside the bedroom window, Kate could see the tears falling across the bridge of Cass's nose. She took Cass's face in her hands and kissed her softly.

"What's going on?" Kate asked.

Cass cried quietly for a few seconds and then looked at Kate and wiped her tears on the pillow. "I just can't help but think how things could've been different."

"Did Scout say anything about wanting to meet Caroline?"

Cass shook her head.

"You didn't talk about her?" Kate asked, shocked.

"Oh, we did. But she doesn't want to meet any of them. She was super clear on that."

Kate kissed Cass again and said, "I can understand that."

Cass nodded. "Me too. I barely want to speak to them, so I don't see why Scout would want to."

"Does Scout have family? Were any of her foster families OK?" Kate asked.

Cass shrugged. "It doesn't sound like it. I think she's just used to being on her own, you know?"

Kate was quiet for a moment and then said, "Well, she has family now. Maybe I can see if she could come to the wedding. It's not her friends' handfasting, but it could be fun for her, and the trifecta would be game, I'm sure."

Cass pulled Kate closer and whispered with beery breath, "You are the best. I love you," and then kissed her hard as she laughed.

THIRTY-EIGHT

"Wait! Where are the unicorns?" Kate said, looking around frantically.

"What unicorns?" Cass peered at Kate, wondering, not for the first time in recent months, if her girlfriend was imagining things.

"Stop it," Kate said.

"What? What am I doing?" Cass held up her hands.

"You're thinking I'm crazy because I got hit in the head with a softball."

"Well, yeah, OK, I am thinking that. But only because I love you." Cass smiled widely.

Kate shook her head. "I'm not crazy. At least not right now." She waved her hand at the gift table, a gigantic piece of old machinery bookended by two giant metal wheels, a remnant of the past activity at the Ironworks. "There were balloon unicorns. I swear."

"OK. Sure. How about no more pre-wedding champagne for you?"

"Cass. I had one glass. No more. Doctor's orders." Kate pursed her lips. "There were unicorns here. Em wanted them

235

at each end of the table, one for each of the flower kids."

"Well, maybe Em took them? I mean, it's her wedding, right?"

"Em is checking on the cakes with Grace, see?" Kate pointed to the other side of the room, where Em was standing, her hands on her hips, watching Grace and Kerry rearrange an impressive array of cake stands made from thrift store china and tea cups.

"Well maybe Steve moved the balloons?" Cass suggested, looking around.

"Nope. Steve's in charge of the ale." Kate gestured at the bar, where Steve was unloading bottles of beer from Postmark Brewing alongside Jeff.

"Hanna?" Cass said.

"With the DJ," Kate said as Hanna and her bandmate, their DJ for the evening, hauled another record box onto the stage.

"I'm running out of people," Cass said, putting her hands up. "There just aren't enough people at poly weddings these days."

Kate laughed and then furrowed her brow. "Em was really excited about the unicorn balloons. Sonia's husband made them."

"They'll show up," Cass said. "I mean, unicorn balloons don't just fly away, right?"

Cass looked around, and then spotted a rainbow striped ribbon and followed it upwards. She laughed. "Um, I guess unicorns do fly." She took Kate's hand and pointed their fingers up towards the collection of balloon unicorns nestled into the rafters.

"Oh. Well, that's not good," Kate said. "Sixteen-foot ceilings are great until you factor in balloons."

"Never fear, my love," Cass said, and went over to talk to Steve and one of the venue staff. She came back with a grin on her face and a pole with a grabbing arm on the end. Cass started to unscrew the pole so it could be extended to reach

236

up to the rafters.

Kate jumped out of the way and said, "Don't get any ideas!"

Cass hopped up onto a chair, climbed onto the gift table, hauled the chair up onto the table and then climbed back onto the chair, asking Kate to hold her steady.

"Cass! Be careful!" Kate called. "It doesn't matter!"

Cass steadied herself on the chair and used the pole to carefully snag a ribbon and pull down a balloon. She handed it to Kate then proceeded to rescue all six unicorns.

"Just another day at the mystical wildlife refuge," Cass said, screwing the pole back down to a more manageable size.

"Thank you. You're ridiculous," Kate said, kissing Cass.

"Hey, I'm not the one who wanted balloon unicorns at my handfasting ceremony. I thought Em was vegan now, anyway?" Cass grinned and Kate scowled at her. "Did she not get the memo on balloon animal exploitation?"

The room grew suddenly quiet and Cass ducked behind Kate and whispered, "It's the vegan police. Save me!"

"Shut up, you," Kate said. "It's just time to go get dressed." She clapped her hands together and looked over at Em, who was wringing her hands and staring over at Kate. Em beckoned Kate over, wide-eyed.

"Ready?" Kate said, kissing Em lightly on the cheek, being careful not to smudge her makeup.

"Oh god. What am I doing?" Em said, her hands shaking.

"That's the spirit."

"I think I need some spirits," Em said. "Got any whisky?"

"There's champagne in the dressing room. Let's go get you a glass to take to the beach."

"Is everything set up for after?" Em asked.

"We're all set. We just rescued the unicorns. Little terrors tried to make a break for it." Kate smiled, then said, "Never mind. It's all fine. Champagne?"

THIRTY-NINE

A sharp wind ruffled the hair of the gaggle of guests who had already congregated at the end of the wharf. Some of the guests clutched at their hats, warily eyeing the mist lurking across the Burrard inlet between them and the North Shore mountains.

"Whose idea was it to have an October wedding outdoors in Vancouver?" Grace muttered to Janice, who laughed.

"Well, you know Em: ever the optimist," Janice said.

"Oh, there's Scout. I didn't realise she'd be here. I should go say hi," Janice said, waving at Scout, who had just walked onto the creaky decking alongside Drew. After several months of not speaking to each other, Janice had run into Scout and Drew at the farmer's market and they had endured an awkward few seconds of silence before Drew introduced herself and then became conveniently engrossed in the task of finding a special kind of fingerling potato.

Janice and Scout began talking across each other, trying to apologise for how things had ended between them. They gave up and busted out laughing, then called a truce and arranged to go for coffee. Scout told Janice that she had started seeing Drew shortly after the breakup, and Janice felt sad at first and wondered if she should have committed to dating Scout. The feeling quickly disappeared, though, as they ran out of things to say to each other. Their connection in the bedroom didn't seem to help them find a conversational rhythm and after finishing their drinks they had both suddenly remembered they had urgent errands to run.

Janice walked over to say hi to Scout and Drew, happy that they were at least on friendly terms now. Grace called after her, "Isn't that Cass? Did her and Kate break up?" Grace frowned, her question had been lost to the wind and Janice hadn't heard, but the woman standing next to Grace laughed.

"That's Scout, Cass's niece," Alice said, leaning over to help Grace out. "It's a long story." Grace stared at her and Alice said, "Sorry for butting in. I figured I'd pipe up and nip any odd wedding gossip in the bud!" She held out her hand and said, "I'm Alice. And this is my fiancé, Jeff."

Grace shook their hands and smiled. She was about to ask how they knew the happy couple, then stalled, not knowing quite how to phrase things.

Alice saved her by saying, "I'm a nurse at VGH. I met the trifecta there."

"Is everyone calling them that now?" Grace said, laughing. "I thought that was just Em's joke."

Alice smiled and said, "It's pretty handy though, right?"

Jeff started to ask how Grace knew everyone, but his voice was drowned out by the propeller noise of the helicopter at the helipad next to the pier. When the helicopter was far enough away, the sound of the first few bars of *The Knot*, by Jill Barber, caused everyone on the wharf to turn around.

Kate was standing on the gravel, holding a bouquet of red gerberas, interlaced with red Russian kale from Hanna's balcony garden. She started walking carefully down the aisle created by the guests, and was followed by Steve's brother,

Hanna's brother, and then by Kerry, who was guiding a slightly startled Thunderpuss on his leash. He was wearing an elaborate purple saddle with a ring pouch sewn to the top, and when he veered off into the crowd of guests, Kerry bent down and scooped him up carefully, trying not to get muddy paw prints all over her dress as she hurried down the aisle to join Kate.

Steve, Em, and Hanna followed them, walking each other down the aisle and taking up their positions in front of Abigail, the officiant, as the last notes of the song blew out across the waters of the inlet.

The diminutive officiant started to speak but stopped suddenly as a gust of wind snatched her pork-pie hat up into the air. Steve leapt up to get it and handed it back to Abigail with a smile.

Everyone laughed and Hanna tugged at a spare pin she had stuck in her dress earlier after helping Kate pile up her hair. She offered the pin to the Abigail, who slid it into place to secure her hat. She smiled, composed herself and began again.

"We stand before this company, on this beautiful, if blustery, fall day, to witness the joining of Emilie, Hanna, and Steven." She looked at the three of them in turn and said, "You are aware of the reality of the vows you are about to speak to one another, and of the responsibility that comes when a partnership is created. If there is any reason within your hearts that this ceremony should not continue at this time, I charge you to voice it now, for marriage is based in honesty and trust, and only with those things can you successfully create a partnership."

The trifecta squeezed each other's hands and beamed at Abigail, saying nothing.

"Emilie, Hanna, and Steven, you stand before me and this company, having desired the bond of marriage. Do you do this of your own free will, coming here today without coercion or pressure from other persons?"

240

They all nodded, "Yes!"

Abigail turned to face Em, who gave her shoulders a little shake to compose herself. She glanced at Kate, wide-eyed and Kate smiled, wiping away the tears already running down her face. Em turned back to Abigail and nodded.

"Emilie, will you seek to do Hanna or Steve harm?"

"I will not."

"And if harm is done, will you seek to repair it?"

"I will."

"Will you seek to be honest with Steve and Hanna in all things?"

"I will."

"Will you support Hanna and Steve in times of distress?"

"I will," Em said, and squeezed Hanna's hand and Steve's.

"Will you temper your words and actions with love?"

"I will."

"These things you have promised to your partners, before this company. May you ever be mindful and strive to keep the vows you have spoken."

Abigail handed Em a long green ribbon and Em took the ribbon and tied it first around her wrist, then around one of Steve's wrists and then around one of Hanna's wrists. Finally, she tied the ribbon around her own wrist again to close the circle, taking care to leave a long length of ribbon.

"And to that promise you are bound," Abigail said, before repeating the vows with Steve. As he spoke, he tied the ribbon to Hanna's wrist, fumbling as his hand shook, and then tied Em's wrist to Hanna's and then to his own.

Abigail repeated the vows with Hanna, who tried to swallow her giggles as she struggled with the last bit of ribbon, pulling on the wrong loop and almost untying Em's first knot. Em whispered, "I'd help, but I'm a little tied up right now."

The three of them began to shake with laughter, but Hanna got a hold of herself and tied the last knot.

Kate sighed, realising she had been holding her breath

for longer than she thought she could. She was dizzy with delight, and mild hypoxia, as Abigail looked up to face the guests.

Abigail held out her hands to the guests and said, "As these three people are joined, so are your families and friends united through them. It has been their decision to bind themselves by marriage, and their lives will be blessed and enriched by the support you give. Will you encourage and bless Emilie, Hanna and Steve in their union? Will you celebrate their marriage, standing beside them in rough times?"

"We will!"

"Me too!" cried a man none of them knew, as he just happened to be walking his dog along the path by the beach when the party of guests suddenly yelled into the wind.

Abigail laughed and turned to Em, prompting her to speak her vows.

"I, Emilie, do ask you, Hanna and Steven, to be my partners in marriage. I ask that you accept my strengths and my faults as I promise to accept yours; I ask for your support and strength when mine own does fail me, as I promise my strength and support in your times of need. I bring you, with best intention, my love, my understanding, all that I have and all that I am."

Steve and Hanna repeated the vows, and then Abigail nodded to Kate for the rings. Kate retrieved the rings from the pouch worn by Thunderpuss and then held out three slender wooden rings to Em, Hanna, and Steve. They slipped the rings onto each other's fingers.

Steve's brother and Hanna's brother also retrieved two sets of three rings, and the trifecta slotted these together, each ring a slightly different hue from its two counterparts.

"These rings, tokens of your love for one another and for the love between the three of you, serve as a reminder that all in life is a cycle: all comes to pass and passes away and comes to pass again."

242

Abigail raised her hands slightly to feel the breeze through her fingers and said, "May the Winds of communication blow ever between you; may the Fires of love sustain you; may the Waters of life heal and soothe you; and may the strength of the Earth bind and steady you throughout your time together." She put out her hands to hold onto the circle created by Em, Steve, and Hanna and said, "By the Winds that bring change, by the Fire of love, by the Seas of fortune and the strength of the Earth do I bless this union."

Abigail stepped back and the trifecta kissed each other, then she said, "You have witnessed the promises made by Emilie, Hanna, and Steven, one to another and another, and the exchange of the symbols of their union. They are now connected to experience together whatever life may bring them."

Abigail turned them to face their guests and held out her arms behind them, saying, "I am happy to present to you, Steven, Emilie and Hanna. May you never hunger. May you never thirst."

The crowd gathered on the pier cheered and applauded, and the trifecta readied themselves to jump the broom that Kate placed in front of them. Hands still tied together, Em, Steve, and Hanna counted down from three and then leapt over the broom. Em looked up at their guests and cried, "Onto the cakes and ale!"

FORTY

"So how's your week been?" Cass asked, handing Scout a beer as she got back to their table.

"I just signed a lease for a goddamn mansion," Scout said, then laughed at Cass's expression of disbelief. "No lie. Me and Afra are moving in with this poet I know and two social work students Afra met at some protest they organised. They both seem pretty cool, but it's still weird to think that I'm actually voluntarily moving in with social workers."

"Social workers can be nice. Sometimes," Cass said. "I've dated a few good ones."

"Social workers and librarians, man. What's with that?"

"I know, right? It's like the easiest way to flag your queerness to a careers counsellor," Cass said, laughing and thinking about the last librarian she dated, who went back to school to be a social worker. She looked around the room and spotted Drew stuffing a cake into her mouth. "What's up with Drew?" Cass said. "I just saw her demolish three of those cakes like she hasn't eaten in weeks."

Scout grinned. "She's four months' pregnant."

Cass sipped her beer slowly, then placed the glass gently

on the bar. There was a moment of silence.

Scout shook her head at Cass and asked, "Well, aren't you going to say congrats or something?"

"I don't know. Should I?"

Scout's voice hardened, "I believe it's traditional, yes."

"But is this what you want? Isn't it a bit sudden, even for queers? Are you happy?"

"Fuck off. Drew's happy. She has wanted this for so long. The least you could do is be fucking happy for her."

"But is it what you want? I mean, that's great for her and all, but it changes things for you."

"Not really. I'll be around, but the kid is her kid."

"But you've been seeing each other for a while. So, what, now she's pregnant you're just going to stop dating?"

"No, but it's not that kind of a relationship. We're not like, well, you and Kate, you know? And she was already doing the baby thing before I met her. It's really nothing to do with me." Scout's face was flushed and she was gripping her glass hard enough that her knuckles were white.

"I don't get it. Aren't you going to move in and be a real family?" Cass asked.

"Hell no. A real family? What does that even look like? Do you think that's what Drew even wants?" Scout scoffed, "How do you think that'd go, if I got down on one knee and proposed to fucking Drewwww? You've met her, right?"

"I get it. You don't think you're important enough to have goals or ambitions, that everything you ever do will inevitably fail, so what's the point. Everyone leaves and everything goes wrong, right? So why even bother thinking about what you really want. People like us can't have it anyway, so it's better to pretend we're happy being fuck-ups who live moment to moment. We don't disappoint because no one expects anything of us, least of all ourselves." Cass gulped down her beer, punctuating the monologue.

"What the fuck, dude? Where did that even come from?" Scout yelled at Cass, drawing some looks from the other side of the bar.

"I know you don't want to hear it. I didn't want to hear it either, but -"

Scout put down her glass and waved her hands across each other, signalling a time-out.

"Look, you're not my mother; no one is, remember? And you don't get to decide what's best for me, just because you finally have all your shit figured out and are going to be some wonderful do-gooder. I'm not you, Cass. I didn't grow up like you and I don't want to be like you or to have dinner parties with my wife, or a mortgage, or a kid."

"But -"

"No. You think you've outgrown fucking around and having fun, and so now you're being all, like, ugh, douchey and think that your way is the way everyone should go."

"Sanctimonious," Cass said.

"What?" Scout asked, shrugging her shoulders.

"The word you were looking for, in addition to calling me douchey, is sanctimonious," Cass said.

"Yeah. That." Scout glared at Cass, wishing that they didn't look so goddamn alike. "You're not me. I'm not you. Get it?"

Cass nodded, "I get it. I'm sorry. I -." She closed her eyes and took a breath. "I'm sorry. I see you flailing about and I know how that feels and I want to fix it."

"You can't. You can't fix me. It's not your job." Scout continued in a quieter voice, saying, "And anyway, I'm not flailing. What the fuck? I'm a lot less broken than you seem to think I am. Don't go making assumptions just because I didn't have the 'benefits' of growing up in your family." Scout scoffed and shook her head.

"You're right. I'm sorry. You're a lot less broken than I've been, that's for sure." Cass smiled, then couldn't resist and added, "Kiddo," the smile turning to a smirk.

Scout gave Cass a little punch on the shoulder. "Fuck off. And, hey, I've had enough enforced therapy to spot
246

someone projecting their own shit."

"Alright. Fair point." Cass drained the last of her beer, then asked, "So, seriously, Drew is having this baby alone? And she's OK with that? And you're OK with that?"

"Yeah. She had already gone five rounds without a pregnancy working out. This was her last lot of sperm and her last real chance at a blood baby, so I'm super happy for her. And anyway, she's not alone, she's spent years figuring out a support system. This kid is going to have more co-parents and babysitters than any kid from a perfect white picket fenced-in family. Sure, it's getting a bit weird now she's started looking pregnant and it'll be even weirder when she actually has the kid, but we've kept our thing casual and fluid and are just adapting as needed. We've got no claims on each other."

"But you care about her, and she cares about you?" Cass asked.

"Well, yeah, but not in an ownership type of a way. We aren't... wait, what did Alice call it? We're not on the relationship escalator, that was it. We're not even in the fucking mall looking at the escalator. We're skipping through some glorious meadow that is infinite on all sides."

Cass laughed. "Way to paint a picture." She picked up her glass and said, "Sorry for being a grouch. Congrats to Drew, and you!" then realised that her bottle was empty. "Hold that thought. Beersies?" Cass tapped her empty bottle to Scout's which was still half full.

"Sure. But the lecture's over, right?"

"Yes. Yes. Find me some photos of this mansion of yours, and we'll talk about that and maybe sports, and not mention relationships and marriage and kids and shit again. How's that for a plan?" Cass lifted her hat and smoothed her hair back under it, and Scout laughed.

"Sounds good. I just hope you're not a Canucks fan." She ducked just in time to miss Cass's half-hearted attempt to throw a napkin at her face. "We've been missing those mad skills on the field!" Scout called after Cass as she walked to the bar, flipping the bird behind her.

As Cass made her way to the bar, she bumped into Em, who was talking to the DJ, saying, "It's to symbolise, in part, that we're sweeping away conventional relationship rules, you know?" Em gestured at the broom propped up on the gift table and said in hushed tones, "And it's made in BC, by the same people who make the Harry Potter brooms. And I just thought that was kind of cool."

Hanna's bandmate, Dia, nodded and looked over at the broom, which was now bedecked with ornaments: little offerings from all the guests to show their love for the happy triad.

"I'll try to find something appropriate to hang on it later," Dia said, frowning. "It's a cool idea."

"No pressure!" Em said. "It'll be hanging in our house for a while, with any luck!"

Cass sidled up beside Em and gave her a hug. "Congratulations!"

Em kissed Cass on the cheek and thanked her, then introduced her to Dia.

Dia smiled and raised an eyebrow. "Oh, we know each other."

Em looked back and forth between Cass and Dia and rolled her eyes, causing Cass to hold up her hands.

"Hey! Not like that. Jeez, Em, what do you think I am?"

"I think you're awesome, and I think you hooked up with a lot of people before Kate, is all. No negative judgement here," Em said, smiling.

"We were in a band together, way back," Dia said, laughing. "Cass sucked and we had to kick her out." Dia grinned at Cass and said, "You still got that bass?"

"Dude, we were fifteen. I sold it for weed and turned my attention to other creative outlets."

Dia laughed and thanked the barman for her beer. She

248

took a sip and turned back to Cass, saying, "Do you still have your decks?"

Em looked at Cass, wide-eyed. "You're a DJ and you didn't even offer to play my wedding?!"

"Woah!" Cass said, taking a step back and putting out her hands. "I'm no DJ. I just messed around for a bit."

"But you had decks and, like, whatever the other stuff is you need?" Em said. "You must've been pretty into it, then, yeah?"

"Cass was an underground phenomenon. She had this knack of choosing records that really spoke to all the super hot, super single, and previously straight-identifying ladies at a party. It was an impressive skill," Dia said, her eyebrows rising as she bit her lower lip.

Cass shook her head and closed her eyes, laughing. She clutched at her heart and said, "Oh, Dia, Dia, how you wound me."

"Hey! I'm saying you were good. You should get up there and help me out."

"Yeah!" Em said, putting her hand on Cass's elbow. "You totally should! That'd be awesome. Play something romantic for Kate. She's a sucker for sentimentality."

"You mean like, 'Can't Touch This'?" Cass said, grinning.

"I have that," said Dia, before suddenly freezing and looking up. "Shit!" she said, and ran away, waving at Em and Cass and yelling, "Song's about to finish!"

"And I heard she was the best," Em said, sighing and then tutting.

"You just can't find good people these days," Cass said, nodding sagely.

Dia made it to the DJ booth in plenty of time to line up another record, and Em and Cass laughed as they heard the frantic drumbeat of Liquor Box's latest single pound out across the room. Em looked around to find Hanna and laughed as she saw her air-drumming, spilling her beer on herself and then looking around to see if anyone had noticed. She caught Em's eye and smiled, then beckoned her over to dance.

Em started making her way to Hanna but someone knocked into her from behind.

"Hey!" Em shouted, losing her footing, and Alice put out a hand to grab Em and stop her from falling.

"Sorry! Didn't see you there!" Alice said, her face flushed.

Em smiled at Alice, then saw Jeff just behind her, and saw the washroom door swinging shut behind both of them.

Em grinned, then narrowed her eyes and started to ask, "Did you just -?"

Alice blushed, but was saved from any further questioning as Kerry and Grace stumbled out of the other washroom holding onto each other and giggling.

They stopped in front of Em, Alice, and Jeff and everyone adopted their best poker faces. Then Em laughed and said, "Is everyone at my wedding having sex in the washrooms?"

Jeff shrugged and said, "Must be something in the cake and ale!"

Alice bit her lip and dragged a grinning Jeff to the bar, and Kerry shrugged her shoulders and pulled Grace onto the dance floor, leaving Em to shake her head and smile to herself.

FORTY-ONE

When Kate got back to the Airbnb, she kicked off her heels and sank into the couch. Cass, still in her oxfords, slumped down next to her and leaned in to Kate's shoulder.

"Ouch!"

"Sorry! It still hurts?"

"No, no, not that. You just snagged my strap and pinched my boob."

Cass sat up and held out her hands like pincers towards Kate's chest. She wiggled her eyebrows.

"How do you have the energy?" Kate said, laughing, and Cass smiled and sat back again, resting her head on Kate's shoulder this time.

"That was a really cute ceremony, and a really fun day," Cass said.

"It was. I'm so glad there were unicorn poop sugared almonds."

"Yeah, that was a nice touch."

"Shame about that second DJ," Kate said, sighing.

"Shut up, you." Cass said, elbowing Kate softly. "I threw a few things in for you."

"Oh, I know. I got it." Kate laughed. "MC Hammer went over particularly well."

"I thought you'd enjoy that."

"There's nothing like a passive aggressive DJ at a wedding."

"There really isn't." Cass grinned. "I had fun, but it was a bit exhausting."

"Only because you were fending off amorous queers all night," Kate said, smiling to herself.

"Oh, was I? I didn't even notice," Cass kept her face straight and her voice even. "Wait, so those hot women who were requesting songs were, oh, they were requesting more than songs?!" Cass clapped her hand to her mouth. "No! The cheek of it!"

"Yeah, yeah. You enjoyed it. All that flirting. You're so well behaved these days." Kate wriggled out from under Cass and sat up. She turned to look at Cass and smiled, then asked, "Do you think about it at all?"

"About what?" Cass narrowed her eyes, wary of the conversation's direction.

"About having what Em and Steve and Hanna have?" Kate asked.

Cass frowned. "No. Do you?"

"Yeah. Well, I mean I've thought about it."

Cass was silent for a second, then whispered, "Really?" She looked down at her hand, holding Kate's and feeling a momentary urge to untangle their fingers. She kept her hand still, but swallowed hard.

"Hey, no. I don't mean that I want to be poly. I just mean that I've tried to imagine what it must be like, for Em, you know, to be so sure about two people that you want to marry them both?" Kate said. "Sorry. I didn't mean to make you think anything else. I love you. And you're more than enough to handle." She kissed Cass, who smiled and kissed her back.

"You can handle me any time you like, sweetheart," Cass said, squeezing Kate's hand.

252

Kate laughed and then said quietly, "I have been wondering if you miss all that flirting you used to do, though. Your life was pretty exciting before you met me."

Cass raised her eyebrows and said, "My life is still exciting, just in a different way. In a happier way." She furrowed her brow and said. "You know I love you, right?"

"I do," Kate said. "I'm just curious is all. I don't want to hold you back from anything."

Cass laughed. "You don't hold me back at all. You help me not to hold myself back! Since being with you, I've started to really see what I want and you make me believe I can get it, instead of assuming I'll fail. That's not something I ever expected to happen with anyone."

Kate turned to Cass and climbed over her, hitching up her dress so she could sit astride Cass on the couch. She cupped Cass's face with her hands and said, "I love you," before running her lips over Cass's lips softly, then kissing her hard.

When Kate pulled back, Cass took a breath and said, "I love you too. And I have something to tell you."

Kate sat back and tilted her head to one side. "Oh yeah?"

"Yeah," Cass smiled.

"Well?" Kate lightly thumped her fists against Cass's chest and widened her eyes. "What? Tell me!"

"So, I know I've been pretty wrapped up in the documentary recently, and that's cool and exciting and everything, but…." Cass grinned, and took Kate's hands in hers before saying, "Since your accident, and with all the stuff I've learnt working with Guy, I've been trying to figure some stuff out, you know?"

"I wondered, but I didn't want to say anything," Kate said. Cass laughed but still didn't explain, so Kate said, "Goddamnit, Cass! I gave you some space, but now you're just teasing me! Tell me what you're plotting already. Are you making another movie?!"

"Ha! No. One is enough for now. In fact, I think this

doc will be my last media foray." Cass smiled, but Kate closed her eyes and wrinkled her nose.

"That's a shame. Em and I were about to ask you to work with us! To help us make videos we can show to hospitals and clinics!"

Cass looked horrified, which led Kate to frown. "What? Does that sound so bad?"

"No offence, but I think we should never work together. Our relationship would survive about two minutes of a business meeting. Anyway, I've got a new plan, and it isn't movies, my love."

Kate grinned. "I imagine you're right. How very wise you have become." She kissed Cass again, then sat back to wait to hear more, saying, "So what's the plan?"

"Well, so I've been trying to figure out how to make myself useful,-"

"Wait!" Kate folded her arms over her chest, saying, "You said you'd finish up your semester and move back to Vancouver. You promised! I can't -"

Cass put her finger to Kate's lips. "Can you please just let me finish? I still plan on doing that. I'll be moving back, stop fretting." Cass reached for her backpack and pulled out a thin white envelope. She handed it to Kate and smiled.

Kate slid out the letter, noting the crest of the University of British Columbia.

"Dear Cassandra McAndrews, Congratulations! We are pleased to invite you to join the Bachelor of Science in Nursing program at the University of British Columbia for the fall 2017 semester."

Kate jumped up and stared at Cass, then at the letter then back at Cass again. "Great smoky mountains! This is fantastic!" She reached out to pull Cass up from the couch and covered her face with kisses. "This is what you've been plotting! This is incredible! I'm so proud of you, and you'll be an amazing nurse! All that practice looking after me and my poor brain."

254

"Stop squeezing my face!" Cass tried to say as Kate continued to kiss her.

Kate stopped, but pulled Cass into a tight embrace and whispered into her ear, "I love you."

Cass grinned and slipped her hands around Kate's waist. She slid Kate's dress up a few inches and whispered, "So you'll let me practice my sponge bath technique with you?"

"Let's get started," Kate said, taking Cass's cue and pulling her dress up over her head.

"Woah!" Cass said, as Kate jumped off her and pulled her up from the couch.

"I'm serious," Kate said, holding Cass's hand as she turned and began walking to the bathroom. Cass let herself be led, then dropped Kate's hand so she could take off her sweater and start unbuttoning her pants. Kate turned on the hot water and waited in the doorway, leaning against the door jam in her underwear and watching Cass strip. She bit her lip and Cass laughed, walking towards her and slipping her hand around Kate's waist.

"What's gotten into you?" Cass said as Kate slipped off her bra and panties and pulled Cass towards the rising steam. "Not that I'm complaining."

Cass lifted Kate up and backed her against the wall of the shower, and Kate gasped at the feeling of the cool tile. She wrapped her legs around Cass and kissed Cass's ear lobe, before whispering, "You know how formal acceptance letters make me horny. That, and the thought of you in scrubs."

ABOUT THE AUTHOR
Leigh Matthews is a queer writer who lives in Vancouver, BC, with a sharp-eyed border collie who is both her biggest fan and harshest critic.

www.ingramcontent.com/pod-product-compliance
Lightning Source LLC
Chambersburg PA
CBHW051422170626
46809CB00006B/2284